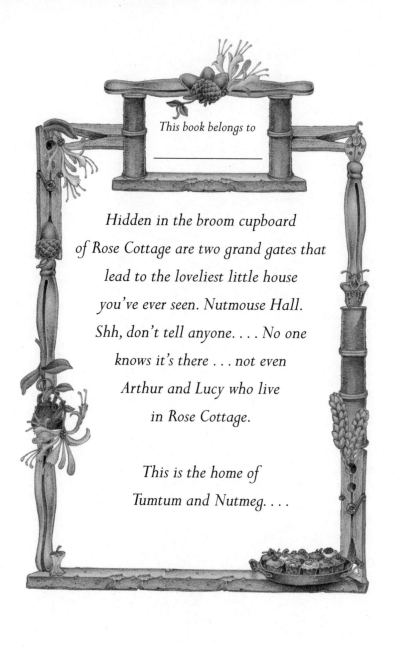

This book belongs to

_____

Hidden in the broom cupboard
of Rose Cottage are two grand gates that
lead to the loveliest little house
you've ever seen. Nutmouse Hall.
Shh, don't tell anyone. . . . No one
knows it's there . . . not even
Arthur and Lucy who live
in Rose Cottage.

This is the home of
Tumtum and Nutmeg. . . .

Stories by Emily Bearn

With pictures by Nick Price

LITTLE, BROWN AND COMPANY

New York   Boston

For my father

Little, Brown and Company

Hachette Book Group
237 Park Avenue, New York, NY 10017
Visit our website at www.lb-kids.com

Little, Brown and Company is a division of Hachette Book Group, Inc.
The Little, Brown name and logo are trademarks of Hachette Book Group, Inc.

First U.S. Edition: April 2009
Book 1 and Book 2 first published in Great Britain in 2008 by Egmont UK Limited
Book 3 first published in Great Britain in 2009 by Egmont UK Limited

Library of Congress Cataloging-in-Publication Data

Bearn, Emily.
Tumtum & Nutmeg : adventures beyond Nutmouse Hall / Emily Bearn; cover
and inside illustrations by Nick Price. —1st U.S. ed.
    p. cm.
Summary: Wealthy, married mice Tumtum and Nutmeg find adventure when
they secretly try to help two human siblings who live in a tumbledown
cottage with their absentminded inventor father.
ISBN 978-0-316-02703-8
[1. Mice—Fiction. 2. Brothers and sisters—Fiction. 3. Adventure and
adventurers—Fiction.] I. Price, Nick (Nicholas R.), ill. II. Title.
III. Title: Tumtum & Nutmeg.
PZ7.B38048Tu 2009
[Fic]—dc22
                                    2008045294

10 9 8 7 6 5 4 3

RRD-IN

Printed in the United States of America

CONTENTS

Tumtum &
Nutmeg

Chapter One

Once there were two married mice called Mr. and Mrs. Nutmouse, and they lived in great style. They had a big, rambling house with a ballroom, and a billiards room, and a banqueting room, and a butler's pantry, and just about every other sort of room a married couple might want. (There were thirty-six rooms in all.)

The house was called Nutmouse Hall, and it was situated in the broom cupboard of a small human dwelling called Rose Cottage. A broom cupboard might not sound like a very grand place for a house, but this broom cupboard was special. It had creamy white walls, mottled red tiles on the floor, and a tiny sash window hidden behind a curtain of honeysuckle.

But the nicest thing of all about the broom cupboard was that no human knew it was there. This is because, a very long time ago, soon after Rose Cottage was built, someone pushed a big Welsh dresser against the kitchen wall, hiding the broom cupboard door from view; and the dresser always stayed there because there was nowhere else to put it.

It was Mr. Nutmouse's great-great-great-grandfather who first discovered the broom cupboard when he crept beneath the dresser and poked his nose under the door. The red tiles and white walls looked so appealing that he decided to build a house there straightaway, and the first thing he had to do was to build a big round mouse hole so that his workmen could get in and out with all their bricks and cement-mixers. Then he fitted the mouse hole with smart iron gates, and as soon as a mouse entered those gates he was on the Nutmouse family's territory.

Nutmouse Hall was built in the middle of the broom cupboard, and it was considered a very fine piece of architecture. The walls were made of pretty pebblestone, and there were gables on the windows and little turrets peeking out of the roof. The front of the house faced south, so the bedroom windows

caught the sun as it filtered through the honeysuckle. The smallest rooms, such as the bathrooms, were the size of a cake tin, while the ballroom was the size of a hamper. (And a hamper-sized room seemed very big to the Nutmouses, since they were only two inches tall.)

Because Nutmouse Hall was so enormous, Mr. and Mrs. Nutmouse did not use all the rooms available to them. Mr. Nutmouse spent most of the time in his library, warming his toes in front of the fire, and Mrs. Nutmouse spent most of her time scurrying about in her kitchen, making delicious things to eat.

Mr. and Mrs. Nutmouse had been married a long time, but they still called each other by the affectionate pet names they had adopted during their engagement. Mrs. Nutmouse called Mr. Nutmouse Tumtum, because he had such a large one, and Tumtum called Mrs. Nutmouse Nutmeg, because she had nutmeg hair. (Tumtum thought this was very exotic, because his family had all been grays.)

In their funny way, the Nutmouses were well suited to each other. Tumtum was a wise, bookish sort of mouse. He

never lost his temper or got agitated, and he did everything very calmly and slowly. Nutmeg was quite the opposite. She did things nineteen to the dozen, and even little tasks, such as putting the icing on a cake, could get her into a terrible dither. But in her hasty way, she was surprisingly efficient. The house was spick-and-span, the bills were paid on time, and the food served at Nutmouse Hall was the envy of all the mice for miles around.

Tumtum looked upon every meal as a celebration. For breakfast there would be eggs and bacon and toast and marmalade; lunch was all manner of cold meats and salads; for afternoon tea there was always a homemade cake or scone; and supper would be a delicacy, such as earwigs *en croute*. Nutmeg had a whole shelf of cookbooks, so she was never short of inspiration.

Tumtum was not as rich as his ancestors had been, and this was because he gave most of his money away. He supported all sorts of charities—charities for homeless mice, charities for arthritic mice, charities for illiterate mice, charities for bald mice . . . he even supported a charity for mice

with hiccups. So one way or another the Nutmouses did not have much money left. They did not employ a butler or a maid, and they could not afford to give banquets in their banqueting room, nor balls in their ballroom.

But since neither of them much liked balls and banquets, they didn't mind a bit; and Nutmeg was such a good house-keeper that life was splendid all the same.

But beyond the broom cupboard, where the humans lived, things were not splendid at all. Rose Cottage was owned by Mr. Mildew, a widower who lived there with his two children, Arthur and Lucy. They were very poor, and they did not have nearly so many rooms as the Nutmouses had. There was one bathroom, which was only a little bit bigger than the bath, and Arthur and Lucy shared a tiny bedroom in the attic with a ceiling that leaked.

From the outside, Rose Cottage looked very inviting. The garden was full of pear trees and wildflowers, and the honey-suckle trailed all over the stone walls and curled along the fat

fringe of the thatch. But inside it was less agreeable. Every room was rife with clutter and chaos; the walls were damp, and the plaster was beginning to crumble. The beams in the living room were full of woodworms, and the carpets were so threadbare you could see through to the floorboards, which were full of woodworms, too. The boiler had packed up long ago, and in winter the wind howled into the kitchen through the cracks in the garden door.

The cottage had been much better cared for when Mrs. Mildew was alive, but she had died long ago, when Arthur was still a baby. He couldn't remember his mother at all, and Lucy could only remember her lying in bed looking very thin and white, with a fat doctor standing over her. She'd been told the name of her illness once, but it had been much too peculiar a word for her to remember.

The Mildew children did not miss having a mother, because they couldn't remember what having one had been like. And yet they knew that there were certain disadvantages to being without one, and they considered living in chaos to be among them.

But Mr. Mildew was such a head in the clouds sort of fellow that he hardly seemed to notice how squalid Rose Cottage had become. He was an inventor by trade, and he spent all his time crashing about in his tiny study upstairs, trying to invent things. Years ago, he had invented a gadget for peeling grapes, which had been sold in a department store in London and had made him quite rich for a short time. But people weren't buying his grape-peelers anymore, so now he needed to invent something else.

And as a result, he didn't think nearly as hard as he might about the housekeeping, which was why Rose Cottage was such a mess. It was all he could do to put meals on the table, and he was so absentminded that he could never remember which meal was which. So as often as not Arthur and Lucy found themselves eating canned spaghetti for breakfast, and porridge for supper.

The Mildews all looked rather scruffy, for they never had haircuts or new clothes, but there was something distinguished about them, too. Lucy was tall and graceful, and she had hair the color of copper; and Arthur had blue eyes and thick black

curls, and he wore glasses with a broken frame, which kept slipping off his nose. Mr. Mildew was the most striking of all—he always dressed in a purple smoking jacket, which was falling to bits, and he had wiry hair, which stuck out of his head like insect antennae.

Less imaginative children might have been embarrassed by Mr. Mildew, but Arthur and Lucy felt proud of him because he was much more interesting and exotic than anyone else's father. And he had plenty of good points. He hardly ever lost his temper, and he never nagged them to do boring things, like cleaning their teeth, or brushing their hair, or tidying their room, or doing their homework. But it wasn't easy living with someone quite so absentminded, and now and again they did feel a bit neglected.

And at the time this story begins they had reason to feel even more neglected than usual. It was the middle of a long, icy winter—they had known weeks and weeks of the sort of biting weather that makes it painful to be outdoors. No one could remember the village being as cold as this. The duck pond was frozen to its depths, the gargoyles on the church were

dribbling icicles, and all the school water pipes had frozen solid. One night, two of them burst.

This was a great drama, and it meant that the school had to be closed for seven whole weeks while something called "essential renovations" took place. Most of the children were overjoyed about this, for it's not every year that one's Christmas vacation is extended until February. But Arthur and Lucy weren't so pleased. For if you have a father who gives you canned spaghetti for breakfast, and you live in a cottage so cold that the butter freezes in the kitchen, then the prospect of being stuck at home all winter long is not especially appealing.

Had they known that there were mice living such gracious lives in their broom cupboard, they might have felt quite envious. They might even have wished they were mice themselves, so that they could move into Nutmouse Hall and live as the Nutmouses did.

And had the Nutmouses been different, they might have turned up their noses at the Mildews and felt quite superior and haughty. But Tumtum and Nutmeg did not feel haughty at all. As a matter of fact, they felt rather uncomfortable.

They were kindhearted mice, and they did not think it right that they should be eating sumptuous meals in a warm house while the Mildew children ate horrid gloop out of cans in their icy kitchen.

The Nutmouses had been concerned about Arthur and Lucy for some time; and the colder the winter became, the more their concern grew. And there comes a point at which a concern grows so big that something has to be done about it.

Chapter Two

A few days after the school pipes burst it started to snow. It was only fleeting at first, and when the Nutmouses poked their noses outdoors after breakfast it looked as if it might not stick. But it snowed all day, thicker and faster, and by afternoon the whole village had been blanketed.

Shortly after four o'clock, Nutmeg visited the Mildews' kitchen to borrow a few bits and pieces for her bread and butter pudding, and there was snow blustering in under the garden door. It was so cold that she could see her breath making little gray clouds in the air.

She didn't linger long, for the Mildews seldom had much worth borrowing, and this afternoon there was even less than usual. There were neither currants nor cinnamon in the cupboard, and nothing on the floor but a bit of squished banana. There was a scrap of fruitcake left on the table, but it was so stale that when Nutmeg bumped into it she stubbed her toe. And when she climbed onto the toast rack to poke her nose down inside the milk bottle, she could see a film of white ice. *Brrrrr!* Drawing her woolen cape tight around her shoulders, she chiseled a corner off a pat of frosty butter, then scuttled as fast as she could back to Nutmouse Hall.

Tumtum was in the kitchen, leaning against the stove. He was hoping for some tea.

"Oh, Tumtum, I don't know what's to become of those Mildews," Nutmeg said forlornly, plonking her wicker basket on the table. "Their kitchen's so cold that the milk's started to freeze, and all the cupboards are bare. They need a fairy godmother to take charge of them."

Nutmeg longed to go through Rose Cottage with her mop and pail, scrubbing and darning and mending and mothering and fussing about from top to bottom, but she was only a mouse, so what use could she possibly be? She couldn't even lift one of the Mildews' saucers!

14

Tumtum looked thoughtful. He knew that Nutmeg was upset about the conditions next door, and he had something to propose.

"How about a little snack, Nutmeg dear?" he said, for he never liked proposing things on an empty stomach.

Nutmeg scurried about the kitchen and laid the table with a dainty blue and white teapot, and homemade gingerbread, and macaroons, and cucumber sandwiches, and scones with butter and jam; but she was feeling too upset to eat more than a couple of mouthfuls.

"Oh, if only we could help them, Tumtum!" she groaned hopelessly, watching him eat.

"Perhaps we can," he replied mysteriously. Then he retrieved a crumpled piece of paper from his waistcoat pocket and studied it through his crescent-shaped glasses.

"I had a look around the attic this morning, while the children were asleep, and I made a list of one or two things we could do," he said. "For a start, I could repair the electric heater—"

"*Repair the heater?*" Nutmeg asked incredulously. "How do you intend to do that?"

15

"Very simply," Tumtum replied, helping himself to a fat slice of gingerbread. "I just need to crawl inside and do a spot of rewiring—it's the sort of thing a mouse can do much more easily than a human." Tumtum was keen on rewiring—he'd once rewired the whole of Nutmouse Hall.

Nutmeg beamed. "What a good idea, Tumtum!" she said. "Then the children won't have to sleep in their winter coats anymore."

"Quite so," Tumtum said, feeling rather pleased with himself. "And there's plenty more we can see to. Arthur's glasses are about to fall apart because there are two screws loose in the frame. So I'll take my drill up to the attic and tighten them again."

"Tumtum, how wonderful!" Nutmeg cried. "And what can I do?"

"All sorts of things," he said reassuringly. "You can darn some of their clothes, for a start. You're a fast sewer, and if you do a small amount each evening, everything will be mended within a week or so. And you can patch their shoes, too, using the leather from that old armchair in my dressing room—

I've never much liked it, anyway; it's rather in the way there. And why not use your clothesline to replace the lace in Arthur's boot? You hardly need it anymore, now that we've got a tumble dryer. . . ."

And so Tumtum went on, suggesting more and more ingenious ways to help.

"When can we start?" Nutmeg asked eagerly, feeling much too excited to drink her tea.

"There's no time like the present," Tumtum said. "I vote we set out tonight."

Nutmeg agreed to this, and that was how the adventures began.

Shortly after ten o'clock, Nutmeg pressed her little brown nose through the front gate, and twitched it back and forth under the dresser. *Twitch! Twitch! Twitch!*

"All clear, Tumtum!" she called back to her husband, who was following behind her carrying a wooden toolbox and a drill, and dragging the bulky leather chair cover. Nutmeg

was carrying her sewing basket and her mop and pail, and also the clothesline, which was wound around her shoulder like a lasso.

They crossed the kitchen floor and crept into the hall, and then they dragged all their clobber up the baseboard, which ran along the stairs, and tiptoed across the landing. There was light glinting beneath the study door, and when they peaked underneath it, they could see Mr. Mildew crouched on the floor amid a sea of brightly colored wires and tiny shards of metal. His face was purple, and he was cursing under his breath: "Awful creature!"

"I wonder what he's inventing now," Nutmeg whispered.

"A battery-operated mouse that gobbles all the crumbs off a dinner table, like a vacuum," Tumtum said knowingly. "I heard him telling Arthur about it. He thinks it's going to make him rich again. It's called The Hungry House Mouse."

"Goodness," Nutmeg said. "What a curious idea! I wonder why it's making him so angry."

"I believe he's got the mechanics wrong," Tumtum said. "Instead of a hungry mouse, he's invented an unusually delicate one. No sooner has it gobbled the crumbs, than it throws them all up again."

"What a waste!" Nutmeg said, shaking her head disapprovingly. "A real mouse would do the job much better."

The mice pressed on and heaved their things up the steep stairs to the attic. The room was bitterly cold, for there were no curtains to keep out the draft, and they had to blow on their paws to stop them from going numb. They had trouble getting their bearings, for it was quite dark at first, but then the clouds scudded in the wind and the moon shone through the window onto the children's beds. Arthur was completely buried under his blankets, but they could see Lucy's hair on her pillow shining red in the moonlight.

The mice worked furiously. Tumtum got the heater going and drilled Arthur's glasses back into shape, and Nutmeg darned three pairs of socks and swept out both the children's satchels; then she climbed into the sink with her mop and polished it until it became so slippery she couldn't stand up again. Tumtum had to throw the plug down to her so she could clamber free up the chain.

Finally she scuttled off into the wardrobe to start mending Arthur's and Lucy's clothes. They were so full of holes that Nutmeg reckoned it would take her weeks to get through them all, and some were so threadbare it was hardly worth mending them at all. As she persevered with her tiny needle, she could hear the children's soft, steady breathing from the other side of the room; they were deeply asleep, quite innocent of all the bustle that was going on.

Nutmeg felt fiercely protective of them. *Mr. Mildew is simply not capable of looking after two children on his own,* she thought sternly, setting to work on a gaping hole in the elbow of one of Arthur's sweaters. *They need a mother, and in the absence of a human one, I will have to do.* And as she set herself the responsibility of mothering the Mildews, Nutmeg felt a warm glow in her stomach. She and Tumtum had never had a litter of their own, and she considered herself very blessed to be able to adopt two human children instead.

The mice toiled away until midnight, when they decided to stop for a rest. Nutmeg had tucked two slices of fruitcake

and a thermos of tea into her sewing basket, and they both felt much in need of them.

"Bother!" she said, unpacking the picnic. "I forgot to pack any plastic cups."

"Never mind," said Tumtum, who could feel his tummy rumbling. "We can swig from the thermos."

But Nutmeg was more particular about such things. "Look, Tumtum!" she cried, pointing toward a tall pink building in the corner. "Lucy's dollhouse! It's sure to have a tea set!"

The mice walked toward it and peered through the living room window. It was not nearly so big as their living room at Nutmouse Hall, but it was prettily furnished, with pale blue curtains and a grand piano. There were two dolls made of pipe cleaners sitting on the sofa, and there was a case full of books by the fire. Something about the house seemed to beckon them inside.

They passed underneath the white awning and pushed the front door. It swung open, leading into an airy hall with a coatrack and a grandfather clock. To the right was the kitchen, in which there stood a long dining table, with benches down each side. There were lots of pots and pans hanging above the stove, and Nutmeg found a whole hodgepodge of mismatched china in one of the cupboards. Everything was mouse-sized.

Nutmeg set the table, and they both sat down feeling very civilized.

"We've still got an awful lot to do," Nutmeg said wearily. "And if we don't finish tonight, we'll have to lug all our stuff back upstairs again tomorrow night."

"We needn't do that, Nutmeg," Tumtum replied. "We could leave everything here, in the dollhouse. We can tuck it all away somewhere so Lucy won't find it."

"Oh, Tumtum, what a good idea!" she cried. "Then we can just come back and do more chores whenever we've time."

So they worked for another hour or so, then they crept back to the dollhouse and put the toolbox and the sewing basket in the cupboard under the stairs. The mop and pail wouldn't fit, so Nutmeg hid them behind the kitchen door.

Then, by instinct, she cleared away their cups and plates from the table and put them in the dollhouse sink. There was

no running water, but she could fill it next time with her bucket. "I do so like this dollhouse, Tumtum. It feels a bit like camping," Nutmeg said, and she thought that next time she came she would bring a new tablecloth for the kitchen.

Tumtum was longing to get home, for he was quite exhausted, but Nutmeg found it a wrench to leave. She would have given anything to have seen the children's faces when they woke up to find their heater working, for by now the attic was lovely and warm.

"We could spend the night here," she suggested, but Tumtum was having none of it.

"That would be very rash, Nutmeg," he said. "They might see us!" They both agreed that that would not do at all, for some humans have funny feelings toward mice, so Tumtum took his wife by the paw and they scuttled back to Nutmouse Hall and collapsed into their four-poster bed.

Chapter Three

The Nutmouses became regular visitors to the attic and thought of more and more things to do. Tumtum bought a bag of cement and used it to seal all the little cracks in the attic windowpanes. And he climbed up onto the roof and patched the leak with a big roll of linoleum, which he'd stripped out of one of the bathrooms in Nutmouse Hall. Nutmeg polished Arthur's train set and mopped the children's shoes, and she spent one entire night sorting out their sock drawer. She also left tiny presents under their pillows—silver candlesticks from her banqueting hall, and bars of chocolate the size of raisins.

Day after day, the children woke up to discover some new

delight. Lucy was most pleased about the tidying and the mending, and Arthur was most pleased about the presents—but they were both equally mystified.

Lucy, who was the eldest, said there must be a fairy in the house. But Arthur had given up believing in fairies long ago, and he wasn't at all convinced. Then one day he opened his pencil case and found that all his pencils had been sharpened in a most peculiar way—they looked as though they'd been nibbled. *Well, that can't have been done by a fairy*, he thought. *A fairy would have small, delicate teeth, not sharp, spiky ones that could nibble graphite.*

Later that week, another strange thing happened. On Friday afternoon, one of Arthur's teeth fell out, and before going to bed he put it on the dresser, thinking he'd find somewhere to hide it away next day. But when he woke up, the tooth had gone. In its place, there was a tin the size of a penny, and inside it a cake covered with white icing and walnuts—the tiniest cake either child had ever seen.

"Well, that means it must be a tooth fairy," Lucy said firmly. "Only tooth fairies take teeth away."

"But tooth fairies leave money, not cakes," Arthur said. (The tooth fairy had never come for him before, but it came for his friends, and he knew that they usually got at least fifty pence, and sometimes more.) "And tooth fairies only come when you lose a tooth, but our fairy—or rather our," he corrected himself, "our . . . our whatever it is—it comes all the time."

In truth, neither child knew what to think. If it wasn't a fairy, then it could be a ghost; but that was such a frightening option that neither of them liked to suggest it.

Eventually, Lucy proposed doing something decisive. "I think we should write whoever it is a letter, asking them over for a visit," she said.

"But what if it's a gh—well, what if it's, you know, something funny?" Arthur asked nervously. The thought of confronting their mysterious visitor face-to-face made his stomach feel quite hollow.

"Well, whatever it is, it would be better to know," Lucy said. Arthur wasn't so sure, but he didn't want Lucy thinking he was frightened, so he reluctantly agreed. Lucy went to her desk and tore a sheet of paper out of a workbook. Then, after some deliberation, she and Arthur composed the following message:

To Whoever Has Been Visiting Us,

    Thank you very much for everything you have done.

    If you are a fairy, and not a ghost, then would you like to come and have tea with us here in the attic tomorrow?

    Love,

    Arthur and Lucy Mildew

P.S. Please come at 4 o'clock.

Lucy folded the piece of paper in half, and addressed one side to *The Visitor, The Attic, Rose Cottage*. Then she left it propped up against the mirror on the dresser. Arthur felt anxious all day—something told him that their visitor might not be at all like the fairies he'd seen pictures of in Lucy's books.

The Nutmouses discovered the letter that night and dragged it back to Nutmouse Hall. They sat a long while in their

kitchen with it spread out in front of them all over the table, wondering what to do. Nutmeg longed to accept, but Tumtum forbade it.

"You certainly can't go, Nutmeg," he said firmly. "Imagine what a shock it would be for them to find that their visitor was a mouse!"

Forlornly, Nutmeg agreed. Humans could be so frosty toward mice—there was simply too much misunderstanding between the two species. And what if the children told Mr. Mildew about them? There was no knowing how he'd react. He might try to evict them from their home, even though the Nutmouse family had been living in Rose Cottage much longer than the Mildews had.

But there was another reason why Nutmeg couldn't introduce herself, and that was because conversation would be impossible. For mice have such tiny voices that the human ear can't pick up a word they say. Even when a mouse is shouting and bellowing at the top of his voice, a human hears only a faint squeal.

But Tumtum had an idea. "You must certainly tell

them that you're a fairy, not a ghost, for otherwise they might get frightened," he said. "But say that you can't accept their invitation, because fairies aren't allowed to be seen by humans, and if they are seen, their magic powers stop working. I'm sure they'll understand that."

Nutmeg agreed that this was a sensible solution, so she found a big piece of blotting paper (mouse writing paper would have been too small) and, in much larger handwriting than she normally used, she wrote the following reply:

My Dear Arthur and Lucy,

I am a fairy of sorts. But sadly I cannot accept your kind invitation because my magic powers would fade if you were ever to set eyes on me.

But if there is anything more I can do for you, then just leave me another note on the dresser.

Love,

And she was about to sign herself "Mrs. Nutmouse," but she hesitated, thinking it sounded too mousy. So instead she

put "Nutmeg," which was much more the sort of name a fairy might have. Then, on Tumtum's advice, she added a postscript:

P.S. It is best not to tell anyone else about me, because that would make my magic powers fade, too.

She folded the letter into an envelope, which she addressed to *Arthur and Lucy Mildew, the Attic, Rose Cottage*. Then, before having his bath, Tumtum delivered it for her, tiptoeing back upstairs to leave it on the dresser, leaning against the handle of Lucy's hairbrush.

When Lucy first picked up the brush the next morning she didn't see the note, but then she noticed a tiny piece of paper fluttering to the floor. Nutmeg's writing was very wobbly (like a drunken spider, Tumtum always said), but Lucy managed to decipher it using Arthur's magnifying glass.

"I wonder what a Fairy of Sorts looks like," Arthur said

when she had read it out loud. A Fairy of Sorts didn't sound nearly as frightening as a ghost—in fact, it sounded rather nice—but even so he felt relieved he wouldn't actually have to meet Nutmeg, for he still felt a little unsure of her.

But Lucy was longing to meet her. "I wonder where Fairies of Sorts live," she said wonderingly, and she felt very frustrated to think she might never find out. But as she went to hide the letter in the drawer of her bedside table, where she put all her most important things, something about the dollhouse caught her eye. She knelt down to look more closely.

She hadn't played with it for a whole week and now everything seemed different. The door knocker had been polished, and inside lots of things had been meddled with. The piano lid was open, and the kitchen sink was full of water. There were dishes on the draining board and there was a tiny pair of pink slippers beside the bed upstairs.

Lucy felt a sudden thrill. "Arthur," she said urgently. "Nutmeg has moved in."

The Nutmouses hadn't really moved in, of course, because

they had a very grand home of their own. But they looked on the dollhouse as a bit of an adventure, and as the days passed they had become much bolder about making use of it. When they had been working especially late in the attic they sometimes spent the night there—despite Tumtum's initial concerns. So when the children scrutinized each room in turn, they noticed all Nutmeg's efforts to make it more homely.

There were new gingham curtains in the kitchen, and new cushions on the living room sofa, and there were soft white towels in the bathroom. There were also hairs on the pillows in the bedroom: gray on one side of the bed, and brown on the other.

"She's got funny hair," Lucy said. "It looks a bit mousy."

Arthur did not comment—he never noticed what people's hair was like. But when he saw how nice and cozy the Fairy of Sorts had made the dollhouse, his fears of her at once evaporated. She seemed almost human. "We should leave Nutmeg something to eat," he said. "If she can't visit with us, then we might at least leave her a snack in the dollhouse."

Lucy agreed, so after supper they waited until their father had disappeared to his study, then salvaged the last bit of shortbread from the cookie jar and crumbled part of it on one of the little plates in the dollhouse kitchen. Then they poured a teaspoonful of milk into one of the jugs and laid a place at the table. They even supplied a tiny napkin cut out of a cotton handkerchief. The Mildews never used napkins themselves, but Lucy thought Nutmeg might appreciate one.

Next morning, the shortbread and the milk had gone, and there was a letter on the table in the dollhouse kitchen. Lucy picked up the magnifying glass and read it out loud:

Dear Arthur and Lucy,

Thank you for a most magnificent feast. Your shortbread was superb, and I ate much more than I should have. I must acquire the recipe one day. I hope you do not mind me making use of your dollhouse, but it is very convenient to have somewhere to leave my things.

Love,

Nutmeg

After that, Arthur and Lucy agreed that they should leave Nutmeg something to eat every night. And they both agreed that life was much, much more interesting now that they had a Fairy of Sorts looking after them.

Chapter Four

Arthur and Lucy had been dreading their long winter vacation at home, but it was turning out to be more exciting than they could ever have imagined. Nutmeg visited almost every night, and when they woke up to find her funny little presents under their pillows, it felt just like Christmas, even though Christmas had happened several weeks ago. (And they hadn't had nearly so many presents then as they were getting now.)

But just at the point at which they felt things could hardly get any nicer, something horrible happened. One morning, while the Mildews were all sitting down to a breakfast of canned rice pudding, they heard a car stopping outside in the lane.

Then there was the sound of someone cursing, followed by a sharp rap on the front door.

"I wonder who that could be," Mr. Mildew said anxiously—he always felt unsettled by visitors, even the postman. As he said it, the rapping started up again, cross and impatient.

His children followed him into the hall, and when he opened the door their hearts sank. For there was Aunt Ivy, and a taxi driver was trailing up the path behind her, carrying five suitcases.

"Your doorbell's not working, Walter," she said sourly, pushing past Mr. Mildew into the hall and ignoring the children entirely. Then she went into the kitchen, flung her gloves down on the table, and said something disparaging about the mess.

Aunt Ivy lived a long way away, in a big city in Scotland, and yet somehow the Mildews always saw more of her than they would have liked. She had been married to Mr. Mildew's brother, Hugh, who had run away to Africa several years ago and had never been heard from since. The children thought that if they had been married to Aunt Ivy, they'd have run away to Africa, too, for there was something distinctly off-putting about her. She was tall and spiky-looking, with long elastic-ey arms and dark, menacing eyes.

Since losing Hugh, she had started spending Christmas at Rose Cottage, and she ruined it every time. She always snapped and snarled and gobbled all the chocolates, and her presents got meaner every year. Last time, she'd given Arthur a Ping-Pong ball and Lucy a packet of plastic clothespins. She also had revolting habits, such as clipping her fingernails at the kitchen table and stubbing out her cigarettes in the children's boots.

Mr. Mildew had her to stay each year because of something called "family duty," which makes people put up with all sorts of awkward things at Christmas time. But it wasn't Christmas now, it was January, and they were all very surprised to see her again. Arthur and Lucy stood at the kitchen door, looking at her in dismay.

"Now, do remind me, Ivy—should we have been expecting you?" Mr. Mildew asked, shifting uncomfortably from one foot to the other.

Aunt Ivy looked at him contemptuously. "Are you going

senile, Walter? We arranged everything on the telephone only last week."

Mr. Mildew acknowledged this was possible, for the one thing he never forgot was his own forgetfulness. "Yes, Ivy, of course . . . but do just remind me—"

"*Mice*, Walter," she said, drumming her fingers irritably on the kitchen table.

At last, Mr. Mildew's memory jogged into action. Ivy had seen not one but two mice in her sitting room in Scotland, and the sight had so upset her nerves that she had asked to stay at Rose Cottage while a pest control company took up all her floorboards trying to find them. And he had said yes, just to get her off the telephone.

"Of course, of course. And, er, I've forgotten how long you might stay," Mr. Mildew said, trying to sound more casual than he felt.

"As long as it takes, Walter," she said defiantly. "I've told Pest Persecutors to turn my house upside down until they find those revolting little creatures. If there's one thing I loathe more than anything, it's *mice*."

Aunt Ivy and her five suitcases took over the living room. The sofa was turned into a bed; and an entire shelf of the bookcase was cleared to make way for all her makeup and hair dye. Aunt Ivy took a good deal of care over her appearance. She painted her lips red and her eyelids green; and she dyed her hair jet-black and parted it in a zigzag. She looked quite sinister.

And she didn't do any of the things that aunts normally do. She never knitted sweaters, baked cakes, or listened to cheerful music on the radio. She just sat in the kitchen all day long, filing her nails and looking grim. In order to avoid her, the children spent more and more time in the attic, and Mr. Mildew spent even more time than he usually did locked away in his room.

The Nutmouses went to ground, too, because the very sight of Aunt Ivy made them shudder. When she was last here, Nutmeg had seen her standing at the kitchen windowsill, squishing a fly with the tip of her eyeliner, and Tumtum had seen her pouring boiling water on a beetle.

He had once heard her telling Mr. Mildew how much she

hated mice, and he dreaded to think what she'd do if she ever set eyes on them. So he was determined to make sure she didn't. That morning, when he heard Aunt Ivy's voice ringing from the kitchen, he put a padlock around his gates, then he drew the bolts across the front door and told Nutmeg that she was not to set foot in Rose Cottage except in a major emergency, such as running out of flour.

"It is simply too dangerous to venture out while that ill-tempered creature is here," he said firmly as they sat down to a lunch of cold tongue and potato salad, followed by sponge cake. "We must hibernate until she's gone."

"But what about the children?" Nutmeg wailed. "We can't stop visiting the attic, Tumtum! Imagine how bereft they'd feel!"

"It's not worth the risk, Nutmeg," Tumtum said. "There's something about that woman that makes my spine tingle."

"Oh, I know, Tumtum, she makes mine tingle, too," Nutmeg replied. "But we can't let her make us prisoners in our own home. So long as we wait until she's gone to bed, then it must be safe to move around. A couple of mice have never woken anybody."

Tumtum looked thoughtful. It was true that every house mouse has the right to roam freely after dark. And they especially wanted to visit the attic that night because they had a rather wonderful present for the children—a five-pound note that they'd found shortly before Aunt Ivy arrived, half buried in the snowbank by the lane in front of the cottage. They'd rolled the money into a cylinder, then Tumtum had carried it home on his shoulder. And now it was leaning against their kitchen wall, waiting to be delivered.

"Oh, let's take it tonight, Tumtum!" Nutmeg squealed for the dozenth time.

Tumtum finished his sponge cake, untucked his napkin from his collar, and sighed. "All right, Nutmeg," he said resignedly. "We'll go." But he felt very uneasy about it.

Much later, after supper, the mice tiptoed up to their front gate

and peeped out under the dresser. The kitchen light was still on, and they could see Aunt Ivy's shadow cast across the floor. She was sitting at the table, smoking. They went back to Nutmouse Hall, waited an hour, then crept back to the gate. . . . Aunt Ivy was still there. *Really*, Nutmeg thought disapprovingly. *No wonder she always looks so crazy, if she never goes to bed.*

Eventually, at a very late hour, they came to the gate to find the kitchen light turned off. They let themselves out and scuttled through to the hall, Tumtum carrying the note again on his shoulder. The living room light was on and the door open, but there was no sign of Aunt Ivy.

Tumtum's ears pricked up as he heard water running upstairs. "Come on, dear!" he said, turning to his wife. "She's having a bath. We can sneak up now."

They ran up the baseboard and sped across the landing. They could hear Aunt Ivy splashing about in the bathroom, humming tunelessly. The noise made them both shudder. Finally they clambered up to the attic, and Tumtum

climbed onto the dresser then unrolled the note and left it leaning against the mirror.

Nutmeg wanted to do some cleaning, but Tumtum wouldn't let her. He felt growing apprehension. "Not tonight, Nutmeg," he said. "We must get back to Nutmouse Hall while Aunt Ivy's still wallowing." So they ate the biscuits that the children had laid out for them in the dollhouse, even though neither had much of an appetite, and then they made for home.

But as they were galloping across the upstairs landing, Nutmeg tripped on her apron strings and landed on the floor, all four paws in the air. *Oomph!* It was very painful.

Tumtum pulled her to her feet. "Are you all right, dear?" he asked anxiously.

"Oh, yes, yes, Tumtum! Nothing broken, nothing—"

Then, "Oh, bother!" she said, fumbling in her apron pocket. "I've dropped the key to the gate. Oh, bother, bother, bother!"

Tumtum shone his flashlight around, nervously scouring the carpet. Eventually, Nutmeg saw it glinting behind the leg of the dresser. "There it is!" she said, squirreling it into her apron pocket.

"Now, hurry, dear! Do hurry!" Tumtum said, tugging her by the paw.

But as he did so, the mice were bathed in a brilliant pool of light. The bathroom door had opened, and looming above them was a tall, thin figure wrapped in a white towel.

Chapter Five

The mice froze, rooted to the carpet in terror. Aunt Ivy froze, too. She hated all animals, unless they had been turned into coats or gloves or suitcases. But it was mice that she hated most of all. They made her pulse race, and her stomach turn, and her skin crawl, and her eyes pop. And now there were two of them, confronting her, face-to-face, on the landing. And they were wearing clothes!

Aunt Ivy looked at them in horror, praying that her eyes were deceiving her. One had an apron on, and the other was dressed in a tweed suit, with brown shoes—shoes!—and a pair of glasses strung around its neck. *They're mad mice!* she thought wildly, her brain spinning with fear; then she tightened her grip on the pumice stone in her left hand, raised her arm, and hurled it down upon the Nutmouses as hard as she could.

As the gray missile was released, the mice finally came back to their senses, and they scuttled like they had never scuttled before—over the landing, down the stairs, across the kitchen, and under the dresser, where Tumtum fumbled with the padlock, his paws shaking.

When the gates opened, he pushed Nutmeg inside to safety and bolted the lock behind them. They could hear Aunt Ivy rampaging upstairs. "Walter! Wake up! You've got *mice*! You've got an infestation of *mice* wearing clothes!" She said *mice* with such loathing that Nutmeg's heart fluttered.

Mr. Mildew sounded unsympathetic. "You've been dreaming—now *please*, Ivy, go to bed!" he said. She eventually did, for it was very late, after all. But next morning the mouse hunt began. . . .

From their breakfast table in Nutmouse Hall, the mice could hear her crashing about Rose Cottage, upturning beds and

bookshelves, trying to find their hideaway. When she started banging about in the kitchen, the Nutmouses went to spy on her through their front gates.

They saw her put down two mousetraps, one by the garden door and another next to the vegetable rack. (Aunt Ivy always packed mousetraps when she went to the countryside, and in summer she traveled with flyswatters and wasp traps, too.) Both the mousetraps were baited with little chunks of cheese. *Really!* Nutmeg thought indignantly. *She must think us very silly!*

But Aunt Ivy was not going to wait for them to take the bait—she wanted to find them now. She rummaged in the pantry, then in the cupboard under the sink. She looked in every drawer and in every saucepan; she even looked in the wastepaper basket. Then she approached the dresser.

"Stand back!" Tumtum ordered, pulling his wife away from the gate. The dresser rattled wildly on the other side of the wall as Aunt Ivy turned out the drawers and the cupboards. "Come out!" they heard her mutter. "Come out, you little vermin! I'll show you what happens to mice who wear tweed suits!"

The Nutmouses trembled. If she moved the dresser away from the wall, she would discover the door to the broom cupboard, and she would discover Nutmouse Hall!

"Oh, Tumtum!" Nutmeg said weakly. "What are we to do?"

Tumtum squeezed her paw very tightly. Then the rattling stopped, and there was a sudden glare of light. Aunt Ivy was on her knees, shining a flashlight under the dresser. She was so close they could feel her warm breath blowing around their legs—it smelled of coffee.

The light beam shone back and forth, then rested on the gates. (They were rather fancy gates, similar to the sort one sees in parks, but of course on a much smaller scale.) The beam lingered there awhile, then a red fingernail reached out and poked the bars.

The mice jumped back into the shadows, sweating with fear. Tumtum thought of the tiny iron plaque on the gatepost saying Nutmouse Hall and wondered if Aunt Ivy's eyes would be strong enough to read it.

At that moment, Mr. Mildew came into the kitchen. "Walter, what's this?" Aunt Ivy asked crossly. "Come and have a look!"

Mr. Mildew approached her, and she handed him the flashlight. "Under here!" she said, getting up to make way for him. "What's that metal grille down there?"

Sighing, Mr. Mildew got down on his knees and peered under the dresser. He shone the flashlight about for a moment, then stood up again.

"I've no idea," he said, sounding preoccupied. "A ventilation hole, I suppose. Or maybe it's something to do with the sewage. I think there used to be a lavatory down here once, before I moved in."

"*Eugh!*" Aunt Ivy said, shuddering. They heard her go to the sink and wash her hands. "We'll have to get Pest Persecutors to take up the floorboards, like they're doing at my house," she said.

"I am *NOT* having my floorboards taken up just because you think you've seen a mouse wearing clothes," Mr. Mildew

replied, sounding quite unusually emphatic. "This house is quite chaotic enough as it is." Aunt Ivy huffed and stomped off to the other side of the room to dig about in the ironing pile.

As they heard her retreat, the Nutmouses felt quite weak with relief. "Come on, Nutmeg, we're safe for now," Tumtum said, and led her back indoors to Nutmouse Hall. Nutmeg made a fresh pot of tea, and they needed several cups each to calm their nerves.

The morning had started off much better for Arthur and Lucy, for they of course had woken up to find the money on their dresser. Arthur thought they should spend it all on sweets, but Lucy thought they should save it, in case their father's money ran out altogether.

"If he doesn't make his crumb-gobbling mouse work soon there'll be nothing left for us to live on at all," she said gravely. "I heard him telling Aunt Ivy so. So we should keep the money in case we need it to buy basic things, like bread." Lucy had read a book in which a very poor family lived off bread for a whole month, and she was fully expecting that the Mildew family might soon have to do the same. She'd even cut a recipe for whole grain rolls out of an old newspaper magazine.

"Of course he'll make the mouse work," said Arthur, who tried very hard never to lose faith in his father. "And besides, if he doesn't make it work, then this money is hardly going to stop us all from starving. So we should go ahead and buy sweets while we can."

This might have turned into an argument, but at that moment the children heard a splintering crash coming from the ground floor. They dashed downstairs, wondering what it could be. And when they peered around the living room door, they found their aunt dragging the old oak chest away from the wall. A china lamp had fallen off it and lay smashed to pieces on the floor.

"What are you doing?" Arthur asked.

"Looking for mice," she said sourly. "It's more than my poor nerves can stand. I came all the way from Scotland because I've got mice there, only to find that this place is infested with them.

And yours are different than the ones in Scotland," she added accusingly. "Yours wear clothes!"

"Clothes?" Lucy asked incredulously.

"Yes, clothes!" Aunt Ivy snapped. "I've seen two of the vermin so far, parading around in suits and aprons as though they owned the place. But there'll be two less by the time I'm through."

Lucy looked at her intently, wondering if her aunt were mad after all—she and Arthur had sometimes thought that she might be. "Mice don't wear clothes, Aunt Ivy," she said firmly.

Aunt Ivy hated being contradicted, so this made her feel even snappier. She had had a frustrating morning, and now she wanted to take it out on someone. Looking up, she saw that Lucy was holding a five-pound note.

"Who gave you that?" she asked; her voice had a distinct taunt to it.

"A friend," Lucy said—and it was true, for Nutmeg was a friend, but she could still feel herself going red. Her aunt was eyeing her coldly, almost accusingly.

"Well, you must have very good friends," she said with a sneer. "Creeping into the house and giving you five-pound notes! My foot!"

Lucy looked at her aghast. The implication was quite clear. If Aunt Ivy didn't believe they'd been given the money, then she must think they'd stolen it. But that was a dreadful thing to suggest! And quite unfair!

Lucy was about to turn on her heel and march out of the room, which was what she always did when anyone was being horrible at school—she'd last done it when one of the girls in her class had said that Mr. Mildew looked like a tramp. She found walking away to be much better than getting angry—it left her with the agreeable feeling of having the upper hand.

But Arthur was not so restrained, and Aunt Ivy's accusatory tone was making him feel all hot and tickly with indignation.

"It *was* given to us by a friend!" he said furiously, his voice quivering.

"And does this mysterious friend have a name?" his aunt asked spitefully.

"Yes!" Arthur replied impetuously, almost shouting. "Her

name's Nutmeg! And she's a fairy! She's a Fairy of Sorts and she comes and gives us things all the time. And she tidies our clothes and mends the roof, and cleans the sink, and we feed her in Lucy's dollhouse, and—"

"Arthur!" Lucy said warningly, and then he stopped. But they both knew he had done something awful. Nutmeg had said the magic would not work if he told anyone else about her, and now, of all the dreadful people in the world, he had told Aunt Ivy!

And she was looking at him very beadily. "You feed this little friend—I mean, fairy?" she asked eagerly, struggling to sound friendly, which had never come naturally to her. She no longer cared about the money—this was much more interesting. "What do you feed it with?"

"Nothing," Arthur mumbled, deciding that he had given away quite enough secrets as it was. But Aunt Ivy's mind had started to whirr. Lucy looked at her with a very grown-up, withering expression, then she took her brother by the hand and led him away.

Much later, when the children were outdoors, Aunt Ivy snuck up to the attic to investigate. The ceiling sloped down on both sides, too low for a grown-up to stand up under, so she had to crawl across the room on her knees.

She made straight for the dollhouse. Kneeling down, she peered through its kitchen window and saw the little plate, piled with biscuit crumbs. Then she pressed her nose to the living room window and saw the mouse hairs on the sofa, and she looked in an upstairs window and saw more mouse hairs on the bed.

Ha! she thought. *Fairies, indeed! As I thought, those idiotic children have been feeding mice! And the cheeky little vermin must have been cavorting around in the dolls' clothes!*

Aunt Ivy knelt there, wondering what to do. As long as there was food lying around, the mice were bound to return, so this was clearly the place to snare them. But if she put down a mousetrap, Lucy might remove it. Something more subtle was called for.

Aunt Ivy sat and gnawed her lips for a moment, and then she had an especially nasty idea. *Poison!* she thought cruelly.

Tonight, when Arthur and Lucy have gone to bed, I'll creep back up here and put mouse poison in the dollhouse!

Now mouse poison is a brutal thing, which can take a mouse quite unawares. At first, he does not even realize he is eating it, then it starts burning horribly at his insides, and if he swallows enough there is little chance of recovery, however good his doctor.

Aunt Ivy knew how vicious it was, which is why she thought it was such a good idea. Feeling very pleased with herself, she hurried downstairs, wrapped herself in a long black coat, and went outdoors. She turned left out of the cottage gate and walked purposefully down the snowbound lane, past the duck pond and the war memorial, until she came to the village shop.

As she entered, Arthur and Lucy were just coming out— after all the upset of the morning, Lucy had agreed that they should spend all the money on sweets, after all. But Aunt Ivy did not appear to notice them; there was a strange glint in her eye.

Behind the counter, the shopkeeper, Mrs. Paterson, was slowly replacing the lid on a big glass jar of gumdrops.

"Do you stock mouse poison?" Aunt Ivy asked tartly, glaring at her.

Mrs. Paterson sighed. She did not approve of mouse poison, but she prided herself on stocking everything. She bent her head and started digging in a deep, wooden drawer beneath the till.

"I don't think we do, Mrs. Mildew," she said. "I certainly haven't ordered any myself and—oh!"

Mrs. Paterson stood up again, holding a small red sachet. "You're in luck, love. We've one packet left."

Aunt Ivy paid for it hurriedly and tucked it into her pocket. Then she walked back to Rose Cottage with a skip in her step.

That evening, she bided her time until ten o'clock, then picked up the flashlight from the hall table, kicked off her shoes, and crept upstairs to the attic. As she poked her head over the top step, she could hear Arthur and Lucy breathing deeply, fast asleep. She slithered onto the floor and crawled over to the dollhouse.

She shone her flashlight through its kitchen window and saw the plate of crumbs on the table. Then she reached into the pocket of her skirt and retrieved the crumpled sachet of poison. Tearing off a corner with her teeth, she wriggled her thin hand through the dollhouse window and released a sprinkling of the pale powder onto the plate, mixing it into the crumbs with a long red fingernail.

There'll be two very sick fairies in the morning! she thought nastily, turning off the flashlight.

Chapter Six

The Nutmouses spent the day in Nutmouse Hall, lying low. Nutmeg polished the great oak staircase, which took her mind off things a little, and Tumtum dozed in the library, which took his mind off things, too. Then there was game pie for supper, and afterward Tumtum read Nutmeg an article in the *Mouse Times*, about lady mice in London having their fur dyed blond. It made her laugh so much that she got hiccups.

"Oh, Tumtum!" she said, dabbing her eyes with a handkerchief. "Oh, I do feel so much better! After all, things could be much worse. Aunt Ivy might have moved the dresser, and that really would have been the end of Nutmouse Hall!"

"Quite so," Tumtum agreed. "She's had a good poke around at our gates, and she obviously didn't realize what they were. Our sign must have been too small for her to read. I doubt she'll look under the dresser again. By tomorrow the whole thing will probably have blown over."

Feeling much more cheerful, Nutmeg settled down to some knitting, and Tumtum decided to read some more of the novel he was in the middle of, which was about pirate mice on the River Thames.

He got up to find his jacket, knowing the book to be in its pocket. But he looked in the library, and the hall, and the gun room, and the bedroom, and the bathroom, and the dressing room, and the living room, and the ballroom, and the billiard room, and every other room, and the jacket wasn't there.

That's odd, he thought, trying to remember where he had last had it. Then he struck a paw to his forehead. *Oh, dear!* He'd taken it off last night while they were having their midnight feast in the dollhouse. He would have to go back for it, as it had his wallet in it, as well as his snuff box. He returned to the kitchen, looking rather sheepish.

"I must go tonight, Nutmeg," he said. "If the children find it, they might take things out of the pockets."

Nutmeg looked at him anxiously. "But what if Aunt Ivy's still on the prowl?" she said.

"If I keep in the shadows she won't see me," Tumtum replied. "I'll be there and back in five minutes."

"*We* will be there and back in five minutes," Nutmeg said firmly, for she was not letting her husband out on his own. Tumtum would have argued, but he saw his wife's expression and knew there was no point.

At eleven o'clock, the mice set out. After the dramatic morning, a peace had descended on Rose Cottage. The lights were off and nothing was stirring; when they reached the hall they could hear the sound of Aunt Ivy's soft snoring carrying through the living room door.

Tumtum was carrying a strong flashlight, so as to avoid the mousetraps. As well as the two in the kitchen, they passed one in the hall and three on the upstairs landing.

Nutmeg looked at them contemptuously; she wanted to attach a rude note to one, but Tumtum wouldn't let her.

When they got up to the attic the children were deeply asleep. On entering the dollhouse, Tumtum found his jacket where he had left it hanging on the wooden peg on the back of the kitchen door. He put it on hurriedly, patting the pockets to make sure everything was still in place. An instinct told him to go straight back to Nutmouse Hall, but Nutmeg was looking longingly at her mop and pail.

"Oh, Tumtum! Aunt Ivy's fast asleep, so surely there can't be any harm in my doing one or two little chores, now we're here?"

Tumtum looked uneasy. There was no knowing when Aunt Ivy might wake up. And given her mood this morning, he felt that this was no time for them to be at large. But Nutmeg was so eager, he hadn't the heart to drag her away.

"Oh, come on, Tumtum!" she said, seeing him hesitate. "Aunt Ivy never comes up here! Anyway, I won't be long. I'll just mop Lucy's shoes and dust the bedside tables and darn a sock or two." She tightened her apron strings behind her back and fetched the mop and pail from behind the door. "You sit down and have a little something to eat," she said bossily.

Tumtum weakened. The thought of a little something to eat always mellowed him. He scrutinized the meal left out on the kitchen table of the dollhouse. It wasn't the usual old short-bread—tonight the crumbs were brown and creamy, quite different. He sniffed the plate, and his face lit up. "It's chocolate, dear!" he said delightedly. "They must have bought it with the money we gave them!"

There were few things Tumtum loved more in the world than chocolate. But since Nutmeg worried that it made him fat, she seldom allowed him any. "Are you sure you won't join me, dear?" he asked, licking his lips greedily.

"No, no, Tumtum," she said. "You sit down and eat, and I'll get on with things." Then she happily scurried off to start scrubbing.

Tumtum sat down at the dollhouse table, where the place had been laid. Then he took his novel out of his jacket pocket, put on his spectacles, and opened it in the middle of chapter seven, where his bookmark was. He didn't know what he was looking forward to more—tasting chocolate again, or finding out what happened when the pirate mice stormed the water rats' barge.

He decided to do both things at once. He laid the book on the table by his place and started to read. . . .

No sooner had the first cannonball struck, than the pirates surged forth over the side of the rats' battered vessel, their pistols firing wildly. . . .

Engrossed, Tumtum reached a paw toward the plate. Then he raised a great dollop of chocolaty crumbs toward his lips. . . .

The rats' captain was below deck, distributing muskets among his petty officers. "God be with you, rats," he said as they heard a second cannonball tear into the rigging. . . .

He swallowed a mouthful of crumbs, then automatically reached out for more.

Captain Rattle crossed himself and led his men toward the burning deck. . . .

Tumtum raised his paw back to his mouth and bolted down more of the chocolate, but this time he noticed that it tasted odd. Then, quite suddenly, his arms started to shake, and he saw his book drop to the floor. He was feeling very, very strange.

Chapter Seven

Tumtum could feel a violent, tearing pain in his stomach, as though he had swallowed a piece of barbed wire. Then his head began to pound, as if a hammer were being knocked back and forth inside his skull. And then he began to choke.

Nutmeg was on the top of the dresser when she heard the sudden explosion of spluttering and gulping, and it gave her such a start she knocked over her pail of soapy water. She jumped to the floor like a cricket and hurtled into the dollhouse to her husband's side.

Tumtum's face was purple and blotchy. There was sweat streaming from his brow, and his hands were tearing frantically at his tie. He was shaking, and his breath was coming in painful spasms. Nutmeg started thumping him on the back, and pressed a glass of water to his lips. "P—p— poison, Nutmeg," he whispered, pointing toward the fateful plate of chocolate. "Mouse p— " Then his voice was swallowed by another violent fit of spluttering.

Nutmeg felt a deep dread stabbing through her. *Mouse poison! It can't be!* she thought wildly, for she knew there was no worse horror.

The coughing finally subsided, and Tumtum slumped exhausted in his chair. He raised his face weakly toward the children's beds. "Why would they have done this to us, Nutmeg?" he asked gently. "Surely we never did them any harm." Then his eyes became lusterless, and the lids drooped.

Nutmeg knew she must get him back to Nutmouse Hall at once before he lost consciousness. She put an arm beneath his shoulders and raised him to his feet. "Come on, Tumtum!" she urged, trying to keep the panic out of her voice. "We must get you home. You'll feel better once you're tucked up in bed."

But all the while, Nutmeg's mind was racing. The nearest mouse doctor, Dr. Goodmouse, lived nearly two miles away in the next village. You had to cross a ford and then climb a very steep hill to get there. It was a hard enough journey in fine weather, but even the fittest mouse would be reckless to undertake it in the snow. She would have taken any risk for Tumtum's sake, but if she perished on the journey then he would have no one to look after him at all.

Besides, she knew that when it came to poison there was generally little a doctor could do. It always took several days for poison to work its way through a mouse's body, and there was no medicine that could stop its course. Some mice were violently sick for a fortnight, then went on to recover, but if Tumtum had eaten a lot of it he would be lucky to survive the week. Nutmeg prayed he had consumed only a small mouthful—but then he did so gobble his food.

Her fear deepening, she guided Tumtum inch by inch across the floor. Then she supported him as they stumbled together down the attic steps, but by the time they came

to the main stairs he was so weak that Nutmeg had to slide him down the trim wrapped in her apron, and then virtually carry him across the kitchen floor to Nutmouse Hall.

He was too exhausted to climb upstairs to his bedroom, so Nutmeg made a nest for him in the living room, on the chaise longue. He tossed and turned all night, retching into a basin and whimpering in pain. His breathing was hot and labored, and his complexion oscillated between purple and green.

Nutmeg pressed a glass of water to his lips, but he seemed unable to swallow.

Watching his livid face, she felt a cold tremor going down her spine. She knew then that she wouldn't mind if Tumtum never fully recovered; she wouldn't mind if he was an invalid, and if she had to nurse him for the rest of his life. But she knew she couldn't face him dying.

"You're going to be all right, Tumtum," she kept saying to him, but she didn't feel at all sure.

For the next five days, Nutmeg barely left her husband's

bedside. His condition showed no signs of improving, and any glimmers of hope were short-lived. On Sunday afternoon, his temperature suddenly went down; but by midnight it was up again, higher than before. On Monday morning he managed to eat a few mouthfuls of dry toast and to swallow some milk; but then he was terribly sick, and for the next two days he didn't eat anything at all.

For most of the time, he was delirious. One morning he asked Nutmeg to send a telegram to his mother, who had died before they were married. And the next evening he suddenly sat up and hurled a glass across the room, shouting, "Out! Out!" as if he imagined someone to have broken in.

Nutmeg had never seen him like this. Tumtum was usually such a calm, mellow mouse, and she found his fits terribly unnerving. The anxiety was taking its toll on her, and by the fifth day of Tumtum's illness she had lost nearly half an ounce in weight—almost as much as he had. That evening, she tried to eat some bread and cheese, but her stomach was in knots and she found she could barely swallow.

As the hours ticked by, Nutmeg started to brood,

clutching her husband's paw. She couldn't stop thinking of the children's betrayal. How could they have done something so dreadful? What had she and Tumtum done to incur such hatred? *All we did was to try and make the attic more comfortable*, she thought mournfully. *Surely they couldn't have objected to that?*

Somehow, Nutmeg suspected that Aunt Ivy must have something to do with it, and yet Aunt Ivy could never have known that she and Tumtum were making use of the doll-house unless the children had told her so—and why would they do that?

Nutmeg felt quite weak trying to make sense of it all. Since adopting Arthur and Lucy she had felt for the first time that her family was complete, and the thought that they had turned on her made her feel quite brokenhearted. Since Tumtum had been taken ill, all the excitement and bustle had gone out of her; she was quite a different mouse from what she'd been before.

The night stole away, and still she brooded, feeling too overwrought to sleep. *If only I had some sewing to do*, she thought longingly, for sewing always took her mind off things. But she had left her sewing basket in the dollhouse. She looked at her watch—it was after midnight. *Everyone will be fast asleep*, she thought. *I don't suppose there can be any harm in going to get it.*

At once feeling a little better for having a sense of purpose, she fetched the flashlight from the kitchen and went to the front gate. The cottage was dark and still; no one was stirring. She crept through the kitchen and into the hall, then cocked an ear at the living room door and heard Aunt Ivy snoring. Feeling bolder, she went upstairs.

The moon was shining in the attic window, and Nutmeg could see the children's heads asleep on their pillows. A part of her longed to get close to them and to brush their hair again with her broom, and yet for the first time she felt wary.

The room looked dusty and neglected, for it was more than a week since she'd last cleaned. The dollhouse had been untouched since she and Tumtum's last visit, and it had a sad, abandoned feel to it. Tumtum's book was still on the kitchen floor where he'd dropped it, and her sewing basket was where she always left it, in the cupboard under the stairs.

I must get straight home, she thought, tucking the basket over her arm. *If Tumtum comes to he'll wonder where I am.* She hurried out

of the dollhouse, carefully closing the front door behind her, then picked her way across the attic floor, over a pile of dirty socks.

And she was about to rush back down the steps when some instinct made her shine her flashlight up toward the dresser. And she saw a letter propped against Lucy's hairbrush. It was addressed to Nutmeg.

Nervous it might be another trap, Nutmeg climbed up a pair of blue tights that was tumbling from the top drawer and went to investigate. She looked anxiously toward the children's beds, then unfolded the letter, spreading it out flat on the dresser. The writing was so big she had to take a step back in order to read it.

Dear Nutmeg,

We have missed you so much, please come back. Arthur is very sorry that he told Aunt Ivy about how you visit us, and how we leave you supper in the dollhouse, but he only said it by mistake. And he wouldn't have said it if he thought it would make you vanish.

We wish you could come back and make Aunt Ivy vanish instead.

Love,

Arthur and Lucy

Nutmeg read it once, then she read it again, and then she felt so overcome she had to sit down on the handle of Lucy's hairbrush to compose herself. At last, everything fell into place. If poor, impetuous Arthur had told Aunt Ivy that a fairy came and ate crumbs in the dollhouse, then she might reasonably have suspected that his fairy was one of the mice she had seen on the landing. And then she must have crept up here at night with murderous intent.

Nutmeg felt a great rush of relief as she realized that the children hadn't betrayed them after all. *Oh, bless them, bless them!* she thought. *I knew that dreadful woman must have been behind it all!* She was anxious to get back to Tumtum, but she knew she must leave a reply. There was a red pencil lying on the far side of the dresser. She picked it up and held it with both arms, steadying it against her chest as she scrawled a hurried note on the back of the children's letter:

Dear Arthur and Lucy,

Please do not think I have abandoned you. Now that your aunt

knows our secret it is more difficult for me to visit, but I am still thinking of you.

    Love,

    Nutmeg

Then Nutmeg added a very defiant P.S.:

I will make Aunt Ivy vanish. I promise.

And she vowed to herself to keep that promise. *I must get rid of her*, she thought, feeling a sudden thrill of determination. *And I will get rid of her . . . but how?*

She bounced down the attic steps, ran across the landing, and slid down the banister, her mind whirring. She had magnificent visions of herself chasing a terrified Aunt Ivy down the garden path, snapping at her heels, and driving her away from Rose Cottage, never to return. In her excitement, she quite forgot that Aunt Ivy was several hundred times bigger than she was.

Nutmeg's mind was still galloping as she crossed the hall and ran under the kitchen door. It was galloping so much that she didn't notice the light had been turned on. *We'll show her who's boss!* Nutmeg thought as she sauntered jauntily across the floor. *Tumtum will get better, and then we'll let her know who owns this place!*

She skirted a patch of grease in front of the cooker, then paused to look down her nose at one of the mousetraps. She was feeling quite extraordinarily ebullient.

But then there was a shattering human scream, and in that instant, Nutmeg saw the tips of Aunt Ivy's slippers just in front of her nose, standing between her and the dresser.

Nutmeg stopped dead in her tracks. She knew Aunt Ivy would do something dreadful, yet she felt unable to move. A dark shadow slowly began to engulf her as Aunt Ivy's arm rose upward; then there was a rapid blur as a teapot came hurtling through the air toward her.

It smashed to the floor millimeters from Nutmeg's feet, sending splinters of china ricocheting all around. Senseless with panic, she hurtled right over Aunt Ivy's slippers and

ran straight under the dresser with her sewing basket swinging wildly back and forth on her arm.

Oh, what a fool I am, what a fool! she thought as she wrenched open the gates. *Now she knows where we live! She'll be back for us again! She'll pull out the dresser! She'll find Nutmouse Hall!*

No sooner had Nutmeg turned the key in the padlock than there was a fierce shaft of light. Aunt Ivy was on the floor, shining her flashlight directly on her. Nutmeg threw herself back from the gate, out of sight, but it could make little difference now. . . . Aunt Ivy knew where they lived.

Chapter Eight

Nutmeg stood shaking in the broom cupboard as Aunt Ivy pulled and heaved at the dresser. At one point, she made it lurch so far forward that all the plates fell off and smashed on the floor. Nutmeg saw a splinter of china fly through the gate, and then there was a deep thud as the dresser crashed back against the wall.

Exhausted, Aunt Ivy stood awhile, cursing under her breath. She had seen where Nutmeg went, so she was no longer in any doubt that the funny metal grid was some sort of mouse hole. She wanted to block it up so the mice would be imprisoned in their lair and slowly starve to death, but the dresser was too heavy for her to move.

She pondered awhile, then had an idea, which pleased her so much that she said it out loud. "Gas!" she announced, clapping her hands together with glee. "I'll pump poisonous gas under the dresser, straight into their filthy little hole! We'll see how they like that!" And just thinking about it made her feel much more cheerful.

On the other side of the door, Nutmeg listened in terror. "Gas! Gas!" she said to herself, quaking. She imagined clouds of foul, blue poison being pumped through the gates, curling in under the front door, and advancing through Nutmouse Hall room by room, slowly choking her and Tumtum to death.

Beside herself, she ran inside and locked the front door behind her, putting the draft excluder in place. Then she raced around each of her thirty-six rooms, upstairs and down, locking all the windows and drawing all the curtains. She found a roll of masking tape in the butler's pantry, and darted back to the hall, using it to seal around the frame of the front door.

But she knew it was hopeless—the gas would find its own way in. It would advance through the joins in the window frames; it would creep in through the pipes and belch from the taps; it would diffuse down the chimneys.

We must escape! she thought. But Tumtum was much too ill to be moved—the upheaval would kill him, even if the gas didn't.

Numb with dread, she went back to her husband's bedside. He was sleeping, and his face looked pale and sallow. All night long the distraught Nutmeg sat beside him, wondering what to do.

If only Tumtum were himself, she felt sure he would be able to think of something. But his mind was still wandering, and when he opened his eyes he appeared not to recognize her. *Oh, what is to become of us?* Nutmeg thought hopelessly. *Tumtum's delirious and Aunt Ivy might strike at any time!* She put her head in her paws and closed her eyes tight, trying to shut out the horror. Their chances of survival seemed horribly slim.

But the truth is that Aunt Ivy had no idea what sort of gas to use, nor where to buy it. The only deadly gas she knew about was cyanide, and she imagined it might be hard to come by. Like Nutmeg, Aunt Ivy spent a restless night dwelling on her difficulties, and she was still dwelling on them the next morning when she locked herself in the bathroom.

Aunt Ivy always locked herself in the bathroom for at least an hour, both in the morning and in the evening, usually at just the time everyone else wanted to use it. And she sprayed so many foul-smelling scents and deodorants on herself that whoever went in afterward had to press a flannel over their noses.

This morning she was applying something particularly revolting, a hair spray with a sweet citrusy aroma, a bit like compost. It came out in dense green clouds and it made her hair very dark and greasy, just as she liked it. When she had applied several layers, she looked at herself approvingly in the mirror, then made to throw the empty canister into the bin. But something on the label caught her eye.

DANGER! it said in big red letters. VERY TOXIC! EXCESSIVE INHALATION MAY CAUSE INJURY OR DEATH!

Aunt Ivy started to feel a delicious tingle in her spine. *Why!* she thought. *If this gas could kill a human, then it shouldn't*

be too hard to kill a couple of mice with it! I'll buy some more and gas them to death tonight!

Then she got dressed much more quickly than usual and went down the lane to the village shop. When she arrived, Mrs. Paterson was behind the counter eating a thick piece of toast. There was butter dribbling down her apron.

"Did the mouse poison do the job, Mrs. Mildew?" she asked good-naturedly.

Aunt Ivy did not appear to hear. "Do you have any more of these?" she asked briskly, slamming the empty hair spray down beside the till. "I bought it here last week." As Aunt Ivy leaned toward her, Mrs. Paterson picked up a foul, toxic smell, almost like a gas leak. It made her feel quite queasy.

"Sorry," she said, wrinkling her nose. "I've none in stock. Next delivery comes at noon on Saturday."

Aunt Ivy leaned forward on the counter and looked at her piercingly. "Reserve me two canisters," she demanded icily—but then, as Mrs. Paterson wrote down the order, Aunt Ivy started to wonder whether two canisters would be enough. There might be more mice than the ones she'd seen—they might have brothers and sisters, and aunts and uncles . . . they might have bred! "On second thought, make that five," she said grimly. Then she stomped back outside, knocking over a pile of newspapers.

Chapter Nine

Nutmeg waited all that day braced for a gas attack, but none came. And yet she felt sure that Aunt Ivy would strike soon.

All the while, the promise she had made to the children rang around and around in her head. *I will get rid of Aunt Ivy. I will. I will. I* will. And now she knew that she must—if she could only think how.

By tea time (which had become a meaningless time, since Tumtum was too weak to eat, and Nutmeg too nervous), she could bear it no longer. If she didn't do something soon, she felt she would go mad.

"Oh, Tumtum! We can't just sit here waiting to be gassed by that dreadful woman," she said, anxiously rearranging his blankets. He was sleeping, and much too ill to follow what she was saying, but talking out loud made her feel better all the same. "We must get rid of her. Oh, I wish I knew how!"

As Nutmeg was musing, Tumtum slowly raised one eyelid, then another, then he turned his hollow face toward her. His eyes were sunken deep in their sockets. "Fetch General Marchmouse," he whispered hoarsely, his lips barely moving. Then his eyelids at once drooped shut again.

"General Marchmouse!" Nutmeg exclaimed delightedly, clutching her husband's paw as he slipped back out of consciousness. "Oh, why didn't I think of him before? Oh, Tumtum, you are so clever!"

It was the first sense he had made all week, and Nutmeg wondered if he'd been talking in his sleep, but it was an ingenious idea all the same because just repeating the General's name made her feel a warm glow about her. He was considered to be one of the great military geniuses of the age, and in the past he had delivered the village mice from all manner of threats. He once saw off a rabble of looting rats from the granary, even though they outnumbered his mouse soldiers by three to one. After that the *Mouse Times* described him as "undefeatable," and that was the general view.

He had retired from the army a few months ago and was by no means in the first flush of youth, but every mouse still had great faith in him. *I suppose he's never gone to war with a human before*, Nutmeg thought, feeling a flicker of apprehension. "But anyway," she said to herself firmly, "if anyone can save us, then General Marchmouse can." She decided to go and consult him immediately while Tumtum was sleeping. She kissed him on the nose, then ran to the kitchen and flung on her cape.

The General and his wife lived in a disused gun cupboard in the Manor House, which was owned by an elderly human couple called Mr. and Mrs. Stirrup. The Manor House was just beyond Rose Cottage, on the edge of the village. Nutmeg knew the route well, for she and Tumtum had often dined with the Marchmouses in happier times. Even allowing for the snow she reckoned she could be there and back within an hour.

But as she went to let herself out of the front gates, she heard voices carrying from the kitchen. It was Aunt Ivy and Mr. Mildew, discussing *them*.

"I saw one of them with my own eyes, Walter, disappearing under there." Peering out through the gate, Nutmeg could just see the tip of Aunt Ivy's finger, pointing toward the dresser. "They've got a nest somewhere behind that metal grill."

"Hmmm, that's possible," Mr. Mildew said, sounding preoccupied. The only mouse he was interested in was the battery-operated crumb-gobbler he was inventing. The department store that had once sold his grape-peelers wanted to stock it, so if he could only get it working, it might make him rich again. But he'd been battling with the digestive system for weeks now, and the mouse was still throwing everything up. It was all giving Mr. Mildew the most dreadful headache.

"Can't you help me move the dresser, Walter, so I can get a closer look?" Ivy whined.

Nutmeg stood behind the broom cupboard door, holding her breath.

"No, Ivy," Mr. Mildew replied firmly. "That dresser weighs a ton. It hasn't been moved for years, and I'm not going to break my back just because you think you've seen a couple of mice wearing aprons."

"They weren't *both* wearing aprons—one was in a tweed suit," she retorted crossly. "Anyway, I'll be getting rid of them on Saturday."

"Will you?" Mr. Mildew said vaguely.

"Yes," she replied mysteriously. "Saturday at noon. When my gas supplies arrive!"

"Oh, *really*, Ivy," Mr. Mildew said, picking up his cup of coffee and making for the door. "I've never heard such nonsense."

"I'm going to wipe them out with a toxic hair spray!" she called after him as he went upstairs. "One whiff of that and they'll choke instantly!" Mr. Mildew was no longer listening, but Nutmeg had heard every word.

Saturday at noon! she thought, her pulse racing. *That's the day after tomorrow!* She let herself out of the gates, then belted across the kitchen floor while Aunt Ivy's back was turned, reckless with urgency.

Nutmeg hurtled under the door into the garden. It was a beautiful afternoon; there was no wind, and the snow was shining pink in the twilight. She ran along the edge of the lawn under the cover of the hedge, and then crossed into the Manor House garden. She took her usual route through the apple orchard, into the vegetable patch, over the potato beds, under the lean-to of wintering sweet peas, then up the clematis on the side of the house, and indoors through the broken windowpane in the downstairs cloakroom.

From the sill, she dropped down onto the toilet seat and then to the floor. She crept to the door and poked her nose out into the long, tiled corridor. It had just been bleached, and the fumes made her eyes water. The door to the kitchen opposite was ajar and she could see the two Manor House Labradors curled up asleep together in their basket. When General Marchmouse had first moved in, the dogs had been notoriously ill-mannered and had growled and snapped at the General's dinner guests. But the General had bashed the dogs both on the nose with his rifle, and now they were said to be more docile.

Even so, the sight of them made Nutmeg uneasy.

So she tiptoed past the kitchen door and then ran down the corridor as fast as she could, skidding and scuttling on the polished tiles, until she finally came to the gun room, which was the last door on the right.

The gun cupboard was a handsome oak chest, nearly six feet tall. There were no guns in it now, as Mr. Stirrup had given up shooting when his eyesight started to fail, so the Marchmouses had the whole cupboard to themselves. *Thank goodness, they're at home!* Nutmeg thought, seeing the light from inside glinting out of the keyhole. She crept around to the back of the cupboard where the Marchmouses had carved out their front door.

It was the General who opened it, wearing a blue and white striped apron. He was holding a rolling pin and looked flustered. His face was red; and his whiskers were covered with flour.

"Mrs. Nutmouse!" he said delightedly. "Come in, come in! What a nice surprise!" He drew her into the hall. There were spears and shields hanging on the wall, and above the fire there was a glass cabinet containing a stuffed cockroach that the General had shot himself. He propelled her through to the kitchen, where his wife was whisking eggs; she looked flustered, too. "We're expecting eleven of my brother officers for dinner," the General explained importantly, "and I'm in command of the fish pie."

He sat Nutmeg down at the kitchen table and started debriefing her as to his recipe. "Salmon, cod, king prawns, nutmeg, mature cheddar, a sprinkling of salt and pepper . . ." On he boasted, hardly seeming to notice Nutmeg's distraught expression.

But Mrs. Marchmouse saw it at once. "Hush, darling," she urged her husband. "Mrs. Nutmouse has something to tell us."

The General finally drew breath, and Nutmeg was able to let the whole dreadful story tumble out. Tripping over her words in haste, she told them how Tumtum was lying at home delirious and poisoned, and about the dastardly Aunt Ivy and how she was plotting a gas attack at noon on Saturday. And Nutmeg told them of her fears that in Tumtum's present condition even the slightest whiff of one of Aunt Ivy's grotesque hair sprays might kill him.

Listening to the drama, Mrs. Marchmouse's eyes glazed with horror while the General's eyes began to blaze. *An*

adventure! he thought, feeling his heart stir. The General was a mouse who lived for adventures. They were his lifeblood, his first love, and since retiring from the army he had found them surprisingly hard to come by. *What luck!* he thought as Nutmeg finished her terrifying tale. *A war zone just next door, in Rose Cottage!* In his mind, he could already hear the thud of the cannonballs and smell the gunpowder.

"Oh, General Marchmouse—do . . . do you think you could help us?" Nutmeg asked plaintively.

"Oh, yes, Mrs. Nutmouse!" the General said heartily. "I shall assemble an army to repel her. We shall fight from the beams, we shall fight from the rafters! We shall hurl hand grenades from coffee cups, we shall fire machine guns from the fruit bowl! We shall never surrender!" Then he thumped his rolling pin down on the table with a mighty crash.

Nutmeg felt very reassured. He sounded like a mouse who meant business.

Chapter Ten

The General had never taken on a human before and, for all his high spirits, he knew he had quite a fight on his hands. Now that he was retired he kept little ammunition about him, and he would be hard-pressed to get hold of any more at such short notice.

And even if he could, he suspected it would be of little use. The Royal Mouse Army's guns would be much too small to wound a human—a whole round of machine-gun fire would barely even scratch an adult's skin.

If he were to launch a sustained attack on the Rose Cottage living room with bombs and hand grenades and cannons, he could probably send the enemy's bed up in smoke. But then the whole cottage might burn down, and Nutmouse Hall with it.

That would not do at all, the General thought sensibly, scratching his forehead with a floury paw. *This will require a much more subtle strategy*. He decided to consult his eleven brother officers when they arrived for dinner. They were all army veterans like himself, and between them they would be sure to come up with something.

"You are in safe hands, Mrs. Nutmouse," he said reassuringly. "My colleagues and I have fought mightier enemies than this one." He could not actually think of any, but nonetheless. "Now you run along home to your husband, and we will all discuss the crisis over dinner," he said, patting her shoulder. "And after pudding and port, we will proceed to Nutmouse Hall and set up our military headquarters in the library. Leave your front gates unlocked so we can come straight in.

"And you, Poppet," he said, turning to his wife. "You will accompany us to the Hall and assist Mrs. Nutmouse with the catering. We will bring as much food as we can muster—we must be prepared for a siege."

"Is that clear, ladies?" he asked when he had outlined the plan.

"Oh, yes," they chorused, for the General always spoke clearly.

"Good," he said. "Now, synchronize watches. It is just gone twenty-eight minutes before seventeen hundred hours. Mrs. Nutmouse, you can expect us to arrive at twenty-one hundred hours precisely."

In actual fact, by the time General Marchmouse and his party trooped through the gates of Nutmouse Hall, it was nearly ten o'clock. (Dinner had been later than expected, as the General had forgotten to turn the oven on.) Each mouse was dressed in his red and green military uniform, and carrying a big canvas kit bag and an assortment of ammunition.

General Marchmouse was the most generously armed. He had a pistol in a holster on his belt and a long string of grenades looped around his chest. Another officer, a peppery gray mouse called Colonel Acorn, was carrying a sword in a silver scabbard encrusted with little red jewels. Mrs. Marchmouse was

bringing up the rear, trundling a smart shopping trolley that her husband had made for her out of one of Mr. Stirrup's matchboxes. He'd painted the box blue, and for the wheels he'd used two big yellow buttons borrowed from Mrs. Stirrup's sewing basket.

The trolley was full of provisions—there was bread, butter, milk, eggs, the remains of the fish pie, a cold leg of lamb, a tin of shortbread, two dozen freshly baked scones, and a chocolate cake with crystallized cherries on it. There were also some cans of peaches and pineapples, and a box of strawberry creams.

"Did you have any trouble getting across the kitchen?" Nutmeg inquired, taking their coats in the hall.

"No trouble at all," the General said breezily. "The enemy is lying low." Nutmeg felt a pang of unease at hearing him sound so jaunty; she knew Aunt Ivy wouldn't lie low for long.

Mrs. Marchmouse disappeared into the kitchen while Nutmeg led the men to the library. They swiftly took the place over. General Marchmouse hung a sign saying WAR ROOM on the door, and

then the officers started rearranging the furniture. The sofas and chairs were all pushed back against the wall, and Tumtum's desk was pulled into the middle of the room and covered with toy soldiers. Then the General and his officers started shuffling the soldiers back and forth and helping themselves to Tumtum's cigars.

They were enjoying themselves immensely. It was just like old times, when they had all been in barracks together. But as Nutmeg bustled in and out of the library bearing trays of cake and cocoa, she felt more and more agitated. The night was stealing away, and Tumtum was tossing feverishly on his chaise longue, his health still in grave danger; but the officers in whom she had placed such faith were behaving as though they were on vacation.

"General Marchmouse, what is your plan of attack?" she asked as she cleared away a third round of refreshments.

The General looked slightly put out at this question, because the truth is he had no plan at all. Fighting moles and rats was one thing, but a human enemy required a wholly different strategy. And though he and his brother officers had racked their brains all through dinner, they hadn't come up with one.

As a result, the General felt as though he was on the defensive, and it was a position he disliked. "I am not at liberty to divulge tactics, Mrs. Nutmouse," he said pompously, puffing his chest.

"Oh, of course, I quite understand, General," Nutmeg replied tactfully, taking away his empty mug. "Well, anyway, I'll be in the living room, tending to Mr. Nutmouse, if you need me." General Marchmouse huffed dismissively, but his brow was furrowed. Mrs. Nutmouse was only a housewife, of course, but it occurred to him that perhaps he should have consulted her. After all, she knew more about Aunt Ivy than he did.

"One minute, please, Mrs. Nutmouse," he called after her as she made for the door. "You may be able to assist us, after all."

The General swept a pile of maps off the sofa, and Nutmeg sat down, balancing her tray on her lap. "We are building up a profile of the enemy, Mrs. Nutmouse," he said, standing over her. He was speaking very slowly, for he imagined that Mrs. Nutmouse might find this sort of talk hard to understand.

"We are drawing up a list of her weak points," he continued.

"The things that might frighten her, you understand, the areas in which she might be most vulnerable to attack. I just wondered, Mrs. Nutmouse, if you happened to know of some?" The General looked down at Nutmeg eagerly, for he hadn't been able to think of any himself.

Nutmeg thought very hard. Weak points? Somehow she had never thought of Aunt Ivy as weak. She wasn't physically weak, at any rate—you could tell from the way she had shaken the dresser about.

And what might frighten her? Nutmeg thought. *What would frighten any fully grown human? An elephant, perhaps? . . . A lion? . . . A hurricane?* She pursed her lips in concentration. It was very difficult. But then the answer suddenly dawned on her.

Of course! she thought, remembering the one thing that Aunt Ivy was very frightened of indeed. In fact, it was something she knew her to be absolutely terrified of—a terror that had been quite clear on that fateful night when Aunt Ivy had seen herself and Tumtum on the landing.

But Nutmeg was worried that the General might think her silly for suggesting it.

"Does anything spring to mind, Mrs. Nutmouse?" he asked impatiently, fingering his whiskers.

"Well, yes, there is one thing, General," she said, blushing. "She's . . . Well, it may sound strange, but—"

"Come on, now, Mrs. Nutmouse," the General urged her. "Time is precious!"

"Well, General," Nutmeg said falteringly. "The truth is . . . the truth is, Aunt Ivy is *terrified* of mice!"

The other officers all looked up in astonishment. "*Mice*, Mrs. Nutmouse?" General Marchmouse repeated, incredulous. "The enemy is afraid of *mice*? Afraid of *us*?"

"Quite so, General," Nutmeg replied. "You should have seen the commotion when she caught sight of me and Tumtum on the upstairs landing. The way she carried on, shrieking and wailing and waking the whole household. Why, you'd have thought she was more frightened of us than we were of her!"

"Were either you or your husband armed at the time, Mrs. Nutmouse?" the General asked. "Were you carrying guns, or what have you?"

"Armed?" Nutmeg repeated, astonished. "Of course not, General! What an extraordinary suggestion!"

"So why was she frightened of you?" the General asked, looking very confused.

"She just happens to be frightened of mice, General," Nutmeg replied. "Some humans are, I'm told, even fully grown ones. I suppose it might explain why they invented mousetraps."

"Hmmm." General Marchmouse was pensive. This changed everything. Forget the grenades and the pistols—the mice could frighten the enemy simply by saying "Boo!" But frightening her was one thing. Driving her away from Rose Cottage, running in terror of her life, might be harder.

General Marchmouse's brain was pounding. He was undefeatable, the *Mouse Times* had said as much, so he must think of something. Failure was not an option. Forgetting all about Nutmeg, he walked over to the desk and gathered the other officers around him. They bent their heads together and started debating earnestly, using all sorts of military mumbo jumbo that Nutmeg couldn't understand.

But as she sat watching them from the sofa, clutching her tea tray, a dazzling idea began to play itself out in her mind's eye, and it became more dazzling by the second.

"General Marchmouse," she cried abruptly, "I—"

"Just a moment please, Mrs. Nutmouse," the General said airily. "We are trying to formulate a plan."

"Well, perhaps you would like to hear my plan," Nutmeg said firmly.

They all turned to face her. "Well, fire away, then," the General said grudgingly, vowing to himself that this was the last time he'd let a woman into his War Room. He drummed his paw impatiently on the table while Nutmeg began.

"Given that Aunt Ivy is afraid of mice, General, I wonder how many mice it would take to make her leave the cottage for good. I mean, she saw Tumtum and me, and now she's determined to kill us. And if she saw all twelve of you, she would probably try to kill you, too. But suppose she were to see dozens and dozens of mice, hundreds of them, flying at her out of every nook and cranny, running all over her, digging into her hair and her clothes, going up her skirt, and under her shirt, and down her sleeves, and under her collar, and climbing up her necklace, and somersaulting from her bracelets, and swinging from her earrings . . . Well—don't you think *that* might make her flee?"

The officers stared at her admiringly, and even the General had to acknowledge that it was a first-class idea.

"A capital plan!" he said ebulliently. "We will overwhelm the enemy with numbers! We will conscript every mouse in the village who is young and fit enough to fight, and we will charge as one!" The General banged his stick on the table, feeling very pleased with himself. This might go down in the history books as his cleverest battle plan yet!

But then he caught sight of Nutmeg, and suddenly remembered that, strictly speaking, it had all been her idea. "I had been about to propose just such a strategy myself, Mrs. Nutmouse," he said chivalrously. "Thank you for prompting me."

Chapter Eleven

Arthur and Lucy had spent the day in a state of great anticipation, wondering when Nutmeg would carry out her promise to make Aunt Ivy vanish. They had no idea what method Fairies of Sorts used to get rid of aunts, but they suspected that Aunt Ivy's disappearance might prove rather dramatic.

"Do you think she'll try and frighten her away?" Arthur asked Lucy when they woke up to find Nutmeg's note on the dresser.

"I shouldn't think so," his sister replied. "Nutmeg must be much too small to frighten her. If she's going to make her vanish she'll have to do it by magic. She'll probably just wave a wand and make her disappear in a puff of smoke."

"Where would she make her go?" Arthur asked.

"Oh, I don't know," Lucy said, trying to sound more laid back about it than she felt. "If she's feeling merciful she might just magic her back home to Scotland—but perhaps there's an especially horrid place where fairies magic away all the people they don't like."

Arthur shivered. It was a terrifying thought. The children spent the day loitering downstairs, monitoring Aunt Ivy around the clock lest they miss the moment of her vanishing. They even trailed after her when she went to the village shop, but they made sure never to get too close, as they expected she might go up in smoke at any minute and they were frightened of getting singed. And yet by supper time she was still there. She spent the evening sitting at the kitchen table, filing her nails and ranting about how she was going to exterminate Rose Cottage's rodents by squirting citrus-scented hair spray under the dresser.

By the time the children climbed up the attic stairs to go to bed they were beginning to feel quite despondent. Nutmeg had had a whole day to make Aunt Ivy vanish, so why hadn't she done it? "You do think she can do it, don't you?" Arthur asked tentatively, but by now even Lucy was starting to have doubts.

It was up to the officers to carry out Nutmeg's promise, and once she had provided them with a basic plan of attack, they sat up late into the night thrashing out tactics. Shortly after midnight, the General and Colonel Acorn went to make a reconnaissance of the ground floor of the cottage, which they now referred to as "the battle zone." They sketched out detailed plans of the kitchen and the hall, then they crept into the living room while Aunt Ivy was sleeping and noted down the exact position of each bit of furniture, even the log basket. When they got back to Nutmouse Hall they pinned their maps up in the library and the General spent the next hour or so sticking red pins in them.

Mrs. Marchmouse scuttled in and out with trays of cocoa, while Nutmeg sat with Tumtum as he tossed and turned on his sickbed, with no inkling of what was going on.

It was not until the small hours of Friday morning that a final strategy was formed. General Marchmouse stood before

his officers, a bacon sandwich in hand, and ran through it point by point. It was a complicated plan, so each mouse took notes in a special Royal Mouse Army code.

At dawn, seven of the officers, led by Colonel Acorn, would leave Rose Cottage and spend the morning enlisting recruits (two hundred or thereabouts) from the village. General Marchmouse and the remaining four officers would mount guard at Nutmouse Hall, in case Aunt Ivy made any premature advances. (The plan did not specify what they would do if she did.)

The new recruits would be marched back to Nutmouse Hall by one o'clock and be divided into eleven platoons, with each platoon under the command of an officer. Then at some point during the afternoon, whenever the coast became clear, the army would march into the Rose Cottage living room and take up position.

One platoon would spread out behind the books on the bookshelf, one would lie in wait beneath the armchair, one would crawl through the tear in the sofa cover and hide in the stuffing. Another would lurk in the chimney, and another in the log basket; there would be platoons in every corner of the room, poised to attack. The General would mount guard behind the flowerpot on the mantelpiece, from where he would have a sweeping view of the battlefield.

And thus would the mice bide their time until evening, when Aunt Ivy finally retired to the living room, and started getting ready for bed. Then the General would fire his pistol, signaling the charge, and they would all race toward her together in one squealing, scrabbling, fearless stampede.

The General could not make any plans beyond that, as he did not know how Aunt Ivy would react. So he adopted a policy of hoping for the best.

"When she sees the size of our army she will run for her life," he said emphatically.

"It's a capital strategy, General!" Colonel Acorn said, raising a mug of cocoa to him. "Quite astoundingly brilliant, even by your standards!"

"Hmmm. I suppose you could argue that it's one of my more imaginative ones," agreed the General, who had by now quite forgotten that the idea owed anything to Nutmeg at all.

And yet one of the officers, a Brigadier with tousled auburn hair and smart leather boots that rose up to his knees, seemed uneasy. "One thing concerns me, General," he said. "When the enemy gets into bed, she might put her light out straightaway. Then she wouldn't be able to see us, and if you were standing on the mantelpiece, you wouldn't be able to see the platoons. We'd be fighting blind."

The General looked pensive; it was keen thinking. "Have you anything to suggest, Brigadier?"

"Well," the Brigadier said, "I suppose we could all carry candles, but they might be something of a fire hazard when the time came to charge."

"Much too dangerous," the General agreed. "We don't want to burn the cottage down."

"Why don't we dress the troops in fluorescent uniforms?" Colonel Acorn suggested.

"It's a good idea, Colonel," the General said. "But how are we going to get hold of two hundred fluorescent uniforms by tomorrow night?"

The officers considered this problem for a moment, and

none could solve it. But then the General remembered the child's bicycle he had seen propped outside Rose Cottage, by the garden door, and he pursed his lips. At that moment, he heard Nutmeg and Mrs. Marchmouse passing outside in the corridor. "Ladies! A moment, please!" he bellowed, calling them into the library.

"Mrs. Nutmouse, does either of the Mildew children possess a cycling jacket?" he asked mysteriously. "You know, the garish sort that humans wear when they cycle on the roads at night."

"Why, yes, General, Arthur has one," she said. "A fluorescent orange one, hanging on the back of the kitchen door."

"And would he miss it if we were to borrow it on a permanent basis?" the General asked.

"I shouldn't think so," Nutmeg said, trying to imagine what this was all about. "He never uses his bicycle because it has punctures in both tires."

"Good!" the General said. Then he turned to Nutmeg and Mrs. Marchmouse, looking very grave. "I need your help," he said. "If we were to retrieve that jacket, could you turn it into two hundred mouse-sized uniforms by thirteen hundred hours tomorrow afternoon?"

"Goodness!" Nutmeg said, and Mrs. Marchmouse shook her head. Two hundred uniforms by lunchtime tomorrow! It was out of the question.

She looked at her husband regretfully. "I'm sorry, darling, but even if we worked nonstop, we could probably only manage five uniforms by then. Sewing trousers and jackets isn't as easy as it looks, you know. There's the legs and the sleeves, and the hems and the cuffs, and the—"

"Yes, yes, I understand all that, Poppet," the General interrupted, even though he didn't really understand at all. "But what about something less ambitious? Armbands, let us say! Could you make two hundred fluorescent armbands by tomorrow afternoon?"

"Oh, yes!" Mrs. Marchmouse said eagerly. "We could run up two hundred armbands in no time, couldn't we, Mrs. Nutmouse?"

"Of course," Nutmeg agreed. "They wouldn't even need hemming."

"Excellent," the General cried, rubbing his hands together. Then he turned back to face the officers. "Very well, gentlemen! From now on, we shall refer to this operation as the Charge of the Bright Brigade, after that glorious human battle that took place in, er, in . . ." The General looked around, hoping someone might prompt him, but everyone looked blank. "Er, well," he said hurriedly, "in the days of Queen Victoria!"

The officers supposed the General was thinking of the Charge of the Light Brigade, which happened not to have been very glorious at all. But they did not like to contradict him, so the Charge of the Bright Brigade is how the operation became known.

"The Charge of the Bright Brigade!" Colonel Acorn cried, raising his sword in the air. And then all the other mice cried it, too, except for Nutmeg, who had already dashed off to find her sewing basket.

The cycling jacket had been left on a coat peg, high up on the kitchen door, but the officers managed to reach it by climbing up the strings of an apron that had been hung beside it. Then they teased it off the peg and dragged it back under the dresser. Colonel Acorn used his sword to cut it into little pieces, small enough to fit through the Nutmouses' front gates, then they carried all the fragments into the living room of Nutmouse Hall, where Nutmeg and Mrs. Marchmouse got to work with their scissors.

The lady mice worked without pause, sitting by Tumtum's bedside. How Nutmeg longed to shake Tumtum awake and tell him that General Marchmouse was going to rouse a whole army to save him, but he was much too weak to take such excitements on board.

Some of the officers managed to grab a few hours of sleep during what remained of the night, stretched out on soft leather chairs in the library, but at the first hint of dawn the hustle and bustle began. Colonel Acorn and his party set off for the village to round up the troops, and the other officers waited tensely for their return, pacing back and forth in the War Room.

As the minutes ticked by, the atmosphere in Nutmouse Hall thickened. By the time the living room clock struck one,

Mrs. Marchmouse and Nutmeg had assembled some two hundred twenty or so armbands (they ran up a few extra ones for good measure), but Colonel Acorn had not come back. And by the time the clock struck two, General Marchmouse had shuffled his toy soldiers back and forth so many times that his eyes were beginning to boggle, and still there was no sign of the troops.

Finally, at ten past three, the officers heard a loud commotion outside. The General straightened his beret and marched out of the front door toward the gates. And through them he saw a great rabble of troops, their cold noses glinting softly in the gloom beneath the dresser. He tried to count them, but couldn't. There were scores, hundreds of them, a multitude of excited, jabbering rodents.

The General peered eagerly into the crowd, picking out faces. There was the baker, armed with a rolling pin! There was the fireman, carrying his hose! There were the school mice, brandishing water pistols! And there was the police mouse with his club! The whole village had turned out on Tumtum's behalf.

It's an army! the General thought ecstatically. *It's an infestation! And I, the undefeatable General Marchmouse, am in sole command!*

"Hello, there, General," Colonel Acorn cried, pressing his nose through the gate. "Quite a crowd we whipped up this morning, two hundred and three at last count. Sorry we couldn't get back earlier, but that Mildew fellow was loitering about in the kitchen, burning toast by the smell of it, and we had to wait ages before it was safe to march everyone across."

"Good work, Colonel," the General replied, brusquely pulling open the gates. The officers came through first, then the village mice surged after them, chattering raucously. They were herded into Nutmouse Hall, then straight through to the ball-room where they were divided into platoons and each allocated an armband. Finally, General Marchmouse climbed up on top of Tumtum's concert piano to make a rallying speech.

"Quiet, please!" he bellowed, stretching back his shoulders. *"QUIET, PLEASE!"* The General did not like shouting; before he retired, he had always had a sergeant to do it for him. He filled his lungs with air, and tried once more. *"QUI-ART,*

PLEASE!" Eventually, the clamor subsided, and the mice turned to face him, all agog as to what was in store for them.

The General cleared his throat solemnly. He always addressed his men before a battle. He felt it good for morale, and he was especially pleased with the speech he was about to make now. He had been rehearsing it secretly in the billiards room.

"Mice," he began slowly. "You are gathered here today to face an enemy greater than any of us has ever faced, and crueller than any of us has ever known. But the purpose of our expedition is not to injure, nor to maim. It is simply to be *seen*. The enemy is deadly, but her weakness is fear. Fear of us.

"And if she sees enough of us, leaping out from the book-case, springing from the windowsill, descending from the chimney, spilling out of the stuffing in the sofa, deluging her from every corner of the room . . ."

The General paused for effect. He needed to make his strategy sound more foolproof than it was. ". . . Well, then she is bound to retreat!"

One of the mice, standing toward the back of the crowd, raised a grubby paw. "Is that why we're wearing these armbands, General? So we can be seen?"

"That is correct, young man," the General replied. "We shall be charging the enemy by night, and her den may be ill lit. The armbands will ensure that every one of us makes an impression. Be he large, or be he small, every mouse among us *must* be seen."

The General hesitated again; he was sure he had planned a much longer speech than this, but he had suddenly lost his thread. Flustered, he started to improvise.

"Mice! You have come here as volunteers, to defeat an enemy, and avenge a friend. As you march into battle, think upon what has befallen our beloved Tumtum, lying wretched and immobile on his chaise longue.

"And think upon the consequences if Aunt Ivy remains untamed. At noon tomorrow, her gas supply will arrive, and what hope for Tumtum then? But remember, above all, that this is not merely a battle of mice against man. It is a battle of right versus wrong. It is a battle of courage versus cowardice. . . ."

General Marchmouse had become very red in the face and was starting to wheeze. He drew his sword from his scabbard and flourished it wildly in the air. "It is *The Charge of the Bright Brigade!*"

A deep volt of electricity surged through the army. Punching the air with their bright orange sleeves, the soldiers chorused back the war cry: "The Charge of the Bright Brigade!" And there was not a mouse among them who was not longing for it to begin.

Chapter Twelve

There followed a tense few hours as the mice waited for an opportunity to march unseen into the Rose Cottage living room. Colonel Acorn and the Brigadier mounted guard at the gates of Nutmouse Hall, monitoring the constant comings and goings on the other side of the wall.

All afternoon, Aunt Ivy sat at the kitchen table, filing her nails and drinking a foul-smelling herbal tea. The children appeared at five o'clock to make some toast, and took it away without a plate. After that Mr. Mildew came and scavenged in the fridge, then retreated back upstairs with some canned ham and half a banana.

"Fascinating, isn't it," Colonel Acorn said, peering through the bars. "These human creatures don't seem to sit down to meals like we do. They graze, like cows." (Colonel Acorn and his wife lived behind the flour bins in the village shop, so he seldom saw humans in their domestic habitat.)

"Yes, most odd," agreed the Brigadier. "But mine aren't at all like that." The Brigadier lived in the airing cupboard of a grand house on the other side of the village, and he was rather proud of his humans. They had dinner in a dining room, by candlelight, and they had a maid to wait on them. "I believe that some humans have higher standards than others," he concluded thoughtfully.

The Colonel agreed this was probably true. And then they both held their noses as Aunt Ivy started smoking a menthol cigarette.

Back in Nutmouse Hall, the ranks were beginning to feel restless. They had been buoyed up by General Marchmouse's speech, but two hours later they were still cooped up in the ballroom. Mrs. Marchmouse was scurrying among them, dispensing cups of cocoa, and as it warmed them up they felt more boisterous than ever.

"When can we be off, General?" was the constant cry, and the General wished he could answer. But there was nothing to do but wait. He checked his watch constantly. Five o'clock . . . six o'clock . . . seven o'clock, and still no go-ahead from the officers at the gate.

Eventually, shortly before nine, Colonel Acorn reappeared. "All clear, General," he reported excitedly. "Aunt Ivy is in the bath; Mr. Mildew is in his study; and the children have gone to bed."

The General turned to face the troops. "Arise!" he roared magnificently. "The time has come to show the enemy what we're made of!" The mice at once scrabbled to their feet, and were briskly marched outside. Nutmeg and Mrs. Marchmouse stood in the hall, watching them go. A lieutenant brought up the rear and slammed the door shut behind them Then Nutmouse Hall suddenly felt terribly quiet and still.

A green felt cap lay on the flagstones in the hall, dropped by one of the school mice, but otherwise the army had left no trace of itself. Nutmeg felt a sudden forboding. *Oh, please bring them all home safely*, she prayed silently. Then, feeling a sharp chill, she went to replace the draft excluder by the front door.

The kitchen light was off when the mice spilled out of the Nutmouses' front gates, but the moon was shining through the window and it made their armbands glow. With the General leading, the army crossed the floor in a tight crocodile, making a detour around a pool of spilled tomato ketchup, and then crept into the hall. The General put a paw behind his ear; he could hear Aunt Ivy splashing about upstairs in the bath.

She had left the living room door open, and a soft reading lamp in the corner was casting long shadows across the floor. The room was cluttered, with lots of places to hide.

The sofa on which Aunt Ivy slept was on the far side of the room, in front of the window, and at either end of it there were coffee tables strewn with books and papers. There were armchairs on either side of the fire, and beside one of them a log basket full of old newspapers. On the opposite wall was

the bookcase, so overladen that the shelves were beginning to sag in the middle, and heaped in front of it were all Aunt Ivy's suitcases—one had a long green stocking snaking out of it.

Seeing the battlefield lying before them, the mice all felt a little awed. Every one of them knew, by instinct, that the thing to do when you saw a human was to run. But tonight they would be charging straight toward one, into hands that could squeeze them to pulp, and toward feet that could kick them so hard that they would go twirling and swirling into the air, until they smacked against a wall. Even the bravest among them felt his stomach flutter.

The General's stomach was fluttering, too, but no one would have guessed it. "Officers, take up your positions!" he barked. Then he flicked his stick under his arm, clipped his heels together, and marched them forward.

Each officer knew where his platoon was to hide, and within five minutes they had all clambered into position. There were mice everywhere, even inside Aunt Ivy's makeup bag, but they were so carefully hidden that there was not a mouse to be seen.

Keeping very still, they settled down to wait. It was a tense time for everyone, particularly for Colonel Acorn's platoon, which had crawled through the tear in the lining on one of the sofa arms. They were hiding in the stuffing, which was thick and coarse; it got up their trousers and under their collars, itching mercilessly.

Things were more comfortable for General Marchmouse, who had hoisted himself onto the mantelpiece, where he was hidden behind a dusty potted plant.

From there, through his field glasses, he had watched the platoons take up their positions, and then, in the deep hush that followed, his sleepless night started to catch up with him, and his eyelids got heavier and heavier.

I must refresh myself before the battle, he thought, beginning to stagger slightly on his feet. He hated being tired, but since retiring he'd become increasingly prone to it. He drew his sword, and, reaching up, cut off one of the soft, green leaves fanning above his head. Then he lay down on it to rest. "Just a quick nap," he said to himself drowsily, and within a few seconds he was fast asleep.

All around the room the eleven platoons crouched stiffly, waiting for the first scent of the enemy, and for the crack of General Marchmouse's pistol signaling them to charge.

Eventually, after nearly an hour, they heard the *thud, thud, thud* of human feet on the stairs. They twitched their noses nervously, and picked up the scent of bathroom unguents. Then Aunt Ivy entered the room. The door made a loud creak as she pushed it to behind her, but not loud enough to wake the General, who was in a deep, deep sleep, dreaming of all the glorious battles he'd won in his youth.

The other two hundred and fourteen pairs of eyes all peeked out of their hideaways, wakeful and riveted. She was dressed in dark green pajamas with a red robe tied tightly at the waist, and she had on a thin gold bracelet and a necklace of fake pearls, each the size of a mouse's head, and a silver lizard hanging decoratively from each ear. (Aunt Ivy always wore a lot of jewelry, even in bed.) The army felt uneasy; she wasn't like the other humans in the village. There was something creepy about her, almost reptilian.

Aunt Ivy walked toward the window and tugged the curtains tighter together. The platoon on the sill cowered back into the shadows as one of her pink fingernails poked through the gap.

Then she walked toward the bookcase and started digging about in one of her suitcases. There was a platoon of mice hiding in the bottom of it, and one of them felt her finger brushing the back of his jacket. Eventually, she found what she was looking for, a tortoiseshell hand mirror and a pair of metal tweezers. She kicked off her slippers and lay back on the sofa, then started plucking the little gray hairs from her chin.

Aunt Ivy did this once a fortnight, and it was very tedious and fiddly. As she held the mirror up to her face she screwed up her eyes, stuck out her tongue, and stretched her legs right out, pressing her feet against the arm of the sofa. Her toes pushed Colonel Acorn's platoon deeper into the stuffing, squashing the mice so tight that they could hardly breathe.

Why the devil doesn't the General give the signal to charge? the Colonel wondered despairingly.

At that moment, Aunt Ivy's big toe wriggled its way right through the hole in the lining, and he saw a gnarled toenail heading straight toward him. The Colonel squirmed, frantically trying to get out of its path, but he was trapped in the stuffing, barely able to move. The nail advanced on him like a tank.

He watched it loom nearer and nearer, dizzy with dread. And then, just as it was about to squash his nose, he opened his mouthand sank his teeth into Aunt Ivy's skin. *Chomp!* He got her just below the toenail, and bit in so deep he had to wrestle his jaw free with his paws.

For a split second, nothing happened, and the Colonel wondered if he hadn't dreamed the whole thing. But then there was a sudden shriek. "Fleas!" Aunt Ivy cursed, rubbing her toe, but she was about to face something much more alarming than that. For her cry had awoken the General, who was scrambling to his feet, frantically fumbling for his field glasses.

Standing beside the flowerpot, he quickly took stock of the battlefield. He saw the Brigadier peeking out from behind a botany encyclopedia on the bookshelf; he saw the glint of a

sword in the log basket, and the soft glow of twelve fluorescent mice crouching up the chimney.

With adrenaline coursing from his head to his tail, the General rushed forward to the rim of the mantelpiece and fired his pistol in the air. The battle had commenced.

Chapter Thirteen

Nursing her toe on the sofa, Aunt Ivy did not hear the General's pistol going off, as the gun was smaller than her fingernail. But the mice heard it loud and clear, and as the explosion echoed around the room they sprang from their hiding places shouting, "Charge!" and ran madly toward her.

She sat mesmerized, her eyes darting left and right as the full might of General Marchmouse's army appeared before her, out of thin air. First, she saw little orange lights on the bookshelf, then a dozen fluorescent mice flew from the shelves. She saw mice bursting from the windowsill, and the wastepaper bin, and the log basket. She saw them spilling out of the chimney and springing from her suitcases, and pouring out from beneath the armchair, like a flood.

This is just a dream, a horrible dream, she thought, desperately trying to calm herself. *Any second now, I am going to wake up. Come on, Ivy! Wake up! Wake up!* But she didn't wake up, and the mice kept coming.

Then she felt something ticklish on her legs. She looked down to see the Colonel's disheveled platoon clambering out of the stuffing and scurrying up her shins. Finally, Aunt Ivy screamed. And she screamed, and she screamed, and she screamed. She batted her arms and kicked her legs, but to no avail. For now there were mice running all over her.

They scuttled up the sleeves of her dressing gown and down the collar of her silk pajamas. They burrowed underneath the towel on her head, tickling her scalp with their claws; they hung from her bracelets; they somersaulted like acrobats on her necklace.

Staggering to her feet, she caught a glimpse of herself in the mirror above the fireplace—there were mice perched on her shoulders, there were mice nuzzling her ears, and there was even a mouse clambering onto her forehead. And there, standing boldly on the mantelpiece, was a mouse carrying a gun! *This must be a dream*, Aunt Ivy thought again. *It must! It must!*

Suddenly, there was the sound of footsteps in the hall. Right under Aunt Ivy's nose, General Marchmouse pointed his pistol in the air and fired it three times, signaling the retreat. His bullets hit the ceiling, but they were too tiny even to graze the paint. The army scampered back to their hiding places so fast that by the time Mr. Mildew poked his head around the door a few seconds later, there was not a mouse in sight.

"Ivy! What on earth's going on?" he demanded. "Anyone would think you were being murdered!"

"I am, Walter! I am!" she shrieked, looking down her body in horror. "I am being murdered by *mice*!"

"Mice? What mice? Really, Ivy, are you feeling quite all right?"

"They were here, Walter," she cried. "They were! They were! There were dozens, hundreds, thousands of them! A whole army of fluorescent mice. And they were *armed*, Walter, they were carrying guns!"

"Ivy," Mr. Mildew said gently, standing in front of the

bookcase, inches from the Brigadier's nose. "It is late, and you are overtired. Try and get some sleep, and then if you're still feeling out of sorts in the morning we'll go to the doctor and get something to calm your nerves."

But Aunt Ivy was not listening to him.

"It's your wretched children," she stammered, ". . . leaving crumbs in the dollhouse, encouraging them . . . giving them ideas . . . breeding an infestation . . . "

"Now go to bed, Ivy," Mr. Mildew said firmly, then he shut the door and went back upstairs. He supposed his poor sister-in-law was having some sort of a turn, but he had spent another frustrating day trying to make his Hungry House Mouse work, so he was feeling less sympathetic than he might otherwise have been.

The General waited tensely behind the flowerpot, and when he heard Mr. Mildew's study door bang shut he stepped forward and let off his pistol again to signal the second charge.

All at once, the mice leaped back out of their hiding places

and raced toward Aunt Ivy. They knew now that she was more frightened of them than they were of her, which made them even bolder. The Brigadier climbed right up onto her long nose, and the Colonel sat on her pointy chin.

When she shrieked, he could see right inside her mouth. *Goodness!* he thought, looking at her huge tonsils and the deep black chute beyond. *If I were to fall down there I might never get out again! I might have to live the rest of my life inside Aunt Ivy's stomach!* He shuddered and jumped down onto her shoulder.

Blind with terror, Aunt Ivy ran to the kitchen and fled through the garden door. "Walter! Walter! Do something!" she shouted as she stumbled across the lawn, her feet sinking into the snow. Then she tripped and collapsed under a pear tree, with two hundred and fifteen fluorescent mice scuttling all over her.

Fearing Mr. Mildew might reappear, General Marchmouse stood on Aunt Ivy's forehead and fired his pistol three times again, sounding another retreat. As the mice were hurtling back into the kitchen, a light flashed on in the attic. Arthur and Lucy appeared at the window, and peered down at their aunt in amazement.

Then Mr. Mildew's head poked out of the window on the upstairs landing. "Ivy, what exactly is going on now?"

"Mice, Walter!" she wailed miserably. "It's those confounded orange mice again!"

"There *ARE NO MICE*," Mr. Mildew said, speaking very slowly and firmly, but not altogether unkindly. "Now come back inside. Please, Ivy. For all our sakes."

The chill night air bit into Aunt Ivy's skin and slowly brought her back to her senses. It was a still, cloudless night, nothing was stirring. She looked down at her dressing gown, at her arms, at her hands. There were no mice there, only a few little hairs, which her eyes were not sharp enough to see. *Perhaps I did imagine it all*, she thought weakly. *Perhaps Walter's right—perhaps I am going mad.*

"Now come inside," Mr. Mildew called down again. Finally, Aunt Ivy got up and limped back toward the cottage. She hesitated a moment at the garden door, her hand trembling on the knob.

"Pull yourself together, Ivy," she said to herself firmly. "There is no such thing as a fluorescent mouse. Walter was right; you are overwrought."

Taking a deep breath, she walked into the kitchen. And from all around the room, she was watched by hundreds of twinkling eyes. General Marchmouse had repositioned his army.

As Aunt Ivy pulled the door shut behind her, she heard a rustling sound coming from the laundry basket. She swung around and saw something orange glinting through the wicker.

General Marchmouse, who was standing on the oven, fired his pistol, and the mice made their third assault, each platoon springing from a different hideaway. They came at her from the sink, from the vegetable rack, from the wastepaper basket, from the teapot on the dresser—one platoon sprang out of a boot.

But this charge was much briefer than the others, for Aunt Ivy seemed so frightened that the General felt it unsporting to carry on very long, and he withdrew his forces after less than a minute.

The army evaporated, but Aunt Ivy remained huddled on the doormat awhile, too fearful to move. Then she walked across the room on tiptoes and gingerly picked up the telephone. The mice watched from their hiding places as

she rustled through the telephone directory, then hurriedly dialed a number.

"Is that Mr. Glengle's Round-the-Clock Cabs? . . . Good . . . I need a car at once. . . . Twenty minutes? No, I need one now! I'll be dead in twenty minutes. . . . Where to? Home, of course. To Scotland. And send me the fastest driver you've got." Then there was a sharp click as she replaced the receiver.

Aunt Ivy thought better of waking Mr. Mildew again; instead she hastily scribbled him a note on the back of an unpaid gas bill and left it on the kitchen table. Then the mice crept after her into the living room and watched from behind the door as she hurled her clothes into her suitcases and dragged them into the hall. When she heard the taxi spluttering to a halt outside, she tossed her black overcoat on over her robe, and went out of the door wearing slippers.

The mice all scrabbled up the curtains onto the windowsill and pressed their noses to the glass, watching avidly. The taxi had its headlights on full-beam, and a tall, thickset driver in a tweed cap got out. Aunt Ivy walked up the path toward him and pointed back toward the cottage, gesturing at him to collect the luggage. They heard him come inside, then saw him return to his car carrying three suitcases. Then he came back for the other two, flung them all into the trunk, and opened the passenger door for Aunt Ivy to get in.

The driver got inside and started the engine. Then there was a belch of exhaust fumes and Aunt Ivy was gone. The mice watched as the headlights faded into the night, and they knew the battle was won. "She's gone!" they cried, waving their orange armbands in the air and jumping up and down with glee. The Colonel was so elated that he made to kiss the General, but then he stopped himself, and they both looked a little embarrassed.

The army trooped back to Nutmouse Hall, singing triumphantly, but the General lingered behind a moment in the living room, surveying the battlefield. Besides some dust that had fallen from the chimney, there was nothing to show that the Charge of the Bright Brigade had ever taken place. No fallen bodies, no bloodied barricades; the General wished all his battles could have been like this one.

He would not let it be forgotten in a hurry. *I must telephone the* Mouse Times *first thing in the morning and make sure it carries a full report*, he thought loftily, beginning to compose what he would say. He decided he would leave out the detail about his falling asleep on the mantelpiece.

Back in Nutmouse Hall, Nutmeg and Mrs. Marchmouse had spent an anxious night sitting by Tumtum's bedside, wondering what was happening in Rose Cottage. They had heard the General's pistol going off, and they had heard Aunt Ivy's terrible shrieking, and they had prayed all the while that the army was winning. It had certainly sounded that way.

It was long after midnight when they heard the first of the troops returning through the front gates. Then the living room door burst open, and the General strode in. "The night is ours, ladies!" he cried delightedly. "Aunt Ivy has been soundly defeated; she's retreated to Scotland in a taxi!"

Mrs. Marchmouse flung herself on him, weeping with joy. "Oh, darling, you are so clever and brave! And to think that I imagined I might never see you again!" The General smiled

broadly, but then he looked down on Tumtum, lying palely on the chaise longue, and his expression turned to one of concern.

"How is the patient, Mrs. Nutmouse?" he asked gravely.

"His temperature is a little down, General, and he's stopped being sick," she said. "There is definitely some improvement. I do hope he wakes up soon—his spirits are bound to improve when he hears that Aunt Ivy has gone."

Even as she said it, Tumtum's head moved stiffly on the pillow. Very slowly and tentatively, he opened his eyes, then he blinked rapidly, like a creature who has lived all winter underground and burst up through the earth's surface on the first day of spring.

"Did I hear you say Aunt Ivy had gone, dear?" he murmured, turning to his wife. He looked anxiously at the clock. "Oh, dearie me. Have I been asleep long? I feel quite ravenous. I hope I haven't missed lunch."

Nutmeg gazed adoringly at him, hardly daring to believe her eyes. He was still very pallid, but the sweat had lifted from his brow, and his eyes were clear and bright, quite unlike yesterday.

"Oh, Tumtum!" she cried joyfully, kissing him on his nose, which was healthy and moist again. "Yes, Aunt Ivy has gone! And you have missed more than lunch! You've missed a week of lunches, and a week of dinners, and a week of breakfasts and teas, and you've got so little tummy left that I'll have to think of another name for you!"

Tumtum looked quite astonished. He patted his stomach and wondered where it had gone. He could remember going up to the attic the other night, and tucking into a plate of chocolate that had tasted rather strange, but since then everything was just a blur.

"What's all that commotion?" he asked, hearing the mice clattering in through the front door.

"That's the soldiers, Tumtum!" Nutmeg said. "You've slept through a battle!"

"Goodness!" Tumtum said, feeling more bewildered by the minute. Then his stomach started rumbling violently, and Nutmeg joyfully raced off to find him something to eat. *The poor troops will be starving, too!* she thought busily. *What on earth can I feed them all?*

But when she entered her kitchen, she found the problem had been solved for her. A pork sausage, a full six inches long, had been discovered abandoned in the Mildews' grille, and the Colonel and the Brigadier had carried it back to Nutmouse Hall on their shoulders. There was also a whole slice of bread, which had needed four mice to carry it, and a knob of butter the size of a golf ball.

Nutmeg instructed the officers to lay out the feast in the banqueting hall. The room had last been used on her wedding day, and this morning her mood was so celebratory that she wanted to see its shutters thrown open again. "Left out of the ballroom, Colonel, then third door on your right—it's the room with the big chandelier and the marble statues," she explained, and then she scurried off to the kitchen to find some mustard.

Two barrels of cider were retrieved from Tumtum's cellar, and then the feast got under way. The Colonel carved the sausage with his sword, and the Brigadier sliced the bread with a cutlass, and there were enough hot dogs for each mouse to eat until his stomach was fit to burst.

Nutmeg took a slice of sausage to Tumtum in the living room, and he wolfed it all down with a cup of strong tea. The General sat with them, giving them a blow-by-blow account of the battle.

"Quite ingenious, General, quite ingenious," Tumtum kept muttering with his mouth full. And Nutmeg and Mrs. Marchmouse laughed until they wept when the General recounted how the mice had swung from Aunt Ivy's earrings, and turned somersaults on her pearl necklace. "Oh, poor woman!" Nutmeg cried, dabbing tears from her eyes. "Poor, poor woman!" But when Nutmeg remembered the horror through which Aunt Ivy'd put Tumtum, it was hard to feel very sorry for her.

Finally, when the General felt he had been congratulated enough, he made to take his leave. "We'd best be getting home, Poppet," he said, turning to his wife. "It will be dawn before we know it."

"Goodness, yes," she replied, remembering that she hadn't slept for—how long was it? One day, two days? She was too tired to remember, and she suddenly longed for her warm bed in the gun cupboard. *We'll need a hot water bottle*, she thought, thinking that all the fires would have long since died out.

"I'll go and dismiss the mice," the General said, getting to his feet. And yet he found himself oddly reluctant to go. Much as he loved Mrs. Marchmouse, the adventurer in him dreaded returning to his quiet life at home.

"Is there anything else I can do for you, Nutty?" he asked Tumtum hopefully.

"Oh, no, General, I think you've done quite enough," Tumtum replied.

But Nutmeg was blushing. "There is something, General," she said hesitantly. "But I'm afraid it might be asking rather a lot of you—I'm sure you're yearning to get home."

"Not if duty calls, Mrs. Nutmouse," he replied stiffly.

"Well," she went on. "It's just that Tumtum and I have been trying so hard to keep Rose Cottage in order—to mend the radiators, seal the cracks in the windowpanes, patch the leaks in the ceiling, and dust and scrub and all that so that the children can live decently. But it's all proven too much for us. I'm sure you noticed what a pitiful state the place is in. But with a whole army of you here, and all so healthy and strong,

I thought, perhaps . . . Well, perhaps you could have a go at getting the place shipshape."

The General beamed, delighted to be given another chance to take command. "Leave it to me, Mrs. Nutmouse," he said. "Give us an hour or so, and we'll have Rose Cottage looking fit for a mouse! My army numbers a plumber, and an electrician, and a carpenter, and a window glazer, and an engineer, and a thatcher, and a plasterer—"

"But would they be able to tackle human-sized things?" Nutmeg asked doubtfully.

"Of course they would," the General replied. "I called the engineer around to the Manor House just last week to fix the overhead light in the gun room. He broke into the fuse box and sorted it out in no time; he said it was only a tripped switch. And when a pipe started leaking onto our gun cupboard, the plumber climbed up and patched it for me with some of his wife's old copper saucepans. If humans had any sense they'd always employ mice for the fiddly jobs like that."

"Quite so!" Tumtum agreed. "We could put every human laborer out of business!"

"Hmmm! No wonder they're so wary of us then," the General said, making for the door. Then he marched off to the ballroom to start bossing everyone around.

From Nutmouse Hall, the Nutmouses and Mrs. Marchmouse could hear the distant hum of activity as the army advanced through Rose Cottage, putting things to rights. At one point, there was a loud *hiccup*, followed by a deep whirring noise. "Sounds like they've got the old boiler working again!" Tumtum said admiringly. Then there was a great crashing and rattling in the kitchen as dozens of mice scrambled about scouring the stove.

They went through each room, mending and scrubbing; and when they found the tin mouse in Mr. Mildew's study, they took it apart and gave it a whole new digestive system so that it could keep down all the crumbs it gobbled. They tested it on Mr. Mildew's desk, which was always covered with crumbs, and it worked very efficiently. *I must get one for the gun cupboard,* the General thought. *Much better than a vacuum cleaner.*

Last of all, they carried out a lightning attack on the attic. The plumber unblocked the sink, the engineer repaired the engine on Arthur's train set, and the carpenter sawed little pieces off one of the shelves in the wardrobe and used them to board one of the broken windowpanes where Tumtum's repairs had come undone. The Colonel had discovered half a sack of coal in the wood shed, and the army carried enough lumps upstairs to light the attic fire.

Just as the flames were beginning to flicker, two great human fists emerged from Arthur's bed and stretched slowly into the air. With a start, the General realized that dawn had crept up on them; the sun was pouring through the window.

"Downstairs, quick!" he ordered, and all at once the army started hurtling toward the attic steps. The General brought up the rear, and had Arthur sat up and opened his eyes a moment sooner, he would have seen an elderly mouse charging across his bedroom floor brandishing a pistol.

Chapter Fifteen

It was the most wonderful day in Rose Cottage. When Arthur and Lucy woke up they discovered that Nutmeg had been back with a vengeance, lighting fires and mending trains, and then they went downstairs and found the whole cottage transformed. But the best surprise of all came when they opened the living room door and realized that Nutmeg had carried out her promise after all: Aunt Ivy had vanished.

"Do you think she's gone for good?" Arthur asked, hardly daring to believe it.

"It looks like it," Lucy said joyfully, for all their aunt had left behind was a pair of tweezers. (She had also left a lizard earring, which had fallen off during the fray, but the General had taken it back to hang in the gun cupboard as a souvenir.)

"Nutmeg said she'd do it, and she sure has." As the reality sank in, they both fell silent for a moment. They hadn't realized Nutmeg was quite so influential.

"I wonder what she did to make her so frightened," Arthur said, for they'd both heard Aunt Ivy shrieking in the night. "You don't think she *really* sent hundreds of fluorescent mice to attack Aunt Ivy, do you?"

"Of course not," Lucy said firmly, for that was too terrible a thought. Even Aunt Ivy didn't deserve that. But Nutmeg moved in such mysterious ways, that secretly Lucy thought she wouldn't have put anything past her. But somehow neither of the children felt it right to question Nutmeg's methods; they just felt very happy she had come back.

Presently, Mr. Mildew appeared. "Good morning," he said cheerfully. He was holding his tin mouse and looking immensely pleased with himself. He'd expected to spend another day struggling to get it going, but when he'd turned it on after he woke up, it was gobbling beautifully and keeping everything down. He couldn't for the life of him remember how he'd done it—but now he was going to rush out to the post office

to have it couriered to the manager of the department store in London. *I might be rich again*, he thought, and the idea made him feel just a little bit giddy.

"There was some sort of racket last night, wasn't there?" he asked, pulling a pair of boots on over his pajamas and trying to remember what it was all about.

"It was Aunt Ivy," Lucy said. "She ran into the garden, screaming that she was being attacked by orange mice. I should think everyone in the village must have heard her. And now she's gone."

"Gone?" Mr. Mildew repeated disbelievingly. He looked in the living room, then in the hall, then in the kitchen, and Aunt Ivy wasn't there. Then Lucy spotted the note Aunt Ivy had left on the table, weighted under the milk jug. The writing was scrawled and messy—it had clearly been written in a great hurry. Mr. Mildew sat down and fished his glasses from his pocket, then read it out loud.

Dear Walter,

Your cottage is infested with wild mice—hundreds and thousands of them, possibly millions. They are armed and they are orange and they are out to kill. They are living in the bookshelf and the sofa and the sink and the laundry basket—they are everywhere. They have colonized the entire cottage. I am leaving for my own safety—I advise you to do the same.

Ivy

"Poor old Ivy," Mr. Mildew muttered. "Orange mice, indeed!"

In Nutmouse Hall, the army had returned to the ballroom, where Tumtum was doing the rounds, thanking each mouse in turn for rescuing him. He was walking cautiously, with a stick, but he was already feeling much stronger.

The mice finally disbanded, crossing the kitchen floor while the Mildews were poring over Aunt Ivy's letter. The General was the last to leave, hovering awhile at the Nutmouses' front door. "I could stay here and stand guard," he suggested to Tumtum. "Just in case—well, in case of any further trouble . . ."

"Oh, no, General," Tumtum said kindly, taking him by

the paw. "You have saved my life and I am not going to let you do anything else for us. But please take this——"

Tumtum walked stiffly toward the oak chest by the fire and picked up a long brass telescope. "It belonged to my great-great-great-grandfather," he said, presenting it ceremoniously to the General. "He served in the Royal Mouse Navy—he traveled far and wide along the stream, all the way to the next village, I'm told."

The General was very stirred. "Thank you, Mr. Nutmouse," he said solemnly. "I will always treasure it." Then he closed his eyes and sent up a silent prayer that there might soon be another battle, so he could have occasion to use it. And he prayed the same thing all the way home to the gun cupboard . . . but not out loud, for fear of upsetting Mrs. Marchmouse.

When the Marchmouses had gone, Tumtum and Nutmeg shut their front door and retreated to the kitchen. It was breakfast time, so Nutmeg boiled a kettle for tea and made some buttered toast, a big pot of porridge, two boiled eggs, and a round

of pancakes. Then she laid the table and they sat down to eat, thinking how nice it was to be alone again.

"He's a strange fellow, that General Marchmouse," Tumtum said philosophically. "Anyone would think he actually enjoyed going to war, and risking life and limb and all that."

"Well, I suppose some mice crave adventure," said Nutmeg. "But I hope we don't have another one, Tumtum. I don't feel I'm quite cut out for them."

"Oh, I don't think there'll be any more adventures coming our way, dear," Tumtum said confidently. "We've had more than our share. From now on we'll just live happily ever after." Nutmeg agreed with him, and then they sat down to breakfast and put all the trouble from their minds.

The Great
Escape

Chapter One

At Nutmouse Hall, the day had begun much like any other. Nutmeg had leaped out of bed at dawn and raced downstairs to bustle and bake and clean. And Tumtum had stayed tucked up under the covers until he heard the bell ring for breakfast.

He tumbled down to the kitchen in his dressing gown. "Good morning, dear!" he said dozily as Nutmeg helped him to porridge and toast and scrambled eggs and bacon, and a pancake or two. "Now, let's see. What shall we do today?"

Tumtum always asked this, even though he knew quite well what the answer would be. For although they lived in a big, grand house, the Nutmouses led very simple lives.

For the most part, Nutmeg spent her days scuttling and bustling in the kitchen, preparing delicious things to eat. And Tumtum spent his days in the library, reading the *Mouse Times* and toasting his toes in front of the fire.

So Tumtum knew what Nutmeg's answer would be. "I think I'll scuttle and bustle in the kitchen, dear," she said.

"Good idea!" he replied. "And I think I'll retreat to the library and toast my toes by the fire."

Nutmeg approved of this plan, so they both settled down to eat, looking forward to another peaceful day at Nutmouse Hall.

But just as Nutmeg was refilling the teapot, there was a loud *Rap! Tap! Tap!* on the front door.

"I wonder who that could be?" Tumtum asked warily. Nutmeg followed him through to the hall, feeling just as puzzled. The post mouse was the only person who tended to visit at this hour, but today was a Sunday.

Before Tumtum had time to draw the bolts, the *rap tap tapping* started again. Then they heard a loud voice on the other side of the door.

"It's General Marchmouse!" announced General Marchmouse, speaking in a very General Marchmousely way.

"The General!" Nutmeg whispered, looking at Tumtum in
astonishment. "What on earth can he want?"

"I can't imagine, dear," Tumtum replied. For it was most
unlike the General to visit so early.

"What a nice surprise, General!" he said when he opened
the door.

And in some ways it was, for the Nutmouses were
very fond of the General. (Who was known to everyone as
General, on account of him being rather Generalish.) But in
other ways it wasn't, for while Tumtum and Nutmeg were very
quiet mice, the General was an unusually noisy one.

And today he was at his noisiest. He marched into the hall
and thumped two leather suitcases on the floor. "Hello!" he
said heartily. "Would you be so kind as to let me stay a night
or two?"

"Why, er—of course, General!" Tumtum stammered,
feeling he couldn't very well refuse.

"Good," the General replied. "Mrs. Marchmouse has gone

to stay with her old nanny for a week and I was feeling lonely racketing about the gun cupboard on my own. Now that I'm retired from active service, time can hang a little heavy, you know. So I thought to myself, *How jolly it would be to spend a few days with my dear friends the Nutmouses, at Nutmouse Hall!*

Tumtum and Nutmeg both groaned inwardly. There was no hope of a quiet day now.

"What's that?" Nutmeg asked, noticing that the General was carrying a fat silver pole.

"That is a pogo stick," the General replied proudly. "The Royal Mouse Army's new secret weapon."

"Whatever do you mean?" Tumtum asked.

The General looked down his nose at him, thinking him very ill-informed.

"Haven't you read the *Mouse Times*, Nutmouse?" he asked. "The army is being modernized. The soldiers are no longer going to ride squirrels—oh, squirrels are old hat! From now on, the cavalry will bounce into battle on sleek, silver pogo sticks, just like this. Stand back, Nutty, and I'll show you how it's done!"

Then the General mounted his stick, and started to bounce—*boing! boing! boing!*—around the hall. Then he bounced—*boing! boing! boing!*—around the living room, and the billiard room, and the ballroom. And so he went on, bouncing all around Nutmouse Hall, knocking into lamps and tables and stuffed cockroaches, and generally making a thorough nuisance of himself.

By the time he reached the kitchen, he was bouncing so high that he biffed his head on the ceiling. He sat down to breakfast feeling quite dizzy.

"We mustn't let him out of our sight for a minute," Tumtum whispered to his wife. "We don't want him giving us away."

Nutmeg nodded anxiously. Any mouse visiting Nutmouse Hall had to come and go very carefully, for it was a secret house, which no human knew about. It was built in the cupboard of the Mildews' kitchen, and since the broom cupboard was hidden away behind a big wooden dresser, none of the Mildews knew it was there. The Nutmouses' front gates were just behind the dresser, and they were forever creeping in and out across the Mildews' kitchen floor.

But the Mildews had never seen them, because Tumtum and Nutmeg crept very quietly. And they did most of their creeping at night.

At night they crept all over the place. They crept into the pantry and into Mr. Mildew's study, and sometimes they crept up to the attic, where Arthur and Lucy slept, and did all sorts of helpful things. Nutmeg darned the children's clothes, tidied their satchels, and polished their shoes with a mop; once Tumtum had mended the wings on Arthur's model plane.

After Aunt Ivy's visit, the children and Nutmeg had continued to write each other letters, which they left on the dresser in the attic. But the children still had no idea that Nutmeg was a mouse. She had told them in one of her letters that she was a fairy—so that is what they thought she was. The Nutmouses knew that Arthur and Lucy must never learn the truth. For some humans have funny feelings about mice and think they shouldn't be allowed in the house.

And imagine what the children might think if they saw the General bouncing about on a pogo stick.

"We must keep him constantly entertained," Tumtum whispered to Nutmeg. "Then he might just forget about this pogoing nonsense."

"What would you like to do this morning, General?" he asked jovially, turning to his friend. "We could have a game of chess!"

"Later, perhaps," the General replied, dabbing scrambled egg from his whiskers. "First I shall go exploring. The broom cupboard's not big enough for a mouse on a pogo stick. I want to have a bounce around the Mildews' kitchen floor and see if they've left any good pickings."

This was not what Tumtum wanted to hear.

"Now, look here, General. I don't think that's wise," he said. "You'll only draw attention to yourself. And besides, the Mildews never leave good pickings. They eat horrible things like canned spaghetti. That's why we have our food delivered by the grocery mouse."

"Well I'd like to try canned spaghetti," the General said carelessly. "Anyway, I won't be gone long. Just a quick breath of fresh air, and I'll be home in time for lunch."

Tumtum looked stern. (He did not often look stern, but when he did he looked very stern indeed.)

"General, so long as you are our guest, Rose Cottage is out of bounds," he said firmly. "Now please promise me that you will not set foot outside the broom cupboard. We've thirty-six rooms here in Nutmouse Hall—surely that's enough for any mouse to bounce about in."

"Oh, all right then," the General said reluctantly. "I promise. I shall pogo around here instead."

As far as Tumtum was concerned, the matter was closed. For a promise is a promise, after all.

But General Marchmouse found this particular promise very hard to keep.

The General was a mouse who craved adventures, but since retiring from the army he'd found them in increasingly short supply. He was starved of danger—and he had a feeling that by pogoing around Rose Cottage he might finally find some.

And yet he was a mouse of honor, so of course he could never go back on his word. That would be out of the question.

Huff! How tiresome to have to stay indoors! he thought crossly, helping himself to the last piece of bacon. He was still full of energy, so when breakfast was over he mounted his pogo stick again and started crashing about in the ballroom.

"Whoopee!" he cried as he went smack-bang into a marble statue. "I'll make as much noise as possible, then Nutty will get so fed up he'll let me go!"

But though Tumtum could hear the racket from the library, he said nothing, which made the General even more frustrated.

"Now, come on, Nutmouse. Surely it wouldn't do any harm if I went out for a few minutes?" he began as they sat down to a light lunch of earwig pie. But Tumtum would not back down.

"I have already made my feelings clear, and I have no more to say on the matter."

"All right, all right," the General muttered. Then he finally let the subject drop.

But after lunch, when Tumtum had disappeared to the library and while Nutmeg was bustling in the kitchen, the General found himself wandering into the hall with his pogo stick tucked under his arm. He stood there awhile, looking longingly at the front door. "You gave your word," the Generalish side of him said. But the adventurous side said, *Go on!*

And so on he went.

He crept out of the door then tiptoed toward the Nutmouses' front gates. He let himself out and fumbled his way through the cobwebs underneath the dresser. Then he marched out into the kitchen, feeling a delicious thrill of adventure now that he was out of bounds.

It was a foolhardy time to set out, for it was broad daylight, and someone might easily have spotted him. But the General could hear Arthur and Lucy outside, playing in the garden. So he assumed he would be safe.

"I'm king of the roost!" he cried, bouncing gleefully across the kitchen floor.

He had visited Rose Cottage several times before, and he knew exactly where he wanted to go. He bounced into the hall, then, gritting his teeth, he bounced up the stairs and onto the landing. Then he stopped suddenly, hearing something clattering in the study.

He hopped across the carpet and poked his nose under the door.

Inside, Mr. Mildew was sitting on the floor amid a sea of tiny wires and twisted bits of metal. He was trying to invent a mechanical frog that could be programmed to catch flies in its mouth. But like most of Mr. Mildew's inventions, it was all going wrong. And as a result he was pounding his fists on the floor in a hopeless rage.

The General watched for a moment, then he turned around and bounced across the landing, until he was standing beneath the steep flight of steps leading to the attic. He flung his pogo stick onto the bottom step and heaved himself up after it.

I'll have all the toys to myself, he thought excitedly as he huffed and puffed his way upstairs. *I'll make castles out of building bricks, and tie up the teddy bears! Oh, lucky old me!*

But even the fearless General Marchmouse might have hesitated a moment had he realized just what sort of adventures were in store.

Chapter Two

The General finally hoisted himself over the top step, onto the attic floor. He was drenched in sweat, and the belt of his camouflage trousers was cutting into him. "You must go on a diet, Marchmouse," he muttered, searching in his pocket for a humbug. He got to his feet, crunching it noisily. But then he saw something that made him suck in his breath.

He was looking straight into the barrel of a rifle!

The General was so frightened he could feel his knees wobble. Standing before him was a figure in red uniform, with a visor hiding his face. It wasn't the uniform of the Royal Mouse Army—and though the soldier was the size of a mouse, he didn't have a tail.

"Do you know who I am?" the General demanded, trying to disguise his terror. "Well, I'll tell you. I am General Marchmouse . . . So . . . er, well . . . So there you have it!"

The soldier ignored him, which made the General cross. Generals are not used to being ignored.

"With whose army do you serve?" the General asked briskly, but there was no reply. And that made the General even crosser.

"Where is your commanding officer? I shall report you for insubordination!" he shouted. He was so cross he forgot he was frightened.

But still there was no reply.

"I HAVE KILLED A RAT WITH MY OWN BARE PAWS!" the General roared, determined to impress him.

But the soldier did not respond.

So General Marchmouse did something very unGeneral-ish. He reached forward and punched him in the stomach.

But, to his astonishment, the soldier just toppled over.

The General blushed, feeling very foolish. For suddenly he realized that it was a toy soldier made of tin! And now, looking around him, he could see dozens more of them scattered all about the floor. Some were in red uniforms, and some in khaki. There were tanks, too, and piles of sandbags and grenades, and there were machine guns the size of matches.

The General sucked in his breath, hardly able to believe his luck. A whole battlefield stretched before him—and everything was mouse-sized! At last he could come out of retirement and take command! Oh, how he throbbed with delight!

I'll form the men into lines, and command a full-scale offensive, he thought gleefully. *We'll blow up the dollhouse!*

So the General spent a blissful hour ordering his new regiments. The dollhouse was placed under siege and its front door barricaded with a pencil box. The red soldiers were put inside to defend it, firing from the windows and the roof, while the khaki soldiers advanced on the building in platoons. The General commanded operations standing on top of one of Lucy's ballet shoes, shouting, "Fire!" until he was nearly hoarse.

When he had hurled all the plastic grenades, he went to rummage in the toy box, looking for more missiles. He nibbled through the string of one of Lucy's necklaces and scooped the

beads into his kit bag. Then he returned to his post on the ballet shoe and started lobbing them at the dollhouse, one by one. He was not a good shot, so he didn't succeed in breaking any windows. But the beads made a satisfying clonk as they smashed against the wall.

When he'd tired of that, he decided to have a go on Arthur's train set. The tracks, which had been painstakingly repaired by Tumtum, looped all around the floor, and every two feet or so they sloped up and down in steep ramps.

I could get up quite a speed! he thought excitedly. He jumped on his pogo stick and hopped over a bank of sandbags toward the glistening blue carriages.

"Sorry, old boy," he grunted, yanking a toy soldier from the driver's compartment. "But General Marchmouse is taking command."

He sat on the stool and turned the big red switch to On. There was a gentle rumbling noise, then the train slowly heaved into motion.

The General whooped with delight and started grabbing

wildly at the controls, trying to make it go faster. "Faster! Faster!" he roared—but Arthur's train ran on a small battery, and however much the General punched and shoved at the knobs, it kept to the same steady speed.

Let's see what happens if I freewheel, he thought impatiently.

The train chugged around a bedpost and up to the top of the biggest hump in the tracks, which was nearly as high as the dollhouse. The General hunched himself over the gear stick, then gingerly reached out a paw and switched off the engine. The train wobbled a moment, then it lurched forward and started whooshing downhill. The General clung to the wheel, shrieking with glee as the room sped past him in a dizzying blur.

"Clear the tracks!" he shouted, blasting the horn. "General Marchmouse is bringing reinforcements!"

But then he saw the hairpin bend in the track just in front of him.

He grappled in panic for the brake, but the train just hurtled on faster. "Help! Help!" he squealed, cowering into a ball on the carriage floor, his paws pressed to his ears. He felt

the train lurch violently as it hit the curve, and then the driver's compartment skidded off the rails and sailed into the air. The General fell nose-down against the window and saw his tin regiments spread out below him on the floor. "I'm flying!" he trembled.

But the worst was still to come. For the next moment everything went black, as the carriage smashed onto the roof of the dollhouse.

The General lay there, too dazed to move. At first he could see nothing but stars and flashing lights. Then, little by little, the room came back into focus. But everything was upside down.

Gradually, as he came to his senses, he realized what had happened. The carriage had landed on its side, and he was squashed tight beneath the driver's stool, with all four paws in the air. The door was on top of him, where the ceiling should be. So it was no wonder everything looked topsy-turvy.

"Oh, poor old me," he whimpered. "What a pretty pickle!" But as he was lying there, feeling as sorry for himself as any mouse can feel, he heard something that made everything much worse. Arthur and Lucy were coming up the stairs.

Chapter Three

The General listened in terror as the children's voices got closer and closer. He knew he was in dreadful danger. Arthur would be astonished enough to discover that his train had been derailed. But what would he do when he found a mouse at the wheel? The General did not know Arthur as well as the Nutmouses did, and he imagined there might be terrible punishments in store.

Gritting his teeth, for he was very sore, he grasped his pogo stick and used it to smash open the door above his head. Then he wriggled free of the steering wheel and pulled himself upright. Peeking outside, he saw that the carriage was stranded high on the dollhouse roof, lodged between two chimneys.

He gripped the door frame and hauled himself out onto the rooftop, wincing with pain. He tried to run, using his pogo stick as a crutch, but the roof was steep and he kept slipping. He floundered about desperately, but there was nowhere to hide. "I'll never surrender!" he vowed—and as Arthur and Lucy entered the room he tossed his pogo stick down a chimney and dived after it headfirst.

The children got a terrible fright when they saw the soldiers pointing their guns out of the dollhouse windows and the train lying on the roof.

Lucy assumed it must have been Arthur's doing, and Arthur assumed it must have been Lucy's doing, and there were some cross words exchanged. But Arthur pointed out that it couldn't have been him, because he'd been outside all afternoon. And Lucy pointed out that it couldn't have been her because she'd been outside all day, too.

So who was it? Surely not Nutmeg, for fairies didn't do things like this. And it couldn't have been their father, for fathers don't crash their children's trains.

"There must be another fairy, as well as Nutmeg," Arthur said. "A bad fairy, who makes a mess. You know what I mean— a sort of elf."

The children considered this awhile. Neither of them would have believed in any sort of fairy a year ago, but since acquiring one of their own they had become more open-minded.

"I wonder if Nutmeg knows," Lucy said. "Do you think we should tell her?"

"I suppose so," Arthur said. "Let's leave everything as it is so she can see for herself what whoever it is has done. Imagine how surprised she'll be when she finds soldiers firing out of her dollhouse."

They both considered it to be Nutmeg's dollhouse because she had redecorated it from top to bottom with new curtains and carpets and cushion covers. She had even made a tapestry cover for the piano stool. And though they had never seen her, they suspected she sometimes spent the night there, for she kept a pair of slippers in its bedroom.

So Lucy found some paper, and the children sat together on the floor and composed a letter:

Dear Nutmeg,

We think an elf has been in the attic while we were outside. He crashed Arthur's train, and broke Lucy's necklace, and he attacked the dollhouse with tin soldiers. And he's eaten all the biscuits we left out for you. What do you think we should do?

Love,

Arthur and Lucy

When they had finished, Lucy folded the letter in half and left it propped against the mirror on the dresser. "I hope she does something to stop it," Lucy said.

"So do I," Arthur agreed. He was beginning to feel quite hostile to whoever had crashed his train.

While all this was going on, the General was in considerable discomfort. By a stroke of misfortune he had dived down the living room chimney, which was the longest of all the chimneys in the dollhouse. His pogo stick had clattered down to the hearth, but he was too fat to follow, and he had gotten stuck halfway down.

He wriggled and squirmed, but he couldn't budge—he was wedged upside down, with his stomach squashed tight against the chimney bricks.

In this undignified position, he had listened to the children's conversation, feeling crosser and crosser.

"An *elf*!" he fumed, kicking his legs. "I'll teach you to refer to the great General Marchmouse as an *elf*!" But though he protested loudly, the children couldn't hear a thing, because mice have such small voices that even when they are shouting they only make a tiny squeal. And besides, the General's shouts were muffled by the chimney.

By the time the children went downstairs for lunch, the General could shout no more. He pulled in his stomach, trying to calculate how tightly he was stuck. *I'll have to lose at least half an ounce before I can squeeze out of here*, he thought miserably. *And that would mean starving for three days!*

It was a very glum thought.

Chapter Four

It had been a peaceful afternoon in Nutmouse Hall. After lunch, Nutmeg had scuttled to the sewing room to start work on a velvet smock for one of Lucy's dolls, and Tumtum had pottered off to the library to put his feet up.

I shall have a nice long read, he had thought, flopping in an armchair in front of the fire. But the fire was so warm, and Tumtum's tumtum was so full of lunch, that it wasn't long before he had fallen fast asleep.

All through the house, there was not a sound to be heard save for the *tick tock* of the big clock in the hall. Nutmeg was so absorbed in her work that she hardly noticed the afternoon slipping by.

"Goodness," she said eventually, looking at her watch. "It's gone four o'clock, and I haven't even iced the fairy cakes." So she hurried downstairs. But when she reached the hall, she noticed that the front door had been left open.

That's odd, she thought, for she knew that Tumtum was very particular about closing it. And all of a sudden a horrible thought occurred to her.

"Oh, surely not," she whispered. "*Surely* the General wouldn't have broken his promise!" But something made her go outside and check the front gates.

And they were open, too.

She raced back indoors, calling the General's name, and, getting no reply, she ran upstairs to look for him in his room.

But neither the General nor his pogo stick were there.

"Tumtum! Wake up! Oh, wake up! The General's gone!" Nutmeg cried, bursting into the library.

"Gone, dear?" Tumtum muttered sleepily, rubbing his eyes.

"Yes, gone, dear!" Nutmeg cried. "Gone bouncing around Rose Cottage, dear!"

"But he can't have gone," Tumtum said. "He promised he wouldn't leave the broom cupboard."

"Oh, promises, promises!" Nutmeg wailed. "He's gone, Tumtum. We must get him back before he's seen!"

Tumtum raised himself to his feet and followed his wife to the front gates. Just as Nutmeg had said, they had been left wide open, swinging in the draft. And from the other side of the wall the Nutmouses could hear Mr. Mildew talking on the telephone.

"Well, we can't set out to look for him now," Tumtum said firmly. "Three mice would be much more conspicuous than one. The General will come home as soon as he gets hungry, we can be sure of that. We must just pray that no one sees him bouncing back under the dresser."

Nutmeg agreed, but there followed an agonizing wait. They sat in the kitchen, listening hopefully for the sound of the General *rap tap tapping* at the front door. But supper time came and went—and still there was no sign of him.

"It's most unlike him to miss a meal," Nutmeg said eventually. "He must be in some sort of trouble."

"I suppose we'll have to go and look for him—he's been

gone for ages," Tumtum said. "But we'd better wait another hour or so, then everyone will have gone to bed."

"He may be injured," Nutmeg said. "I'll bring some bandages in case he needs patching up."

So at ten o'clock, after an anxious cup of cocoa, the Nutmouses finally set out to track the General down.

Tumtum held Nutmeg's paw as they groped their way under the dresser, for he knew it made her shiver to feel the cobwebs brushing against her legs. Nutmeg was a little wary of the Rose Cottage spiders, for some of them were bigger than she was.

When they stepped out into the Mildews' kitchen it was very dark. The curtains were closed, and the downstairs lights had been turned off.

Tumtum shone his flashlight around the room, to be sure that there was no one lurking. Then they scurried through every nook and cranny, calling the General's name. They looked for him in the cupboards and the cutlery drawers, and in the saucepans and the teacups; then they hunted in the laundry basket and the vegetable rack. They even looked inside Arthur's boots.

And when they had searched the kitchen they searched the hall, then the living room, then the upstairs landing, and then the bathroom; and drawing a blank there, they crept into the study and searched that, too—while Mr. Mildew lay snoring on the sofa, clutching one of the legs of his mechanical frog.

"We'd better check the children's room," Tumtum said finally. "There's nowhere else he could be."

So, with much huffing and puffing, for they were getting very tired, the Nutmouses climbed up the long steep steps to the attic.

Arthur and Lucy were sound asleep, for it was long past their bedtime. But the Nutmouses entered the room on tiptoe just in case. When Tumtum was sure the children were sleeping, he turned on his flashlight and shone it over the floor. And they were both astonished at what they saw.

"Oh!" Nutmeg cried, gazing around her in dismay. She

had tidied the room only last night, but now it looked like a battlefield. "Whatever could have happened?" she asked.

Tumtum put his arm around her, feeling equally bewildered. It didn't occur to them that the General could be responsible for such a mess.

They stood in silence, surveying the chaos. Then suddenly they heard a noise that made them jump. It was the sort of noise a ghost might make—a long, muffled *Aaaaah*. They both stiffened and pricked their ears. There was a brief silence, then they heard it again, louder this time.

"It's coming from the dollhouse," said Nutmeg. "Look! The door's been left open!"

They crept toward it, glancing warily at the tin soldiers firing from the windows. Then they poked their heads into the hall. The moaning had started up again and it sounded much closer now.

"It's coming from in there," Tumtum said, gesturing toward the living room. They tiptoed together through the door. "Gracious," Tumtum said, pointing to the hearth. "It's the General's pogo stick!"

No sooner had he spoken than the moaning started again—but this time, instead of *Aaaaah*, it sounded like *Heeeelp Meeeee!* And it was echoing down the chimney.

Tumtum crouched in the fireplace and shone his flashlight up to discover a very wretched-looking General Marchmouse, suspended upside down.

"General!" Tumtum cried. "Whatever are you doing?"

"I am hanging upside down!" the General said furiously. "Can't you see? I've been stuck here all afternoon. Now pull me down, won't you? Pull me down!"

The General stretched out a paw, and Tumtum grasped it as tight as he could and pulled and pulled. Then Nutmeg held on to Tumtum, and she pulled, too. And finally, with Tumtum and Nutmeg both pulling with all their might, the General thudded into the grate.

"Ooooh!" he moaned feebly. "I thought I'd starve to death!"

"How on earth did you get up there, General?" Tumtum asked, heaving him to his feet.

"I was hiding," the General said miserably, rubbing the bruise on the end of his nose. "I'd had a perfectly pleasant afternoon

commanding the tin soldiers in battle. Then I decided to take Arthur's train for a spin, but the tiresome thing crashed, and just as I was crawling out of the wreckage—"

"So it was *YOU* who caused all this mayhem, General!" Tumtum said furiously. "When we saw the mess, we thought rats had broken in. But it was *YOU*! What a fine way to carry on! You break your word of honor, and then you come up here and wreak havoc with Arthur's and Lucy's toys! It is hardly the sort of behavior one expects from an officer and a gentlemouse!"

The General, who had been expecting sympathy, flushed angrily. But before he could utter a word of protest, Tumtum had thrust an arm under his shoulders and was marching him out of the dollhouse and across the floor.

"I'm sorry, General," he said grimly. "But you're coming back to Nutmouse Hall—under house arrest!"

Chapter Five

As Tumtum was leading his indignant prisoner toward the steps, Nutmeg noticed the letter addressed to her on the children's dresser. She quickly scrambled up to it, climbing by means of the various socks and tights and sweater sleeves tumbling from the drawers.

She was dismayed to think of the children coming home to find all their toys in disarray. And she was terrified they might have caught sight of the General before he flung himself down the dollhouse chimney. So she was anxious to see what the letter would say.

But when she read it, her mind was put at rest.

"An elf!" she chuckled, reading in the glow of Lucy's alarm clock. "So they think General Marchmouse is an elf. Goodness, what would all the mice in the village think?"

Nutmeg at once dashed back into the dollhouse and sat down at the desk in the living room where she kept her stationery. She had her main desk at Nutmouse Hall, but this was the one she used when she wrote to the children. There was even a little light on it, which she needed on nights such as this when there was no moon to see by.

She dipped her pen in the ink pot, unfolded a piece of stiff white paper, and composed the following reply:

Dear Arthur and Lucy,

I am sorry for all the mess the naughty elf has caused, but I will come and tidy it up tomorrow night. I believe I know the elf concerned, and I promise he won't come back. You need not do a thing.

Love,

Nutmeg

She put the letter in an envelope and addressed it *To Arthur and Lucy Mildew, The Attic, Rose Cottage.* (Her writing was so small that the children always had to read her letters

with a magnifying glass.) She stuffed it in the pocket of her apron, then climbed back up the dresser and propped it against Lucy's hairbrush. After that, she rushed off to catch up with Tumtum, who had already dragged his prisoner back to Nutmouse Hall.

The Nutmouses were determined to keep Nutmeg's promise, and to prevent the General from ever returning to the attic. So Tumtum padlocked the front gates, and he kept the key to the padlock on a string around his neck so as to be sure the General could not get his paws on it.

They had expected him to be furious at being held prisoner, but he appeared to take it quite well.

On Monday, which was the first day of his captivity, he seemed restless, and pogoed around and around the ballroom. But on Tuesday he was much calmer, and by Wednesday he gave the impression he was enjoying his quiet life. He helped Nutmeg make a stew in the morning, then he ate a magnificent lunch and spent the afternoon dozing in the library.

"I do so like these peaceful spring days," Tumtum said as he led his guest into dinner that evening.

"Quite so," the General agreed. "A peaceful day is just the sort of day I like."

Tumtum was very pleased to hear this. But in actual fact the General hated peaceful days, and he was not feeling nearly as settled as he would have Tumtum believe.

The General was secretly still fuming at being held hostage, and was longing to get back to the attic. He may have been battered and bruised by his adventures, but every bone in his body ached for another ride on Arthur's train set, and another chance to lob toy grenades at the dollhouse.

So his relaxed manner was just a ploy while he plotted his escape. He had been thinking of all sorts of bold and foolish schemes. He could smash through the Nutmouses' gates with a battering ram! Or blast them open with gunpowder!

But since he didn't have a battering ram, nor any gunpowder, he was unlikely to succeed.

Then finally, shortly before dinner, he had come up with what he considered to be a much more sensible plan. . . .

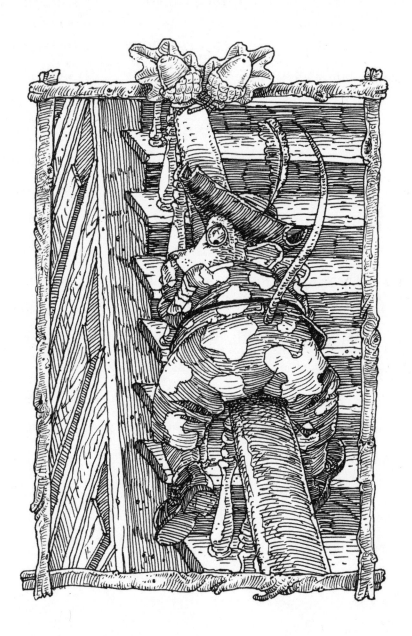

"How about a game of Scrabble?" Tumtum asked when they had finished dessert.

The General yawned theatrically. "Truth be told, I'm feeling a bit sluggish," he said. "I think I'll go to bed and read a learned book."

"Good idea!" Tumtum said approvingly, thinking he might do just the same. "Sleep tight, then."

"Sleep tight," the General replied. Then he walked upstairs, humming a little tune. But instead of going to his room, he loitered on the landing. And as soon as he heard the Nutmouses going into the library with their tray of cocoa, he slid gleefully down the banister and slipped out of the front door. He had hidden his pogo stick among the croquet mallets. He picked it up and started hopping purposefully across the broom cupboard floor.

But he did not head for the gates, for he knew they were locked. Instead, he bounced around Nutmouse Hall toward the broom cupboard's back wall. High up in that wall was a little window, and it was through that window that the General intended to escape.

It was far above his head, and the wall much too smooth for him to climb. But the General had an ambitious plan.

Pressing down on the footrest as hard as he could, he pogoed back and forth on the floor, each bounce carrying him higher and higher, until he was bouncing so high he could see a fly cruising in the air below him.

And then the General bounced higher still—and when he was level with the window he let go of his pogo stick and grabbed the sill with both paws. He clung to it for dear life and heard the stick clatter to the floor beneath him. Then, slowly, he heaved himself up onto the ledge.

No one can make a prisoner of me! he thought as he stood looking down triumphantly on the rooftops of Nutmouse Hall.

He wriggled out through the little crack in the window-pane, then clambered down the honeysuckle to the ground. "General Marchmouse strikes again," he chuckled as he marched along beside the wall. Then he held in his stomach and crawled into Rose Cottage under the garden door.

Chapter Six

Mr. Mildew was sitting at the kitchen table, but the General crept across the floor behind him and reached the hall unseen. The children were in the living room—he could hear their voices carrying under the door. "Good!" he said, thinking that once again he would have all the toys to himself.

But when he arrived in the attic, he found that everything was amiss. The soldiers he had lined up in battle had all been swept to one side. And his sandbags had been dumped in the toy box.

What *nerve!* he thought, furious that the children should have interfered with his battle scene. He rolled up his sleeves and began to drag his troops back into position. He arranged the khaki soldiers in crescents around the floor, then he hauled the red ones into the dollhouse.

He was dripping with sweat, and his camouflage uniform felt unbearably hot. There was only one thing for it. He would have to strip off.

No one will see me, he thought, hastily removing his jacket and trousers. He undressed down to his underpants and felt much more comfortable.

"Back to work!" he grunted, and started lugging a soldier up the dollhouse stairs. He stood him on the landing, shooting down toward the front door. Then he heaved another into the bedroom. "Pow! Pow!" he shouted, pointing its rifle out of the window—

But then he reeled back in fright. For peering in at him was a huge, human eye.

It was Lucy, and she got a fright, too, as any child might who discovered a mouse playing in her dollhouse.

"Oh!" she cried.

But though she was very taken aback, she was still quicker-

witted than the General. While he stood rooted to the spot, she shot out a hand and shut the bedroom window then snapped the latch down on the outside.

"Arthur, look what's in here—a mouse wearing underpants!"

The General panicked and stumbled out of the bedroom toward the stairs, but by the time he got to the ground floor Lucy had secured the other windows, too, and bolted the dollhouse door.

He was trapped.

Arthur came and crouched next to his sister, and they both peered inside, watching in astonishment as the little brown mouse stamped his feet in rage, demanding to be let out.

"He's the one who's been playing with my soldiers!" Arthur said, seeing the tin man on the dollhouse landing and the sandbags piled by the door. First a fairy, and now a mouse in underpants! There seemed to be no end of extraordinary things going on in the attic.

The General was rattling the windows now and kicking furiously at the front door. "We mustn't let him go," said Lucy. "He might cause even more damage."

"But we can't just leave him in the dollhouse," said Arthur. "He'll keep us awake all night scrabbling."

The children sat in silence a moment, wondering what to do.

"I've got an idea!" Lucy said finally. "Just for today, let's put him in a biscuit tin. We can pierce holes in it so he can breathe, and give him some food and water. And we can leave the tin in the kitchen overnight so he doesn't keep us awake. Then tomorrow morning we'll take him to school and put him in Pets' House. He'll have a lovely time there."

Arthur at once agreed, for Pets' House was a very agreeable place. It was a big wire cage, and all sorts of animals had lived in it. Once there had been a guinea pig called Sam, but eventually he'd died of old age, and then two hamsters had moved in. But one vacation the hamsters had gone to live with the principal, Miss Page, and she had gotten along with them so well that she'd decided to keep them at home. And after that two gerbils had arrived, but they'd had lots of children, and some of their children had had children, too, so at the present time there were twelve of them living in the cage.

"Good idea. He's bound to like living with gerbils—they're just the same size as him," Arthur said confidently. "I'll go and look for a tin."

Hearing this, the General became even more frantic. "Gerbils!" he cried in horror, hurling himself desperately against the front door. "They're sending me to live with *gerbils*! Oh, the shame of it!"

Lucy stood guard at the dollhouse, making soothing noises, while Arthur raced downstairs. A few minutes later, he returned carrying a purple tin with SCOTTISH OATCAKES written on the side. He poked three holes in the lid with a compass, and Lucy made a bed inside out of old socks. Then the children took two bowls from the dollhouse, and filled one with breadcrumbs and the other with water.

"He'll be very comfortable in there," Lucy said. Then she opened the living room window and reached a hand inside.

The General cowered behind the sofa with his paws over his eyes. "Not a biscuit tin!" he begged. "Oh, please don't put me in a dark, dank biscuit tin!" But his protests went unheard. He felt a sudden brush on his spine, and next thing he knew he was being carried into the air, in Lucy's fist. Then everything went dark as he was dumped in his tin prison, and the lid shut on him.

"Let me out! I demand to be let out!" he cried furiously as the children carried him downstairs to the kitchen. "Do you know who I am?"

But of course the children didn't know, and though the great General Marchmouse shouted with all his might, they heard only a tiny squeak.

Much later, when he'd squealed and ranted all he could, the General collapsed on his bed of socks and sank his head into his paws. He thought longingly of his wife, Mrs. Marchmouse, and of their comfortable little home in the gun cupboard, and he wondered if he would ever see his own bed again.

And when he remembered what was in store for him the next day, he felt quite cold. "*Gerbils!*" he kept muttering in horror. "*Gerbils!* I'm going to be sent to live with *gerbils!*" The General had never met a gerbil before, but he'd been told that they were savage creatures who went around naked and ate with their paws.

He didn't like the sound of them at all.

Chapter Seven

The General spent a wretched night tossing and turning in his tin prison. He kept shouting for Tumtum and Nutmeg, praying they would come out looking for him again as they had a few nights earlier. But his cries were in vain, for the Nutmouses were sound asleep in Nutmouse Hall, with no inkling of what was going on.

And when Nutmeg went downstairs next morning to cook breakfast, she still didn't suspect a thing. The General had seemed so weary after dinner last night, she supposed he was sleeping in.

That will be just what he needs, she thought approvingly, melting a pat of butter in her frying pan. *No doubt he'll wake up when he smells the kippers cooking.*

But at eight o'clock, when Nutmeg rang the bell for

breakfast, the General did not appear.

"I'd let him sleep in if I were you," Tumtum said, sitting down hungrily. "He must have worn himself out with that silly carrying on in the attic."

"But if he doesn't come down soon his breakfast will spoil," Nutmeg fussed. "I've an idea. I shall take him a cup of tea in bed. That should wake him up."

So she laid a tray with a pot of tea, a jug of milk, and a bowl of sugar, and made her way upstairs.

But when she knocked on the General's door, there was no reply.

I hope he's not unwell, she thought.

She knocked again. And when he still didn't answer she opened the door a crack and peeked inside.

And what she saw gave her such a start that she dropped her tray. "Tumtum!" she shrieked, racing downstairs. "Tumtum! *The General's gone!*"

"Whatever do you mean, dear?" Tumtum asked as she burst into the kitchen. "He can't have gone; I locked the front gate."

"Well, he's not in his room, and he clearly didn't sleep

there last night," Nutmeg cried. "The bedcovers aren't even rumpled."

"Well, he won't have got far," Tumtum said. "He can't have opened the front gate without the key. And there's no other way out. So he must be here somewhere."

Tumtum at once abandoned his breakfast, and they started racing around Nutmouse Hall, looking for the General. But though they searched in each of their thirty-six rooms, he was nowhere to be found.

Then they went out of the front door and saw his pogo stick lying on the broom cupboard floor under the window. And the same incredible thought occurred to them both.

"He couldn't have bounced that high, surely . . . it would be . . . it would be quite impossible," Tumtum stammered.

"Nothing is impossible for General Marchmouse," Nutmeg said despairingly. "He must have made a great bounce for freedom after dinner, when he told us he was going upstairs to read in bed. I'll bet he's spent the night in the dollhouse, and now he's most likely running amok with Arthur's soldiers. Oh, I do hope he hasn't been seen!"

"Let's go and find him now," Tumtum said. "It's as good a time as any—the children will be at school, and Mr. Mildew will be working."

They set off at once, letting themselves out of the gates, then creeping underneath the dresser. But when they poked their noses out into the kitchen Arthur and Lucy were still there.

The Nutmouses waited while the children packed their satchels and buttoned their coats before finally making to leave by the garden door.

"I wonder what she's got in there," Nutmeg said, seeing the biscuit tin under Lucy's arm.

"Oh, I don't know, dear," Tumtum replied, not thinking it of any significance.

As the children were going, Mr. Mildew appeared in the kitchen. "Have you remembered your captive?" he asked them.

"He's in here," Lucy said, pointing to the tin. "You do think he will be happy at school, don't you?"

"Oh, very happy. Very happy indeed," Mr. Mildew mumbled, pouring cornflakes into his coffee cup. "We certainly don't want him in the house, at any rate."

The Nutmouses looked at each other in horror. "Captive?" Nutmeg whispered. "Surely they're not talking about the General?"

"We'll soon find out," Tumtum said grimly.

When Mr. Mildew's back was turned, they flew across the kitchen floor and raced up to the attic.

They realized at once that something was wrong—for there had been the most dreadful scuffle in the dollhouse. The crockery was smashed, and all the furniture upturned, and two of the banister rails were broken. "Look, the children have left us a letter," Nutmeg said, pointing to the dresser. The mice scrambled up to read it, dreading what it might say.

Dear Nutmeg,

We have found the elf and he's not really an elf at all. He's a mouse! But he is very sweet, and we like him. We have taken him to school in a biscuit tin, and he's going to live with the gerbils in Pets' House. He will be very happy there, because he'll have lots of friends to play with. And so now there won't be any more mess in the attic for you to clear up.

Love,

Arthur and Lucy

"He's been captured!" Nutmeg cried. "Oh, how terrible! Just think of it! What will Mrs. Marchmouse say? She'll be quite beside herself with grief. They may never see each other again! Oh, Tumtum, we have to save him!"

"We will, dear," Tumtum replied bravely. "Now, come on! We must follow the children to school at once!"

Knowing there was not a moment to lose, they both hurtled downstairs to the kitchen, then slithered outside under the garden door. The mist was still clearing, and as they beat a path through the grass their coats got soaked in dew.

The school was just a few hundred yards or so from Rose Cottage, down the lane that led past the village shop. The mice had often walked as far as the school gates, for they had friends who lived in a mailbox a little way beyond them.

But in the past they had always made the journey at night, when there was no one about. This morning it took them longer, for there were several people milling in the lane and a cat prowling menacingly. So instead of going along the tarmac, they climbed up onto the bank and scrambled along under cover of the hedgerow.

It took them nearly an hour to reach the school gates. The playground was deserted, for the children were in a morning assembly. So they ran straight toward the school building, then crawled inside through an air vent. They came out in the middle of a corridor full of bags and coats.

It was a small school, but to the Nutmouses it seemed as big as a town. The children's wooden lockers were the size of houses, and the tiled corridor, lit by bright neon lights, stretched before them like a long road.

For a moment they felt quite dazed. "Come on," Tumtum said eventually, taking Nutmeg by the paw and pulling her across the corridor. "Let's try in here."

He led her under a door with ROOM 3A written on it. On the other side, they found themselves in a room full of wooden

desks, taller than Nutmouse Hall. "How disgusting!" Nutmeg said, seeing a big glob of chewing gum stuck under one of the desktops.

The Nutmouses went all around the room, shouting the General's name. But there was no sign of him.

So they hurried back into the corridor, and tried the next door along.

This one had ROOM 2B written on it, and as they wriggled underneath they became aware of some sort of to-do going on inside. At first they could just hear shouting and shrieking. But then, rising above the din, came the unmistakable voice of General Marchmouse.

"I'll have you know that I am an officer in the Royal Mouse Army, you little ruffians!" they heard him roar; then there was a chorus of jeers.

"That's him all right!" Tumtum said as he and Nutmeg crept into the classroom. But what they saw gave them a horrible fright.

In the far corner of the room there was a big wire cage on a table. And inside, the General was imprisoned with a crowd of naked gerbils.

The room was otherwise deserted, so the Nutmouses ran straight toward them. As they got closer, they could see that one of the gerbils was flicking the General with bits of straw. The cage was lined with filthy bedding and, to Nutmeg's horror, the food had been served in a communal trough.

The gerbils were making such a racket that the Nutmouses had to shout to get the General's attention.

"Oh, Mr. and Mrs. Nutmouse!" he cried out in relief when he finally heard them calling up to him from the floor. "Oh, thank heaven you've come! I have been most hideously abused! I've not even a blazer to my name! Oh, the shame of it!"

"I want to take a look at the bars on your cage, General," Tumtum shouted back. "I might be able to cut through them with a hacksaw. But I can't climb the table—the legs are too slippery. Is there anything you can throw down?"

When they heard the word *hacksaw*, the gerbils fell silent.

They had lived all their lives in captivity, but they still hadn't given up hope of escape. And the thought of getting their paws on a hacksaw made their hearts tremble with excitement.

"Hold there, whoever you are!" one of them squeaked down to Tumtum. "We'll make you a ladder out of straw."

The gerbils all worked together, and in what seemed like no time they had plaited a sturdy ladder out of their filthy straw bedding. They tied one end of it to the bars of the cage and tossed the other down to Tumtum and Nutmeg, who climbed it hurriedly. Tumtum went first so he could help Nutmeg up onto the tabletop.

But when they reached the cage, they realized that the General's predicament was much worse than they had feared.

The cage bars were nearly a quarter of an inch thick; it would take the Nutmouses weeks to saw through them. And the door was secured with a padlock twenty times the size of the one they used on the gates of Nutmouse Hall. They would never be able to break it open.

The gerbils looked on intently as Tumtum and Nutmeg walked around and around their cage, looking for any possible escape routes. The General, who was usually so good in a crisis, was slumped miserably on the exercise wheel.

"I just can't understand it," he moaned. "This classroom is commanded by a teacher called Miss Short, and before she led her troops into assembly I told her who I was, and demanded in no uncertain terms that I be let out. But she ignored me! *She ignored me!* And all the children seemed to think it a great joke that I was wearing underpants. 'A mouse in pants! A mouse in pants!' they all squealed, as though they expected me to be entirely naked! I have never felt so misunderstood."

"Who keeps the key to this cage?" Tumtum asked, ignoring this self-pitying speech.

"The janitor," the General replied glumly.

"Where does he keep it?" Nutmeg enquired.

"On a big key ring around his belt," the General said. "He wears it at all times, except when he's opening the door. And he's a giant of a fellow. You haven't a hope of getting it off him."

"And when does he open the door?" Tumtum persisted.

"During the lunch break, when everyone else is in the cafeteria," piped up one of the gerbils, who had known the same routine all his life. "But he only opens it for a few seconds—just long enough to stick his fist in and dump more food in the trough."

"And do the children ever take you out for exercise?" Nutmeg asked.

"Never!" another gerbil replied. "Miss Short won't let them, because we give her the creeps—I've heard her say so. So the children just poke their fingers through the bars and tickle us. And when there's a special occasion—a parents' day or some such—they decorate us."

"How?" Nutmeg asked, astonished.

"Oh, all sorts of things," the gerbil prattled. "Last time, they tied pink ribbons around our necks and—"

But at this disclosure he was interrupted by a great gulping sound. To everyone's astonishment, General Marchmouse was weeping.

"Oh, the shame!" he cried wretchedly. "The shame of it all! Can you imagine if the *Mouse Times* finds out about this! I can see their front page now: 'General Marchmouse has been captured. He is imprisoned in a school cage, with a pink ribbon tied around his neck.' I shall never live it down!"

Even the gerbils were touched by this, for there is something very upsetting about the sight of a grown mouse crying, no matter how badly he has behaved.

But try as they might, there was nothing anyone could say to console the General that morning.

Chapter Eight

The General was still sobbing when the mice heard the children making their way back from the assembly.

"I'll think of something," Tumtum promised him. Then he and Nutmeg fled back down the ladder.

As soon as they reached the floor, the gerbils hoisted it back up into the cage and hid it beneath their bedding. Then the door opened and Miss Short came in, followed by the children.

"Quick, this way!" Tumtum shouted, pulling his wife toward the wall. They ran along the baseboard, searching for somewhere to hide. But there was not a mouse hole to be found.

In desperation, they dived into a satchel lying open on the floor. Once they were inside, it felt oddly familiar. The canvas had been patched with gold thread, and there was a wooden pencil case with the initials *A.M.* scratched into the lid.

"Why, it's Arthur's satchel!" Nutmeg exclaimed. "I repaired it only last week. What luck, dear! This must be his classroom."

"And we must be sitting under his desk," Tumtum said. The Nutmouses crouched at the bottom of the bag, among the crumbs and the candy wrappers. All around, they could hear the sound of chairs and chattering voices. Then Miss Short clapped her hands, and the room fell silent.

"Now, class. I have an announcement to make," she said.

Nutmeg wrinkled her nose. She didn't like the tone of Miss Short's voice.

"As you know, I have been wondering what to do about the gerbil problem," Miss Short continued. "When they came to live with us, there were only two gerbils. But now there are twelve! *Twelve gerbils*, children! Just think of it! If they continue to multiply at this rate, we shall have seventy-two gerbils by next term, and four hundred and thirty-two gerbils by the term after that. And in a year, they will number *two thousand five hundred and ninety-two*!" (Miss Short was a math teacher, so she enjoyed these sorts of calculations.)

There were gasps all around the room as these extraordinary statistics sank in.

"But two thousand five hundred and ninety-two gerbils wouldn't fit in the cage," someone said.

"That is correct," Miss Short replied. "And it is for that reason that I have decided to find our gerbils a new home."

There was a chorus of groans at this announcement, for the children had become quite attached to them. But Miss Short was adamant. "Now don't be sad," she said briskly. "They will all be well looked after."

"Where are they going, Miss Short?" someone asked. The Nutmouses, still hidden in Arthur's satchel, listened anxiously for her reply.

"I am happy to announce that they are going to a pet shop in town!" Miss Short said brightly, as though this was a special treat, like going to the cinema. "I am going to take them there myself on Saturday when I go to return my library books."

"Will they be kept together?" one of the children asked.

The gerbils—who, like the Nutmouses, had been following every word—all held their breath.

Miss Short hesitated. Until that moment, she had not considered whether the gerbils would be kept together or not. She did not think it of any importance.

"I imagine they will be split into different cages and sold in pairs," she said finally. "I doubt anyone would want to buy all of them together."

The gerbils did not like the sound of this one little bit. When they heard that their family was to be separated, they protested violently, hurling themselves against the bars, shouting and squawking as loudly as they could.

"Goodness!" Miss Short said irritably. "What a nasty noise they make. It's just as well we've found another home for them."

"What will happen to the mouse?" someone asked. Tumtum and Nutmeg recognized the voice at once. It was Arthur's.

"The pet shop will find him a home, too," Miss Short replied. "Perhaps they'll even find him a mate. I'm sure there

will be much demand for a mouse wearing underpants." The Nutmouses bristled with anger, willing Arthur to protest.

And he did, for Arthur wanted the General brought home, too. It was *his* mouse, because it had been found in *his* cottage. It had been rather a nuisance there, it was true, and yet he felt protective toward it. And he didn't see why Miss Short thought she had the right to sell it.

"I can take him home with me again," he said helpfully. "He may as well go back where he came from."

But Miss Short was not keen on this idea. "Don't be silly, Arthur," she replied. "You told me yourself that you have no cage for it, and imagine what destruction it might cause if it were to run free. Just think—it might *multiply*."

"But I want to take him home with me," Arthur persisted. "I wouldn't have brought him here if I'd thought he was going to be given away."

"Now that's enough, Arthur," Miss Short said crossly. "These creatures are all going to the pet shop, and that is the last I am going to say on the matter."

There was a sudden racket from the cage as the General shouted something very rude at her—but Miss Short did not hear.

"Now, children," she said briskly. "Let's get out our math books, shall we?" And though Arthur felt very indignant, he hesitated to say any more.

Meanwhile, Tumtum and Nutmeg huddled in the bottom of Arthur's satchel, their brains spinning. The town was ten miles away—if the General was taken there to be sold, he would never be seen again.

"We must think of something!" Nutmeg cried.

"We will, darling," Tumtum said, but he felt a deep foreboding. Saturday was the day after tomorrow—they had little time. He squeezed his wife's paw, trying not to show his fear.

"Oh, think, Tumtum! Think!" Nutmeg pleaded.

And think they did. There they sat in Arthur's satchel, thinking all through the math lesson, then all through the English lesson, too. And then they thought all through the spelling test;

and when the bell rang for break they were still thinking so hard they both jumped. But they still hadn't thought of a plan.

They waited until the children had gone outside—less noisily than usual, for they were all subdued at the thought of losing their pets. Then, as soon as the room was quiet, the Nutmouses climbed out of the satchel and ran toward the cage.

The gerbils tossed down the ladder, and when Tumtum and Nutmeg appeared they all threw themselves against the bars, clamoring for help.

"Do something, Mr. and Mrs. Nutmouse!" they cried. "If they split us up our whole family will be destroyed. We'll never see each other again. You must help us. You're our only hope!"

Tumtum and Nutmeg tried to reassure them, but the situation was very bleak. The only consolation was that the General appeared to be back to his old self again. He had stopped his boo-hooing, and instead was standing with one foot on the feeding trough, spitting with rage.

"A pet shop!" he fumed. "A pet shop! How dare that

wretched woman presume to dispatch the great General Marchmouse to a pet shop!"

Tumtum turned to him as a sudden inspiration struck. "Do you think it might be worth calling in the Royal Mouse Army, General?" he asked. "They could launch an attack on the janitor next time he opens the cage."

The gerbils all pricked up their ears at the mention of the Royal Mouse Army—but the General was dismissive.

"Pah! Do you imagine I hadn't thought of that already?" he snorted. "I am confident, of course, that the Royal Mouse Army would send every soldier it could muster to rescue *me*. But there's no point trying to summon it. All the troops are undergoing a week's intensive pogo-training at Apple Farm— it's nearly two miles away; they'd never get back here in time.

"And besides," he went on, "there's nothing the army could do against the janitor. He's huge—if you fired a cannonball at him, he wouldn't even feel it." (This was probably true, for the Royal Mouse Army's cannonballs were the size of raisins.)

As this one ray of hope was extinguished, the gerbils

looked even more wretched. Some were hugging each other now and sobbing, dreading the parting to come.

Meanwhile, Tumtum and Nutmeg went on thinking. But even after thinking for another three whole minutes, which is a long time in a mouse's life, they still hadn't thought of what to do.

Chapter Nine

Eventually, just as Nutmeg was thinking she could think no more, an extraordinary idea began to play itself out in her mind. She squeezed her eyes tightly shut, feeling a shiver run down her spine.

"I've had a brainstorm!" she announced.

"What is it, dear?" Tumtum asked eagerly. Nutmeg's brainstorms were not always sensible, but they were often spectacular. And he felt they were all in need of something spectacular just now.

"We must summon Miss Tiptoe's ballet school!" Nutmeg said.

Everyone looked bewildered. They had all heard of Miss Tiptoe's ballet school, of course, for it was the most famous ballet school in the land. It was situated in the church vestry, and smart young mice came from far and wide to board there for a term or two. If you went to a mouse ball you could always tell the mice who had been trained by Miss Tiptoe, because they moved around the dance floor much more gracefully than anyone else.

But what possible use could Miss Tiptoe and her ballerinas be against the giant janitor?

"*The ballet school*, Mrs. Nutmouse?" the General said witheringly. "I suppose this is your idea of a joke."

"Oh no, General. I wouldn't joke at a time like this," Nutmeg replied excitedly. "Our only hope of setting you all free is to get hold of the key to the padlock. But Tumtum and I can't do that if the janitor's wearing the key ring on his belt—"

"Yes, yes," the General interrupted. "So how will your dancers save the day?"

"Just listen," Nutmeg said impatiently. "You said that the janitor removes the key ring in order to open the padlock— so that's when we must snatch it. But Tumtum and I could never do it alone; we wouldn't be strong enough. And even if we managed to tug it from the janitor's hands, he'd catch us before we could run away with it.

"But imagine if Miss Tiptoe's ballerinas were assembled in the wings, hiding behind a desk, or a wastepaper basket . . . and imagine if each ballerina was mounted on a pogo stick, waiting until the janitor came to unlock the cage. And then imagine if they all bounced silently toward him on their sticks, bouncing higher and higher, until they were bouncing so high that they could snatch the keys from his hands and bounce away with them! I've seen Miss Tiptoe's ballerinas performing in the church, and they're so nimble and light-footed that the janitor would hardly know what had happened until it was all over!"

Everyone looked stunned. Nutmeg's proposal was so extraordinary that it took awhile for it to sink in. They tried to picture the incredible scene she had described. A troupe of tiny ballerinas, ambushing the colossal janitor! Could it really work?

The gerbils weren't at all sure. But they had to believe in it. It was their only hope.

"I think it's a splendid plan!" one of them declared. "Quite splendid! Quite ingenious! I wish I'd thought of it myself!"

This was all the encouragement the other gerbils needed. With a great roar of approval they rose to their feet and started cheering, "Hooray for Mrs. Nutmouse!" Tumtum clapped his wife on the back, feeling very proud.

But the General still looked scornful. "If the janitor's keys were snatched, he'd run after them," he said. "The ballerinas wouldn't stand a chance."

"You underestimate them, General," Nutmeg said. "Miss Tiptoe's mice are the nimblest in England. They're so light, they can almost fly. When they've snatched the key ring, they'll drag it into the corner of the room before the janitor's recovered his wits. Tumtum and I will be waiting for them, and we can unhook the key to the cage."

"He's got hundreds of keys on his belt. How will you know which it is?" the General asked.

"It's the small green one," one of the gerbils replied. "He paints his keys different colors so he can tell one from the other."

"Good—and when we've removed it, we'll tie the key ring to the girls' pogo sticks," Nutmeg went on eagerly. "Then the entire dance troupe will bounce out into the corridor, with the bunch of keys clattering behind them. While the janitor runs after them, Tumtum and I will climb up the ladder and unlock the cage."

"But what if the janitor catches the ballerinas?" Tumtum asked, voicing everyone's worst fear.

"He won't," Nutmeg answered firmly. "They will move much too fast for him, especially if they're on pogo sticks. As soon as we've opened the cage, we'll sound the all-clear. Then the ballerinas can simply drop the keys and bounce back into the playground through the air vent."

"Where do you intend to get hold of the pogo sticks?" the General asked, determined to find some hitch in Nutmeg's plan.

"You said that the Royal Mouse Army had a big supply of them—we'll borrow some from the barracks," she replied. "Surely they're unlikely to refuse if you write us a letter of authorization."

The General considered all this for a moment, stroking his whiskers. He supposed it might just work; and it was certainly better than having no plan at all. And yet something about it made him uneasy. The truth was that his pride had been deeply wounded by his imprisonment, and the thought of being rescued by ballerinas was more than he could bear. Imagine if one of the gerbils snitched about it to the village— he'd be a laughingstock!

But, as he mulled things over, a more cheerful picture began to appear.

Perhaps it needn't be so humiliating, so long as I take sole command, he mused. *I might be behind bars, but I can still issue orders, and I can still take all the credit if it works. Why! This could turn out to be one of my greatest battles yet!*

The General felt a quiet flutter in his stomach. How impressed everyone would be if he won! In his mind's eye, he could already see his picture on the front page of the *Mouse Times*, accompanied by a glorious report: "The Great General Marchmouse conquers against all odds. He escapes, Houdinistyle, from a gerbils' cage, and sends a giant school janitor fleeing for his life."

The involvement of Miss Tiptoe's ballerinas could be glossed over entirely.

"How soon can the dancers be mobilized?" he asked.

"We shall have to find out," Tumtum replied, relieved that his wife's plan had been accepted. "Nutmeg and I have got a lot to do. First we must get to the barracks and collect the pogo sticks. Then we'll go and see Miss Tiptoe and persuade her to lend us her dancers. And that mightn't be easy—it's a risky enterprise, and she'll probably have grave misgivings about them taking part."

"Not when she learns that it is my freedom that's at stake," the General said grandly.

Tumtum ignored this and looked at his watch. It was nearly twenty past eleven; the children would be returning from break at any moment. "We must go at once," he said, turning to his wife.

With not a moment to spare, the Nutmouses quickly

shimmied down to the floor. And just as the gerbils were whisking the ladder back into the cage, the door burst open and the members of Room 2B started pouring into the room.

"We'll be back tonight!" Tumtum called over his shoulder as he and Nutmeg hurtled behind Miss Short's desk and under cover of a filing cabinet. They waited until the children were all seated and had their heads in their books. Then they crept out under the door, and across the corridor toward the air vent.

"Bring me my field glasses and my compass and my pistol and my whiskey flask and my military uniform and something decent to eat!" the General called after them—but the Nutmouses were already gone.

Chapter Ten

The General would have been tickled to know that Arthur and Lucy had spent the whole of break time thinking about him. As soon as the bell rang, Arthur had rushed into the playground to find his sister and tell her all about Miss Short's plans. As he had expected, Lucy thought it all just as unfair as he did.

"It's bad enough her selling the gerbils, but she's got no right to sell our mouse!" she said crossly. "We brought him here thinking he would have a happy home. But if he goes to the pet shop he might end up with someone horrible—someone who forgets to feed him."

When they had found the mouse in the dollhouse, they had not felt nearly as protective of him as they did now. They had just been annoyed that he had made so much mess, and that he had eaten Nutmeg's biscuits.

But when they had seen him looking so unhappy in the gerbils' cage they had felt a pang of remorse, thinking it might have been kinder to have kept him at Rose Cottage. And now that he was to be sent away forever, they felt even worse.

"What will happen if he goes to the pet shop and no one buys him?" Arthur asked.

"I suppose he might be put down," Lucy said glumly.

"*Put down?*" Arthur whispered, not liking the sound of this. "What do you mean, put down?"

"Oh, I don't know," Lucy replied, not wanting to upset him further. "I just mean we must rescue him before something awful happens."

"How can we rescue him if we can't open the cage?" Arthur asked. "The janitor's got the keys."

"Well, we can just ask him to open it, then," Lucy said, not knowing what else to suggest. "He opened it when we wanted to put the mouse *in* the cage, after all."

"I know, but he's not going to let us take him out again without Miss Short's permission," Arthur said defeatedly. And Lucy knew he was right.

"Well, we should tell Nutmeg, then," Lucy said. "And ask her to come to school and rescue him for us."

"Do you think she'd come all this way?" Arthur asked doubtfully. Somehow he didn't like the idea of Nutmeg coming to his school. She was their secret, and he felt they should keep her to themselves.

"Of course she would," Lucy said confidently. "The school's not far from Rose Cottage, after all, and she can come at night when there's no one here."

"I suppose so," Arthur said. But he still felt uneasy.

Later that day, before going to bed, he and Lucy sat down and wrote a long letter to Nutmeg, telling her all about Miss Short's plan to sell their mouse, and asking her to return him to Rose Cottage.

. . . If you bring him home again, we'll find him a nice big bucket

to live in, and we'll let him out for runs in the bath. We'd look after him very well,

they concluded.

Meanwhile, Nutmeg's day had been most eventful. After leaving the school, she and Tumtum had made straight for the Royal Mouse Army's barracks to see if they could borrow some pogo sticks. They needed thirteen, for Miss Tiptoe always had thirteen ballerinas in her school. It was something she was very particular about.

The barracks were on the other side of the village park, in a dugout underneath the war memorial. It had formerly been a fox's lair, but the Royal Mouse Army had taken it over some years ago, and now it was a warren of underground dormitories and ammunition stores.

Tumtum and Nutmeg arrived at the main entrance to find two sentries playing poker. When Tumtum showed them General Marchmouse's letter, requesting that the pogo sticks be released immediately, they were not at all helpful.

One said that all the pogo sticks were locked in a store-room, and that he didn't know where to find the key. The other said he thought he might know where the key was, but that he couldn't go and look for it because he had a sprained ankle. And then the other one said he had a sprained ankle, too, at which both sentries started cackling.

Tumtum became exasperated. "Now look here," he said crossly. "I happen to be on lunching terms with your commanding officer, Brigadier Flashmouse and—"

Suddenly, both the sentries became more cooperative. One offered Tumtum a slug of whiskey from his hip flask, while the other went inside and returned with thirteen pogo sticks, each with the Royal Mouse Army's initials, *R.M.A.*, engraved near the tip. Tumtum signed for them, then the Nutmouses hurried on their way.

They made straight for the ballet school, crossing the lane at the top of the green, then climbing up the steep verge that led into the churchyard.

"Hang on!" Tumtum said, suddenly noticing three women coming up the church path with bundles of flowers. He and

Nutmeg waited until they had gone into the porch, then followed behind.

There were more women inside the church, arranging big bouquets of lilies. But they were concentrating much too hard on their work to notice two mice scuttling down the aisle toward the vestry.

The entrance to Miss Tiptoe's school was through a little mouse hole, hidden behind an old oak chest. There was no door, just a frayed velvet curtain to keep out the draft. The Nutmouses dumped the pogo sticks on the floor and went inside.

The school was in a big, chilly cupboard with dark red walls and a flagstone floor. Long ago, it was where all the church silver had been kept. But then the silver had been sold and the cupboard wasn't needed anymore. So Miss Tiptoe had taken it over.

The school was lit by candles borrowed from the church, which gave only a dim light, and it took a moment or two for Tumtum's and Nutmeg's eyes to become accustomed to the gloom.

They could just make out the ballerinas in the far corner, practicing at the bar. All thirteen of them were present, dressed in white tutus with gold braids in their hair. Miss Tiptoe was sitting next to them at the piano, playing soft, tinkling tunes. Tumtum knew the piano well—it had once lived in the drawing room of Nutmouse Hall, but he had given it to Miss Tiptoe when her last piano had got dry rot. (Miss Tiptoe's pianos often got dry rot, for the cupboard was rather damp.)

The Nutmouses waited until Miss Tiptoe had finished playing before approaching her. She was surprised to see them, for mice seldom visited her school unannounced. But their expressions clearly told her that something was wrong.

"Take a rest, girls," she instructed her class. Then she got up and led the Nutmouses to her desk, which stood in a corner of the cupboard, raised on a red hymnbook. She walked with a stick, but her back was as straight as a ruler. She sat on a big throne-like chair, while the Nutmouses faced her perched on tiny embroidered footstools.

Miss Tiptoe was very beautiful and composed, and everyone found her a little intimidating. She was tall and thin and

gray—and astonishingly old. No one knew how old, but one of Nutmeg's sisters had been taught by her when she was a young girl, and she had seemed very old then. And now of course she was even older.

She listened silently while Tumtum told her all about the General's capture, and explained the amazing role they hoped her ballerinas might play in his and the gerbils' release.

The Nutmouses had expected that she might be shocked at their request, but she had a calm, wise expression on her face. Miss Tiptoe had seen many odd things in her life, and she knew the strange and wonderful plots of all the classical ballets, so it took a lot to surprise her.

"I'm . . . er, I'm sure your ballerinas would look most elegant on pogo sticks, Miss Tiptoe," Tumtum concluded, feeling rather awkward.

Miss Tiptoe looked at him piercingly. "Imagine that you were in my position, Mr. Nutmouse," she said, speaking in a very clear voice. "Would you risk your pupils' lives for the sake of the General?"

Tumtum said nothing, but his silence was as good an answer as any. For of course, he knew that if he had a daughter he wouldn't want her risking her life on account of anyone.

Miss Tiptoe's expression softened. "Is the General a close friend of yours, Mr. Nutmouse?" she asked kindly.

"I suppose he is," Tumtum replied. "I know he can be exasperating, and a bit above himself, but there is a side to him which is good and loyal, too. And he is a great hero, of course."

Miss Tiptoe nodded. She did not know the General well, but like all the mice in the village, she felt a certain loyalty to him. For whenever there had been trouble, such as when rats had invaded the village grain store, he and his troops had always risen to save the day. So now that it was his hour of need, was it fair to desert him?

She looked pensive a moment, for she was still wavering. But her conscience told her what to do. "Bring your pogo sticks inside, Mr. Nutmouse," she said calmly. "My ballerinas will do what is required of them."

Tumtum and Nutmeg both let out a cry of relief.

"Oh, thank you, Miss Tiptoe! Thank you!" Nutmeg gulped, leaping up to embrace her.

But by the time Nutmeg had found her feet, Miss Tiptoe had already glided back to her pupils. "Come along now, girls!" she cried, rapping her stick on the floor. "We have a new routine to rehearse!"

Chapter Eleven

None of the ballerinas had used a pogo stick before, but they took to them at once, leaping into the air as gracefully as gazelles with Miss Tiptoe accompanying them on the piano. Before long, they were bouncing so high they could touch the cupboard ceiling.

When she felt they could bounce no better, Miss Tiptoe sent the girls off to have tea, which was served next door, in a flour bin in the vicarage kitchen.

"Oh, Miss Tiptoe! They were splendid!" cried Nutmeg, who had been watching, spellbound. Miss Tiptoe smiled graciously. Then she listened as Tumtum spelled out the plan of attack.

"We'll come back early in the morning, and escort you and your girls to Room 2B before the school opens," he began.

"That way you can familiarize yourselves with the classroom, and take instructions from the General before any of the children turn up. Then you can find somewhere to hide away until the janitor comes on his lunchtime rounds. It will be a long wait, but it's important that all the dancers are out of sight before school begins."

Miss Tiptoe raised her eyes when Tumtum mentioned taking instructions from the General. But she made no comment.

"I will entrust you with the refreshments, Mrs. Nutmouse," was all she said. "If my girls are to spend all morning cooped up underneath a filing cabinet, they will need something to nibble."

"Of course," Nutmeg replied eagerly, and she at once began planning a sumptuous picnic.

By the time the Nutmouses left the vestry, the flower arrangers had long gone. The lights had been turned off, and the church was almost dark. As they walked back down the aisle hand in hand, they heard the clock strike five.

"Five o'clock, Tumtum!" Nutmeg sighed. "And we've so much to do. I have to prepare the picnic, and then we'll have

to go back to the school and tell the General what's happening and—"

"There is no need to go back to the school tonight," Tumtum said firmly. "We've a busy day tomorrow, and we must go home and rest. We'll see the General first thing in the morning."

The thought of rest was very tempting to Nutmeg, for all the excitement was beginning to take its toll on her. Her eyes felt heavy, and her ankles were starting to ache. As they walked home to Nutmouse Hall, she leaned wearily on Tumtum's shoulder.

They had only been away for a day, and yet the house had a deserted feel to it. The big rooms seemed empty and echoey now that the General had gone.

Nutmeg felt quite forlorn as she set about in the kitchen making a meatloaf and a mushroom quiche and a salmon mousse and a lemon cheesecake and two dozen jam tarts for the ballerinas.

While she worked, Tumtum put his feet up in the library. He felt forlorn, too.

"What if our plan doesn't work?" Nutmeg said anxiously as they finally sat down together to supper in the kitchen.

"It will work, dear," Tumtum replied reassuringly. "You saw how high those ballerinas could hop on their pogo sticks. They'll have no difficulty bouncing up and snatching the janitor's keys."

"But what if he catches them?" Nutmeg fretted. "Oh, those poor young girls. If he were to hurt them, I'd never forgive myself!"

"Now don't fuss, dear," Tumtum said. "They'll be bouncing so fast the janitor won't even see them coming."

"I do hope you're right," Nutmeg said. But she could feel a dread rising in her stomach.

It had been her idea to enlist the help of the ballet school, and it had seemed such a splendid idea at first. And yet as the time of the rescue operation drew nearer, she had a horrible feeling that something was to go horribly wrong.

Perhaps the General was right, she thought. *Perhaps the ballerinas simply aren't up to it!*

Nutmeg worried all through supper, and then she

291

worried while she washed up, and she was still worrying when she and Tumtum sat down in the library to drink their cocoa. She knew she would never get to sleep, so she decided to go and tidy Arthur and Lucy's bedroom.

"I don't want them thinking I'm neglecting them, and this morning I noticed that Lucy's sweater needs darning," she said when Tumtum protested. "And I still haven't cleared up all the mess the General made in the dollhouse."

"Very well, dear, but don't be long," Tumtum said, stifling a yawn. "We both need an early night, and you've already done quite enough bustling for one day."

But when Nutmeg reached the attic, she found the children's letter. And that made her even more anxious. For even if she managed to get the General back from the school, she knew she couldn't possibly let Arthur and Lucy keep him in a bucket. He wouldn't like that at all.

She sat a long while at her desk in the dollhouse, nibbling the end of her fountain pen and wondering how best to reply. The letter she finally wrote went as follows:

Dear Arthur and Lucy,

I intend to rescue your mouse tomorrow. This will be a very difficult mission, and I cannot guarantee that I will succeed. But if I do, perhaps it would be best if we were to set him free again. For I happen to know the mouse in question, and I doubt he would much enjoy living in a bucket.

Love,

Nutmeg

Then, while the children slept, she darned the elbow of Lucy's sweater, and the toe of one of Arthur's socks, and she scrubbed the dollhouse kitchen and put all the furniture back to rights in the living room. And finally, feeling more tired than she could ever remember, she limped back to Nutmouse Hall and collapsed beside Tumtum in their four-poster bed.

Everyone in Rose Cottage slept soundly that night. But there was no such peace for the General. After the Nutmouses had left him, his day had gone from bad to worse.

After break, there had been a nature lesson, conducted by a gangly teacher called Mr. Greaves, who had asked the class questions such as what field mice do in winter, and where squirrels sleep at night. The General had shouted all the answers loud and clear from his cage, but the teacher had ignored him.

Then there had been a math lesson during which the children had recited their times tables. The gerbils turned out to know them all perfectly. But when the General tried to join in he'd got in the most dreadful muddle, and said that three times three was thirty-three, and that six times six was sixty-six. And then his cell mates had mocked him all the more.

By the time the children filed off for lunch, the General was feeling more homesick than he'd ever felt before. Even when he had been away at war for whole days on end, he had never felt as homesick as this. Then the janitor had turned up to give the prisoners more revolting seeds to eat, and the General felt sicker than ever.

There was something off-putting about the janitor. He was so tall he had to stoop almost double to open the door of the cage. And his fist was so wide that when he reached inside to dump the food in the feeding trough, the animals had to press themselves back against the bars so as not to be crushed. He was a curious-looking man, too, with thick tufts of black hair coming from his nostrils, and red veins in his cheeks.

The General made clear his displeasure at the luncheon being served. "Take away this filthy birdseed and bring me some decent roast beef!" he shouted. But the janitor just slammed the cage door shut on him.

"How can you digest that muck?" the General asked sullenly, watching the gerbils crowd around the trough. But it had been a whole day since they had last eaten, and the gerbils were too busy eating to reply.

As the afternoon wore on, with a history lesson followed by a spelling test (to which the gerbils recited all the correct answers, and he all the wrong ones), the General began to feel more and more wretched. And then a new crisis arose.

Shortly after the children had gone home, the janitor appeared at the door of ROOM 2B. He found Miss Short in the room, tidying her desk.

"Can I lock up in here now?" he asked her.

"Yes, I'm just going. And I'll be taking these beastly things with me," she said, nodding toward the cage. "I was going to get rid of them on Saturday, but I'm seeing my sister in town tonight so I might as well take them now."

"What'll you do with them?" the janitor asked casually.

"I'll take them to the pet shop," she replied.

"I wouldn't do that," he said. "I know old Mr. Dye who runs it, and he won't be wanting a cageful of flea-bitten old rodents like this. He sells fancy things—carp and budgies and the like."

Miss Short sucked in her breath. "Well, if the pet shop can't take them, I'll have to think again," she said crisply. "I'm sure the vet could dispose of them for me."

At this the gerbils let out a collective cry of horror and started scrabbling frantically, desperate to get out, while the General clutched the bars, swearing furiously at his captors. Then the floor lurched beneath their feet as the cage was hoisted into the air.

Chapter Twelve

Tumtum and Nutmeg set out early next morning to collect the ballerinas. The milkman had not yet stirred, and the church spire was still shrouded in mist.

When they arrived in the vestry, they found Miss Tiptoe and her class waiting for them outside the cupboard. The girls were dressed in beige tutus, which had their names embroidered on them in silver thread. The Nutmouses studied them amoment so that they might remember who was who. There was Trixibelle, who had the long, beautiful ears . . . There was Millicent Millybobbette, who was the shortest . . . There was Lillyloop, who was the tallest . . . There was Horseradish, with the pink braids in her tail . . . and Tartare, with the sharp, silver toenails—

But it was no good. They could never remember so many names; just trying made their heads spin. And they were such odd names, too. In their day mice had been given simple names, like Nutmeg.

"You told me that the school had wooden floors, so I decided beige would be our best disguise," Miss Tiptoe said. She had been up all night sewing.

"How clever of you," Nutmeg replied. She suddenly felt embarrassed by the bright green cape she was wearing and wished she had dressed more discreetly.

Presently, the party set forth. They were a curious convoy, with the girls bouncing along like crickets on their pogo sticks, and Miss Tiptoe gliding elegantly beside them, while Tumtum and Nutmeg straggled in the rear with the picnic baskets.

The girls were in high spirits, and Horseradish shrieked when Tartare tried to bounce away with her earmuffs.

"Young ladies! Please recall that you are representing *my* ballet school!" Miss Tiptoe said sharply, and then they all looked a little chastened.

Before long they reached the school gates and saw the playground stretching before them. The girls all craned their necks as they looked up at the vast steel climbing frame. To them, it seemed as tall as a skyscraper.

"This way," said Tumtum, leading the party toward the air vent. He pushed the pogo sticks through the grille first, then the mice climbed inside.

The ballerinas had never been in a school for human children, and the building felt cold and unfamiliar. They found something ominous about the huge shoes in the lockers and the enormous overalls hanging from the pegs on the wall. It was all so different from their own little school in the vestry.

They kept close together as they followed Tumtum under the door of ROOM 2B. It was dark, for the blinds were shut, and they couldn't see as far as the cage. Everything was deathly quiet. "The prisoners must still be asleep," Tumtum said, leading his party across the room.

"General! Gerbils! We're back!" he called up from beneath the table. "Throw down the ladder!"

But there wasn't a sound.

He called again, wondering why they didn't reply. Then, blinking, Nutmeg let out a cry: "The cage! It's gone!"

The Nutmouses stood motionless, stunned by this discovery. They couldn't understand it. Miss Short had said that she was taking the gerbils to the pet shop on Saturday, but Saturday wasn't until tomorrow.

"The cage must have been moved to another part of the school," Tumtum said urgently. "We'll search all the classrooms. Miss Tiptoe—you and your girls head down the corridor to your left, and look under every door. We'll try the rooms to the right."

The mice hurtled back out of ROOM 2B, and dispersed down the corridor, shouting the General's name. Miss Tiptoe's ballerinas bounced high and low around the gymnasium, the art room, and the kitchen. And the Nutmouses scuttled around ROOM 3A, and ROOM 1C, and all around the staff room, and the music room—but the cage was nowhere to be seen.

"He must have gone to the pet shop!" Nutmeg wailed. She

had a sudden vision of Mrs. Marchmouse living the rest of her life alone in the big, rackety gun cupboard with no one to keep her company—and she started to weep.

"I will take my girls back to the vestry, since it seems there is no use for us here," Miss Tiptoe said tactfully.

The subdued rescue party made its way back down the corridor toward the air vent. The girls walked quietly, pulling their pogo sticks behind them. None of them had met the General before, but the thought of any mouse being taken to a pet shop was enough to take all the bounce out of them.

But just as they were about to climb back outside, Tumtum suddenly stopped in his tracks. "What's that?" he said, motioning the party to be still. They all stood quivering, their ears pricked. They could hear faint squeals.

"Over there! They're in there!" Tumtum cried, pointing to the cupboard door across the corridor. Miss Tiptoe's dancers had passed by it—they'd looked in all the classrooms, but they hadn't thought of exploring the cupboards, too.

As Tumtum wriggled under the door, he could hear the gerbils howling. And rising above them was the voice of a most indignant General Marchmouse: "We're here, you fools! Let us out! LET US OUT!"

"Where?" Tumtum shouted, fumbling for his flashlight. "It's pitch-black. I can't see a thing."

"Here!" squeaked a dozen voices. "HERE!"

"Where?" Tumtum called again.

"*Up here!*" they chorused impatiently.

Tumtum craned his neck and shone his flashlight back and forth along the shelves. At first all he could see were cardboard boxes.

But then, on the lowest shelf off the ground he noticed a big lump covered with a filthy gray blanket. He shone his flashlight over it, trying to make out what it was. All of a sudden, the corner of the blanket tweaked, and the straw ladder came tumbling to the floor.

"Quick! I've found them!" Tumtum shouted under the door. The rest of the mice raced after him and they all clambered up to the prisoners.

"Uncover us!" the General shouted furiously; and with the Nutmouses and Miss Tiptoe and the thirteen ballerinas pulling

and tugging as one, they eventually managed to drag the blanket from the cage.

When Tumtum shone his light on the prisoners, it was clear that there had been quite a commotion. The exercise wheel had been snapped in two, and everyone was badly bruised. The General had a black eye and was in an especially ill humor.

"Why the devil didn't you come back last night?" he asked furiously. "We've been sentenced to death, every last one of us!"

Each prisoner had a different version of what had happened, and everyone talked at once, so the story was rather hard to follow.

But it seemed that after Miss Short's threat to transport them all to the vet, the General had become quite wild with anger. And when she'd picked up the cage he'd sunk his teeth deep into her finger—drawing blood, or biting it right off, depending whose account you believed.

Miss Short had then dropped the cage on the floor, and it had landed with a great crash, which is what had caused all the cuts and bruises and black eyes. She had shrieked a good deal, using words that had made the lady gerbils cover their ears—

but the upshot was that she was too frightened to go near the cage again. And she had told the janitor that she would not take it in her car, nor did she want it to remain in ROOM 2B.

So the janitor had offered to get rid of it, saying that he would dispose of the gerbils over the weekend. Miss Short had not inquired how he intended to do this, but he had muttered something about having a friend who kept owls—and that had made all the prisoners quake, for they knew that owls liked nothing more than a succulent little mouse or gerbil to nibble.

And then the janitor had dumped them in the dark cupboard, out of Miss Short's sight. He had thrown the blanket over them in order to muffle their protests, and left them to await their terrifying fate.

"The worst of it was thinking you'd never find us, Mrs. Nutmouse," one of the gerbils said pitifully.

Nutmeg said nothing. For she was terrified that her plan might no longer work. It wouldn't be nearly so easy now that the cage was in a cupboard instead of in the classroom. And besides, the janitor's routine might have changed. There was no knowing what time he'd come and feed the gerbils now—or if he would come at all.

"Our plan will still succeed so long as everyone follows my commands to the letter," the General said bossily, reading her thoughts. Then he looked at Tumtum and started giving orders.

"You and all the dancers must hide on the other side of the corridor, under the shoe lockers, until the janitor comes to feed us," he said. "When he opens the door and removes the keys from his belt, I'll give the order to hop. But nobody is to move until I issue it!"

"When do you think the janitor will come?" Tumtum asked.

"Oh, I don't know!" the General snapped. "But if he wants to feed us to the owls, then it's in his interest to fatten us up. I should think he'll come soon enough."

"Very good, General," Tumtum said, looking at his watch. "We'd better hurry up and hide. It's nearly eight o'clock and the school will be opening soon."

"We're starving!" one of the gerbils cried. "Did you bring us anything to eat?"

"Oh, I don't think you'll be short of things to eat," Tumtum said, shining his flashlight over the labels on the cardboard boxes. "You've been locked up in the school's candy cupboard!"

Chapter Thirteen

There was a great whoop of joy from the gerbils when they read the words on the boxes. They had been locked away with a lifetime's supply of lemon drops, candy bars, lollipops, and potato chips! Even the General managed a cheer when he saw the enormous carton of chocolates.

The Nutmouses spent a frantic few minutes nibbling through all the cardboard packaging and distributing the food. Tumtum pulled out a bar of hazelnut chocolate and passed chunks into the cage; then he wrestled the cap off a tube of Smarties and showered them down onto the prisoners. Nutmeg handed them chips and gumdrops and long strands of strawberry licorice.

The ballerinas were looking longingly at a box of jelly beans, for it seemed an eternity since breakfast. But Miss Tiptoe did not approve of sweets and promptly shooed them all back down the ladder.

When the prisoners had been given all they could eat, the Nutmouses scurried down after the others. Then the mice lay in wait on the other side of the corridor beneath the long row of lockers.

A few moments later, a bright light came on, and they felt the floor quake as the children charged into the building. The ballerinas huddled together, watching the huge feet thundering by. One of the children stopped just in front of them to hang up her coat, and the tips of her shoes poked under the locker, brushing Horseradish's tutu. Then suddenly a bell clanged, and the children disappeared into their classrooms.

After that, the mice had a long, anxious wait for the janitor to appear. The hideaway was cramped and dusty, and had it not been for their picnic they would have felt very glum.

Arthur was having an uneasy time, too. The moment he

had walked into Room 2B, he noticed the empty table where the cage had been and felt a sense of foreboding.

"Where have the gerbils gone?" he asked Miss Short, who was sitting at her desk eating a jelly sandwich.

"I will explain to you when we are all sitting down," she replied annoyingly.

It seemed a very long wait until everyone had settled, and Miss Short had gone through the attendance sheet.

"Now, children," she said eventually, speaking with forced cheerfulness. "Some of you may have noticed that our large family of gerbils is no longer with us."

"Where have they gone?" they all cried.

"They have been *removed*," Miss Short replied. She spoke as though referring to something distasteful, like a rotten egg. "And I will tell you why," she continued, raising her voice as the children bombarded her with more questions. "Last night, I learned that our gerbils were not the timid creatures we assumed them to be. . . . One of them bit me!"

Miss Short paused a moment while this information sank

in. To force the point, she raised the first finger of her left hand to show off a small bandage.

"How come?" Arthur asked suspiciously, for he knew that Miss Short never went near the cage.

"It bit me when I tried to give it something nice to eat," Miss Short lied. "And when I discovered how dangerous the little creatures were, I knew I must remove them at once, for we wouldn't want any of you being injured, would we? I didn't dare put the cage in my car, so the janitor kindly agreed to deliver the animals to the pet shop for me."

"Has he taken them already?" Arthur asked anxiously.

"I sincerely hope so," Miss Short said. "I have told him that I do not wish to see them inside the school building *ever again*."

The children were shocked by this development, and they felt that the story didn't quite add up. But when they pressed Miss Short for more information she got very angry and told them that she never wanted to hear any mention of the beastly gerbils again.

Arthur was so upset he couldn't concentrate on any of his lessons. Then at break time he rushed to find Lucy on the playground to tell her what had happened. "So she *hopes* the janitor'salready taken them, but she didn't say he definitely had," he explained.

"But he must have," Lucy said miserably. "They're not in any of the classrooms, and they can't be in the staff room because Miss Short said she didn't want to see them again."

The children sat down together on the bench beside the basketball court, feeling wretched. They wished they had never brought their mouse to school.

"We could go to the town, find the pet shop, and *buy* him back," Arthur suggested. But even as he said it, he knew it wouldn't work. For the town was ten miles away, and their father had no car to take them there. Besides which, they had only eighty-eight pence between them, and a mouse would surely cost more than that.

They felt so downcast that it was almost a relief when the bell rang to mark the end of break.

But as they were making their way back inside, they saw the janitor walking toward them. He had come from the direction of the shed in the corner of the playground where

he kept all his things. He was carrying a brown sack.

"That's the gerbils' food," Arthur said in surprise. "I've seen him with it before. Come on, let's follow him and see where he goes."

The children waited until he had gone inside, then crept after him down the corridor. But halfway along it, he disappeared into the boiler room.

"Surely he can't be feeding the gerbils in *there?*" Lucy said, thinking it a very odd place to hide them.

They waited outside, pretending to be looking for something in one of the lockers. They should have been back in their classrooms by now, but they had to see what happened.

Presently, the janitor reappeared, still carrying the brown sack. The children watched, motionless, as he walked on down the corridor, then stopped outside the candy cupboard. He stood there a moment, glancing left and right. He looked nervous, as if he didn't want anyone to see what he was doing. Then he removed the keys from his belt and opened the cupboard door.

As he did so, the Nutmouses and Miss Tiptoe hovered at the rim of the locker, watching his every move. The ballerinas were lined up behind them, mounted on their pogo sticks, poised to advance the moment the General gave the order.

"On your marks, girls!" they heard him bellow from inside the cage. "Get set . . . CHARGE!"

But just as the order was given, Nutmeg issued a counter command. "STOP! STOP!" she shrieked, pointing down the corridor. "Tumtum, look! It's Arthur and Lucy! We can't let them see us!"

"Hold back, girls!" Tumtum shouted.

The janitor fumbled a hand inside the cupboard, trying to find the light switch. He could hear lots of rattling and squealing as General Marchmouse roared commands and shook the bars in the most dreadful rage.

"CHARGE! *CHARGE!*" the General cried. But Tumtum was still holding the ballerinas back. "How dare you disobey my orders!" the General shouted.

At that moment, there was a sudden clack of high heels, and Miss Short appeared. As she walked past the candy cupboard, the janitor looked over his shoulder shiftily. But she took no notice of him.

"Arthur! Lucy! What are you doing here?" she asked crossly. "Break ended five minutes ago!"

The children at once hurried off to their classrooms, and then Miss Short disappeared into the staff room.

Finally, the coast was clear.

"*Chaaaarge!*" the General shouted again. And this time the mice did.

Chapter Fourteen

The janitor was still fumbling for the light switch when the ballerinas sprang from beneath the locker and began bouncing toward him. They moved in perfect unison and made not the slightest sound. It was like a silent ballet, with Miss Tiptoe conducting unseen from the rear.

The General was issuing commands through the bars. "GO! Ambush him now!"

"Stop squeaking!" the janitor muttered, finally finding the switch. As he turned on the light, the ballerinas all bounced straight for him on their pogo sticks, soaring like a flock of birds toward the huge key ring in his left hand.

The Nutmouses and Miss Tiptoe shook with fear. But the dancers were much too agile for the janitor. As they rose into the air, they raised their left paws from their pogo sticks and grabbed at the keys as they sailed by, jerking them from his hand. The whole bunch crashed to the floor, with the ballerinas dropping down silently behind.

Before the janitor had time to look down, the ballerinas had dragged the key ring under the shelf at the back of the cupboard. The Nutmouses were waiting.

"This one!" Tumtum cried, finding a small red key.

"Didn't the gerbils say it was a green key, dear?" Nutmeg asked anxiously.

"No, no—they said it was red," Tumtum replied. He wrestled furiously to unhook it, sweat pouring down his nose.

"Oh, hurry, Tumtum! Hurry!" Nutmeg squawked as the janitor got down onto his hands and knees, searching in bewilderment for his keys. He still had no idea what had hit him.

Finally, the red key fell free.

"Quick! Divert him!" Tumtum shouted to the ballerinas.

Each one of them had a long lace looped around her waist, borrowed from the shoes left in the lockers opposite. Tying one end to the key ring, and attaching the other to their pogo sticks, they all bounced out of the cupboard and made off down the corridor, with the keys clanking and clattering behind them.

The janitor looked on in astonishment as the ballerinas bounced higher and higher, and faster and faster. He thought he must be seeing things. And yet there they were, as clear as day, *thirteen bouncing mice dressed in beige tutus!*

By the time he had gathered his wits and chased after them, they had bounced nearly as far as the gymnasium.

Meanwhile, the gerbils lowered the ladder, and Tumtum and Nutmeg scrambled up with the red key. "Hurry up there!" the General said. "What the devil's taken you so long? Come on. *Come on!*"

The key was nearly as long as he was, and as Tumtum pushed it into the padlock his paws were shaking. He was normally such a calm mouse, but all the excitement had unnerved him.

Nutmeg placed her paws on his to steady him, and together they tried to turn it in the lock. But though they wriggled it and jiggled it, it wouldn't budge. "Oh, do move along!" the General bullied, rattling the bars in frustration.

The gerbils were crowded behind him, desperate to get out. But there was nothing the Nutmouses could do. "We've got the wrong key!" Nutmeg said in despair.

The General turned green. He could hear the other keys clattering farther and farther away down the corridor, and with them his only hope of freedom. "Get them back!" he shouted.

Tumtum skedaddled down the ladder and ran recklessly after the ballerinas. "Come back!" he cried—and hearing him they all obediently turned and raced back down the corridor, pulling the keys behind them.

The girls were at Tumtum's side in seconds. He quickly found the green key and tried to unhook it. But it was wedged tight, and he couldn't pry it off the ring. He could hear the janitor thundering back up the corridor. He would be upon them in seconds.

"Quick! Tie the whole bunch to the ladder, and we'll pull them up!" shouted the General, monitoring events from the cage.

Trembling, Tumtum tied the keys to the end of the straw ladder with one of the shoelaces. Then the prisoners hoisted them up to the shelf, and Miss Tiptoe and Nutmeg dragged them to the cage.

"This one!" Nutmeg cried, finding the green key. She and Miss Tiptoe seized hold of it and heaved it up into the lock. Then they wrenched it clockwise, and finally the padlock gave way.

But at that moment a shadow fell over the cage, and, to their horror, the animals saw the janitor peering in at them. He shot out a hand to snap the padlock shut—but the prisoners moved too fast for him.

"*Charge!*" the General cried, and before the janitor could secure the lock they all stampeded the door together—a dozen gerbils and their commanding officer bursting free with a great, victorious squeal.

They leaped straight onto the janitor and started scrabbling along the arms of his sweater, then cascading down the legs of his pants. He swatted at them wildly, but they clung on tight. On reaching the floor they spread into the corridor, hurtling all over the place.

"Scatter!" the General shouted. "Run for your lives!" The plan had been to retreat through the air vent, but in his excitement the General had forgotten where it was.

Chaos ensued as ballerinas and gerbils flew about the floor, with the janitor trying to stamp on them with his enormous boots. The gerbils moved like tornadoes, amazed at how fast their legs could carry them after their long months in captivity. But the General was so full of chocolate that he was less nimble. "Give me a pogo stick!" he panted, but there were none to spare.

Tumtum and Nutmeg and Miss Tiptoe crouched under a locker, looking on in dismay. They had promised the General they would follow his orders, but they couldn't understand what he was up to. The operation had descended into chaos.

"Why doesn't he beat a retreat through the air vent?" Tumtum asked hopelessly. "If this goes on much longer, someone's going to get trodden on."

Miss Tiptoe decided to take charge. "He is not fit to lead," she said sharply, marching out into the corridor.

"Girls! Gerbils! This way, please," she cried, pointing under the locker with her walking stick. "Follow me through the vent."

The girls at once obeyed and bounced straight toward her. But the gerbils dithered, their loyalties torn. For while they thought the General rather ridiculous, he was an officer, after all, and he was still telling them to scatter.

But then they saw the janitor's boot looming over them—and without dithering a moment longer they all bolted for cover.

At that moment, Miss Short reappeared.

"They've multiplied!" she shrieked, seeing the animals fleeing under the locker. And then all the classroom doors opened at once, as teachers and children poured into the corridor wondering what the commotion was about.

"You've let them out!" Miss Short raged at the janitor. "The whole school will be infested!"

And yet even as she spoke the animals were all escaping through the vent—or at least all but General Marchmouse, for he was so busy shouting commands that he didn't notice the others leaving.

"It's my mouse!" Arthur cried delightedly, seeing the General rushing back and forth in his underpants.

Miss Short let out another shriek as he darted over her shoe.

"Scatter!" the General cried again, wondering where the others had gone.

"Here, General! Follow us!" shouted Tumtum as he helped Nutmeg wriggle out through the vent.

"How dare you leave the battlefield without my permission!" the General retorted. But then he looked up and noticed for the first time the huge pairs of feet—dozens of them crowded all around him. And suddenly he didn't feel quite so brave.

"Wait for me!" he whimpered, and ran full speed after the others.

The children all cheered, delighted that their gerbils had escaped being sent to the pet shop.

But Miss Short was furious.

"You may think it's funny now, but just you wait until they multiply!" she snarled. "They've doubled overnight—I saw at least two dozen of them, and by tomorrow there'll be four dozen, and by Monday there'll be sixteen dozen, and in a few weeks' time there'll be thousands and thousands and thousands of them! And they'll be *everywhere*! You'll find gerbils writhing in your shoes, and burrowing in your pencil cases, and nesting in your coat pockets! They'll take over your desks and your bags! And when they die, you'll find their corpses rotting in your food!"

The children looked alarmed, for much as they liked their gerbils, the thought of thousands and thousands and thousands of them was rather unsettling. And the school food was disgusting enough already, without dead gerbils flavoring it.

For a moment, they were all silenced. But then Lucy noticed something going on outside—it looked as if there were lots of rubber balls bouncing across the playground. She turned and pressed her face to the windowpane.

"It's the gerbils," she said in astonishment. "They're bouncing!" In fact, it was the ballerinas who were bouncing— the gerbils were running by their side. But they were already too far away for Lucy to tell the difference.

The children crowded around the window to look.

"They're on pogo sticks!" one of them said.

"Don't be ridiculous," Miss Short snapped. "Gerbils do *not* use pogo sticks." But the children sensed that this was not her area of expertise. And from that day on the story of the fantastic bouncing gerbils was to become quite a legend in the village school.

Chapter Fifteen

The animals ran and bounced across the playground as
fast as they could, fearing that the janitor and Miss Short
might come chasing after them. It was only when they were
outside the school gates that they dared to look around—but
the playground was empty, and there was no one coming.

"We've made it!" Tumtum cried. And then all the gerbils
started clapping and whooping—for it isn't every day that a
gerbil escapes.

The ballerinas whooped, too—but it was the General who
seemed the most excited of all.

"We're free!" he shouted, punching the air in triumph. "The
enemy has been fooled! Oh, what a brilliant campaign! When

the Royal Mouse Army hears about this, I shall receive another medal!"

"I say three cheers for Miss Tiptoe and her dancers," Tumtum said chivalrously. But the General appeared not to hear.

Seeing as the mood was so festive, Nutmeg decided to invite everyone back to Nutmouse Hall. "We shall have a celebratory feast," she announced eagerly. And they all thought this was a very good idea—especially the gerbils, for now that they had left the cage, they had no home to go to.

So Tumtum led the party back toward Rose Cottage. It was a slow journey, for everyone was rushing around in different directions, and Miss Tiptoe kept stopping to make sure that none of her dancers had been left behind.

By the time they crawled in under the garden door, it was nearly mid-afternoon.

There was no one around, so Tumtum led the party straight across the kitchen floor and under the dresser. Then he held open the gates while they all trooped into the broom cupboard.

When they set eyes on Nutmouse Hall the gerbils suddenly fell quiet. It was like a fairy-tale house, grander than anything they had ever seen, and the sight of so many turrets and windows overwhelmed them.

When Tumtum showed them inside they were even more astonished. For the gerbils had lived all their lives in one room— and the cage hadn't been much of a room at that. But the Nutmouses had dozens of rooms, all stuffed with treasures. Wherever one looked, there were chandeliers, tapestries, pretty vases, silver candlesticks, and gilt mirrors. There was even a grand piano.

It was all so splendid that the gerbils, who were still naked, felt a little out of place.

But Nutmeg had an idea as to how to make them more at home. "I'm afraid the house is rather chilly," she said tactfully, blowing on her paws. "I think I should find you all something to wear."

"*Something to wear?*" they asked nervously. The gerbils had never worn anything except the fur coats they had been born in. The idea of clothes struck them as very strange.

But Nutmeg gave them no chance to protest and promptly shooed them all upstairs for a fitting.

She showed the lady gerbils into her bedroom and supplied them with pretty frocks and smart cashmere shawls. Then she took the male gerbils into Tumtum's dressing room and found them each a fine tweed suit.

Once they were dressed in the Nutmouses' expensive country clothes, the gerbils began to feel more sure of themselves.

"Hooray! You look much more civilized," the General said approvingly as they strutted back into the living room. He barely recognized them from the scruffy little creatures he had shared a cage with.

And the gerbils barely recognized the General, for he had not only got dressed, but had brushed his tail, blackened his eyebrows, and oiled his whiskers. When he was staying in a smart house he always liked to look his best.

The gerbils and the General had a delightful time admiring each other in the living room. And meanwhile Nutmeg set about rustling up a celebratory feast from the odds and ends in her pantry.

She made a salmon mousse, a saffron risotto, a fish pie, a hash, a cockroach roulade, a trifle, a chocolate mousse, and a sponge pudding with a jug of hot molasses sauce to pour on top.

By the time she'd finished it was getting dark, so she served the meal by candlelight in the banqueting room. And she laid the table with all her best silver and crockery and damask table napkins.

This was a little confusing for the gerbils, who until now had always eaten from a trough. But the ballerinas showed them what to do, and explained how knives were for cutting with, and forks for spearing with, and spoons for spooning with— and the gerbils picked it up so quickly that before long one could hardly tell them from the mice.

Many courses later, as Nutmeg was serving coffee and mints, Tumtum tapped his glass with a fork, signaling for quiet. Then he stood up heavily and made an announcement.

"Until you find somewhere to live, you must all stay here with us," he said to the gerbils, who were seated in a long line down one side of the table. "We've plenty to eat and drink, and

we've sixteen spare bedrooms, nine spare bathrooms, a ball-room, a library, and a schoolroom!"

The gerbils raised their glasses and cheered. They were getting so used to all this fine living that their days in captivity already seemed a distant memory.

By now everyone was in such high spirits that no one wanted the party to stop. So after dinner the gerbils and the ballerinas danced together in the ballroom, and it was long after midnight when Miss Tiptoe finally took her charges back to school.

Once the General and the gerbils had gone to bed, Tumtum and Nutmeg made themselves a thermos of cocoa and went to sit in the library. They were unused to entertaining on this scale, and they were both worn out.

"Do you suppose the gerbils will ever move out?" Nutmeg asked, collapsing onto the sofa. She had become very fond of them, but there was a part of her that longed for some peace and quiet again.

"I'm sure we can help them find a proper home of their own," Tumtum replied reassuringly. "Rose Cottage is much too small and crowded—there's not an inch of space left to build in. But there are plenty of nooks and crannies at the Manor House that they could move into. I remember the General telling me about an airing cupboard that the present owners never use. He and Mrs. Marchmouse had been going to make their home in it, but they decided it was too big so they took over the gun cupboard instead. It might be just right for the gerbils."

"Oh, Tumtum, what a wonderful idea!" Nutmeg said happily. "I'll go up to the attic tonight and write the children a letter telling them that all the escaped pets are moving into a new home just down the lane."

Once this problem was solved, the Nutmouses sat silently for a while, watching the fire flicker. They both felt very relieved that all the dramas had come to an end.

"We're such humdrum mice, Tumtum," Nutmeg said eventually. "It does seem unfair that we should have been dragged into another adventure quite so soon. I hope we don't have any more."

"Of course we won't, dear," Tumtum replied confidently. "Life will be a lot quieter once the General's safely back in his gun cupboard."

And Nutmeg hoped very much that Tumtum was right.

The Pirates'
Treasure

Chapter One

It was a fine May morning with not a scent of trouble in the air. The sort of morning, Tumtum noted happily, that bore the promise of a very uneventful day. He rose from his bed and set off for the kitchen—and the kitchen was a long way from the bedroom, for Nutmouse Hall was a big house with long corridors and lots of stairs.

As he went, he remembered all the things he had to do. There was breakfast, lunch, and supper to eat, and a newspaper to read, and a nap to fit in. And that is a lot of events in a day that promises to be uneventful.

Tumtum pressed on, eager to get started. But when he reached the kitchen he found Nutmeg in a terrible fuss.

"Something dreadful's happened!" she cried.

"What, dear?" Tumtum asked, sitting down at the table. Nutmeg often fussed, and usually about the silliest things—such as an upset vase or a broken mug. Even so, it struck Tumtum that this morning she looked more flustered than usual.

"It's the children," she said miserably.

"Why? Is one of them ill?" Tumtum replied.

"Oh, no. Nothing like that. Something much worse."

"Gracious. Have they died?" Tumtum said, looking shocked.

"Oh, no, no. Not that. But something almost—well, something terrible, all the same." She sat down and looked at him very solemnly. "Arthur and Lucy are going to spend the night outdoors. *In a tent.*"

Tumtum looked relieved. Dear Nutmeg! It was just like her to make a fuss and bother about nothing. He took the lid off the serving dish and helped himself to some scrambled eggs. "What's wrong? Why are you so concerned with sleeping in a tent? I'm sure they'll have a lovely time," he said.

"But think about all the things that could go wrong," Nutmeg wailed. "I heard them planning everything just now when I went to borrow some butter from the kitchen, and I'm sure it will end in disaster. They're using an old tent that Arthur found in the garden shed. Well, I wouldn't be surprised if it leaks—"

"If it rains they can come back inside," Tumtum interrupted. "Their father is sure to leave the kitchen door unlocked for them. Now don't look so anxious, dear. I don't see how they could come to any harm camping out in the garden on a warm spring night. Besides, we'll be able to creep outside and check on them."

"No we won't," Nutmeg groaned. "That's the whole point. Oh, don't you see, Tumtum? The children have no intention of sleeping in the garden. They're going to camp by the stream!"

"Are you sure?" Tumtum asked. Now he looked anxious, too. The stream ran along the bottom of the meadow behind Rose Cottage. It was at least a quarter of a mile from the house. And a quarter of a mile would seem a very long way if you were a mouse.

"I am quite sure," Nutmeg said. "I heard the whole conversation. At first they were going to pitch the tent in the garden, then Arthur suggested they go down to the stream. And of course Lucy went along with it, because she thinks it will be more of an adventure. And now they seem to think they're going on a real safari. They want to light a campfire, and fry sausages on it, and boil a kettle to make tea!"

"Don't they have to be at school tomorrow?" Tumtum asked.

"No. They're on break. They don't have to be back at school until Thursday."

"Hmmm," said Tumtum. "What does their father say about it?"

"Oh, you know what Mr. Mildew's like. He wouldn't notice if they stayed away for a month."

Tumtum looked thoughtful. It was true that Mr. Mildew was very absentminded. He was an inventor by trade, and he spent all day long shut away in his study, inventing silly things such as grape-peelers and singing key rings. He had little interest in anything other than his work. As often as not he wouldn't even notice what time of day it was, and then he would get all his meals muddled up and give Arthur and Lucy canned spaghetti for breakfast and porridge for lunch.

Nutmeg was right. He would be too absorbed in his latest invention to worry about what his children were up to.

"When do they plan to set off?" Tumtum asked.

"This afternoon, around four o'clock," Nutmeg replied. "They're going to spend the morning packing."

"Well, if they've made up their minds, then I can't think how we can stop them," Tumtum said. "We shall just have to hope for the best. I can't see that much will go wrong. Lucy's very responsible and— "

"*Hope for the best?*" Nutmeg cried. "I will have you know, Mr. Nutmouse, that I am not going to watch those children set off all alone across that vast meadow, and then just sit here as though nothing had happened, *hoping for the best.*"

Tumtum was taken aback. Nutmeg only called him "Mr. Nutmouse" when she was very, very cross. "Then what do you propose we do?" he asked feebly.

348

Nutmeg started picking at the tea cozy, avoiding Tumtum's eyes. He could sense she was about to say something he wouldn't like. When she looked up, her expression was very fierce. "There's only one thing for it," she said. "If Arthur and Lucy are going camping, then we're going, too."

But, my dear. You don't propose we sleep *outdoors?*" Tumtum asked nervously. He had lived all his life at Nutmouse Hall, which was an unusually grand house with tapestries, and paintings, and a ballroom, and a billiards room, and a banqueting room—and just about every sort of room a mouse might want. So the thought of sleeping outdoors was very strange to him. At home he always slept in a four-poster bed.

"That is exactly what I propose," Nutmeg replied. "We'll follow the children to the stream and set up camp alongside them. Then at the very least we shall be on hand should any trouble arise."

"But we haven't got a tent," Tumtum protested.

"Yes, we have. General Marchmouse gave us one as a wedding present—don't you remember, dear? And it comes with two inflatable mattresses, so we shall be quite comfortable."

Tumtum groaned. He had forgotten all about the General's present, for their wedding had been a long while ago. He had thought it a silly present at the time, for why would he want the tent when he had a house with seventeen bedrooms? He had never been camping before, and he felt sure he wouldn't like it.

"Now," Nutmeg said impatiently, "hurry up and finish your eggs. We've a lot to do."

As soon as the breakfast had been cleared away, the Nutmouses sat down at the kitchen table and made a list of all the things they would need for their expedition.

"Let's see," Nutmeg said, nibbling the end of her pencil thoughtfully. "I shall make sausage rolls and centipede pasties, and a pâté and a soup—dandelion, I think—and a walnut loaf and a ginger cake, and an apple tart and a strawberry pie . . . and we shall need a frying pan and a kettle and the picnic china and two forks and four knives and six spoons . . . oh, and bless me if I'm not forgetting the napkins and the salt and the pepper grinder and the folding chairs and—"

"Hang on! We shall only be away one night," Tumtum said.

"Yes, but we shall be gone for supper and breakfast—and as likely as not for lunch as well," Nutmeg replied, adding a further item to her list.

"Supper and breakfast—and as likely as not lunch as well," Tumtum said thoughtfully. "That's a lot of food. And there's the camping equipment, too. How will we carry everything across the meadow?"

Nutmeg frowned. Tumtum was right, they would never manage it all. But then she had an idea. "The children will have to carry us," she said. "We can hide inside one of their satchels before they set off, and hitch a lift. I shouldn't think they'll notice a few extra ounces."

"It will be more than a few ounces," Tumtum grumbled. But he had nothing better to suggest.

So when Nutmeg's list was completed, they started to get everything ready. Tumtum busied himself in the butler's pantry, filling a wicker basket with crockery, while Nutmeg bustled about in the kitchen, making delicious things to eat.

"If we must go camping, then we might as well do it properly," Tumtum muttered as he polished the glasses.

It was past lunchtime before the Nutmouses were ready.

"We had better get aboard the satchels, or the children might leave without us," Nutmeg said.

"But it's only two o'clock," Tumtum replied. "You said they weren't going to leave until four."

"Yes, but you know what humans are like. They might decide to leave on a whim. Now, come on. We can't risk being left behind."

Tumtum could see there was no point arguing. So he helped Nutmeg drag everything through to the hall, then they staggered out of their front door. Tumtum was bent double, hauling the tent, the picnic table, the two folding chairs, and a mass of plates and silverware. Nutmeg followed behind, heaving the hamper and the cooking pots.

Tumtum locked the door behind him, then they trudged across the broom cupboard floor and through the little iron gates covering their mouse hole. On the other side of the gates lay the Mildews' kitchen and the big wooden dresser that hid the broom cupboard door from view.

The Nutmouses always came and went without a sound so as not to give their hiding place away. So this afternoon they closed their front gates very quietly, and did not make so much as a squeak as they crept out into the dark, dusty patch beneath the dresser.

"Wait here. I'll check there's no one there," Tumtum whispered. Then he went to the edge of the dresser and poked his nose into the kitchen.

The room was empty, but he could hear the children talking outside in the hallway. And he could see their satchels lying beside the garden door. They were already packed very full. One satchel even had a frying pan poking out at the very top.

On the floor beside them was Arthur's wooden boat—a pretty blue yacht, about the size of a man's shoe, with white sails and the name *Bluebottle* written on the stern. Tumtum had seen the boat before. It lived in the attic of Rose Cottage. And now he supposed Arthur intended to sail it on the stream.

He suddenly imagined the boat racing through the icy water, crashing over the pebbles, and he felt himself shiver. Tumtum had never been sailing before, and the very thought of it filled him with fear. He was glad that he and Nutmeg would be staying on dry land.

He took one more look around the kitchen, standing very still and listening to the silence. He felt uneasy. He and Nutmeg usually visited Rose Cottage at night, when the Mildews were asleep. It felt reckless to venture out in daylight, when there was such a risk of being seen.

"Come on," he whispered to Nutmeg. "The satchels are by the door. We can get in now, while there's no one here."

The Nutmouses lugged their things across the kitchen, beneath the towering table and chairs. But just as they were reaching the far side of the room, the floor gave a sudden tremor, and Arthur and Lucy walked in.

The mice froze. They were standing at the base of the first satchel, which rose above them like a hill. In order to wriggle inside, they would have to climb to the very top—and if they did that, Arthur and Lucy would be sure to see them.

The children were standing by the table. They might look around at any moment.

"What shall we do?" Nutmeg trembled. She was so frightened she could feel her heart going thump.

They stood there helplessly, wishing the kitchen tiles would swallow them. Then Tumtum noticed a bulging pocket on the side of the satchel, just a couple of inches above their heads.

"Look, we can hide in there!" he said. "You go first, and I'll hand everything up to you."

He hoisted Nutmeg onto the base of the satchel, then she pulled herself up by a buckle and crawled into the pocket under the flap.

A moment later, her head peeked out, her face full of anxiety. "Hurry, dear!" she urged as Tumtum started passing her all their equipment. There seemed no end to it. First came the picnic hamper, then the table, then the two folding chairs. . . . Nutmeg snatched each item hurriedly, terrified the children might look their way.

"That's everything," Tumtum panted as he handed her the

basket of crockery. Then he scrambled up the buckle and wriggled into the pocket beside her.

There followed a long wait. The Nutmouses could hear the children coming and going in the kitchen, but they seemed in no hurry to set off. The pocket was pitch-black and very stuffy. But the mice dared not lift the flap for fear of being seen.

They sat side by side on the hamper, nervously nibbling a sausage roll. An hour or more slipped by. They started to wonder if the children had decided not to go camping after all.

"Surely there couldn't be any harm if I poked my nose out, just for a second?" Nutmeg asked restlessly.

"No, dear. It's too dangerous," Tumtum replied—and even as he spoke, the children's voices got nearer. Next thing the Nutmouses felt themselves soaring into the air as Arthur hoisted the satchel onto his shoulder.

They could not see out, and yet there were some clues as to where they were going. They heard the back door being slammed behind them as the children went outside. And then they heard the garden gate opening and shutting, and they knew they had entered the meadow.

"Let's go this way," Lucy said. Then she and Arthur started walking downhill toward the stream.

It was horribly bumpy in the pocket, and Nutmeg soon began to feel sick. But the children hadn't far to go—at least, not by human standards. And in what seemed like no time Lucy said, "Let's camp here," and suddenly the satchel fell to the ground with a crash.

"I think we've landed," Tumtum said, feeling very bruised. He slowly picked himself up and peeked outside. "We're beside the stream, next to the oak tree," he reported. "Come on, let's get out of here before the children find us."

While Arthur and Lucy were unpacking their tent, the mice threw all their things out of the pocket, then clambered down to the ground. They felt safer now, for the grass was taller than they were. They would be well hidden.

"Where shall we set up camp?" Nutmeg said.

"How about just over there, under that clump of nettles?" suggested Tumtum. "So long as we're under stinging nettles, the children won't trample on us. But we'll still be close enough to keep an eye on them."

"Good idea," Nutmeg agreed. "And we can light our camp-fire behind that pebble. We shall be completely hidden."

So the Nutmouses heaved their things through the long grass and started setting up camp.

Although Tumtum hesitated to admit it, everything was very luxurious. The General's tent was well proportioned—bigger than the butler's pantry at Nutmouse Hall, and tall enough to stand up in—so the Nutmouses did not have to squeeze together, as some campers do.

Tumtum blew up the inflatable mattresses, and Nutmeg made up their beds with feather sleeping bags and soft pillows. Then they unfolded the picnic table and laid it with plates and glasses and silver candlesticks, and damask table napkins embroidered with the Nutmouse family crest. And after that, Tumtum made a big fire out of twigs while Nutmeg marinated some earwigs for dinner.

It was the most magnificent display of camping you have ever seen. But the children's campsite was another story.

Chapter Three

Everything was going wrong for Arthur and Lucy. They had managed to erect their tent, but it looked much smaller than the one in the instructions. And it was sagging in the middle.

"We can't both fit in *that*," Lucy said, feeling very disappointed.

Arthur shrugged. "You can sleep in it. I'll sleep on the grass. It's the campfire I'm worried about. You are a dummy, Lucy, forgetting to bring the matches."

"Oh, don't start that again. It wasn't me who was meant to remember them—they were on your list."

"No, they weren't."

Lucy was about to say, "Yes, they were." But she thought better of it, because then there would have been an argument, and everything really would have been spoiled.

"There's no point bickering about it," she said. "But whatever happens I'm not going back to the house to get them. If Pa sees us he might not let us out again."

Their father had seemed disapproving when they had asked if they could go camping for the night. And at one stage they thought he might not let them. He had agreed to it in the end, and they suspected that by now he had probably forgotten they'd gone. But if they went back to the cottage to look for matches, it might start the whole thing up again.

"We'll just have to make do without a fire," Lucy said. "It's very warm, it's not as though we need one."

"But how will we cook supper?" Arthur asked. He had been looking forward to cooking supper all day. They had brought pots and pans, and sausages and eggs and sunflower oil, and even a can of macaroni and cheese.

"We'll have to eat the macaroni and cheese cold. And we can have the canned peaches for dessert," Lucy said practically.

Arthur made a face, imagining what cold macaroni and cheese would taste like. But then there was another disaster.

"Where's the can opener?" Lucy asked, emptying both satchels onto the grass. "Don't say you've forgotten that as well."

"I thought you packed it," Arthur said.

"Well I thought *you* packed it," Lucy replied testily. "But since neither of us packed it, I suppose we'll have to go home. If we can't open the cans, then there really is nothing to eat— unless you like raw sausages."

"You can go home if you like, but I'm staying here," Arthur said. He was determined to spend a night outdoors, even if it meant he had to starve. He looked very stubborn.

"Oh, all right, I'll stay, too," she said unhappily, for she felt it wouldn't be right to leave him on his own. "But this is the last time I'm going camping with you—ever!"

The Nutmouses sipped their dandelion soup, observing this unhappy scene.

Nutmeg would willingly have given the children her own supper, but it would have been much too small. They could have eaten the Nutmouses' entire hamper in one bite.

"Couldn't we at least get their campfire going, dear?" she asked. The children had gathered a big pile of wood from under the trees along the stream. It seemed a terrible shame it couldn't be lit.

"It's too big. Our matches could never ignite branches that size," Tumtum said. And he was right, of course, for each of their matches was smaller than an ant.

"But we must do *something*," Nutmeg went on. "We can't just sit here and watch them go without supper."

"Certainly not," agreed Tumtum, who never missed a meal. But he could see this problem was not going to be easily solved. "Let's have a sautéed earwig," he suggested, for sautéed earwigs always helped him think more clearly.

"All right, dear. I'll clear the soup bowls," Nutmeg said. But as she stood up they heard a sudden bang. The children didn't hear it, for it was too quiet for human ears. But it gave the Nutmouses a tremendous fright. It sounded like a gun going off.

Nutmeg clung to her chair. Her face had gone very pale.

"It's probably just a field mouse out hunting," Tumtum said, trying to reassure her. But she could hear the fear in his voice, too. Tumtum stood up and peered warily into the grass, unsure which direction the noise had come from. Then he heard something rustling toward them. Nutmeg heard it, too, and gave a shriek—then all at once a creature sprang out in front of them and shouted, "BOO!"

The Nutmouses both jumped. But they were very relieved when they saw who it was.

"General Marchmouse!" Tumtum exclaimed. "Gracious, what a fright you gave us!"

"That was my intention," the General chuckled. "I spotted you through my field glasses, having a quiet little dinner out-of-doors, so I decided to jolly things up. 'Ha, ha!' I thought. 'I shall let off my gun, then rustle up through the grass and pounce on them shouting, "BOO!" That'll make 'em jump!'"

Nutmeg looked disapproving. She thought it a very silly prank. "What are you doing out so late?" she asked.

"I am beetle hunting," the General replied, patting his rifle. "I've been out since dawn but it's been a rotten day. I haven't shot a single bug. Anyway," he continued, sitting down on Tumtum's chair and helping himself to some soup, "what are you two doing here, more to the point? Babysitting, from the look of things."

"That's right," Nutmeg said. "We came to keep an eye on the children. We heard them planning a camping trip, and we didn't want to let them go out alone. But I'm afraid we haven't been much help. They need matches and a can opener, but we can't give them ours as they are much too small."

The General stood up and studied the children's camp through his field glasses. "What a poor show," he said disapprovingly.

"They're not usually like this," Nutmeg replied defensively. "It's just that they forgot—"

"Leave this to me," the General interrupted. "I'll soon have things shipshape." He took his rifle from his shoulder and stuffed it full of bullets. Then he marched toward the children's tent.

The Nutmouses watched in terror, wondering what he would do. Arthur and Lucy were playing by the stream, so the General was able to approach unseen. He made first for the can of peaches, which was standing upright in the grass beside Arthur's satchels, and aimed his gun straight at it. The General had a seasoned eye, and with an immaculate volley of fire, he blasted the top right off.

Tumtum and Nutmeg pressed their paws over their ears, for the gun made a dreadful din. This first round was quickly followed by a second, as the General blew open the can of macaroni and cheese.

Nutmeg shrieked. But there was more to come. The General reached a hand to his belt and unclipped a grenade. (General Marchmouse always carried a grenade when he went outdoors, on the basis that you never knew when a grenadish situation might occur.)

He removed the pin, and took aim. Then he bowled the grenade full tilt into the children's campfire. And no sooner

had he let it go than he raced for cover, throwing himself flat on the ground behind a tent peg. The grenade was no bigger than a raisin, but it went off with a huge bang— enough to make the Nutmouses' tent wobble. Then there was a brilliant burst of light as the campfire exploded into flames.

When the General finally sauntered back to the dinner table, he was looking understandably pleased with himself.

Chapter Four

The children were beside the stream and did not hear the General's grenade going off. But when they looked around a few moments later, they saw the flames dancing from the campfire.

They were astonished, for fires don't light themselves. They had only been away from the camp for a few minutes, and they could see all the way across the meadow, so they would have spotted someone coming.

"Come on," Arthur said, running back to the tent. "Let's look in the grass. If anyone's been here they'll have left tracks." But though they searched all around the camp, they could find only the tracks they had made themselves, going back and forth to the stream.

Lucy was frightened, for it was odd to think of someone creeping up and lighting the fire, then vanishing without a trace. But she had an even bigger surprise when she noticed that the cans had been opened.

"That's really spooky," Arthur said, examining them very carefully. "They haven't been opened with a can opener."

"Then how have they been opened?" Lucy asked nervously. She could feel herself shiver. It was not yet dark, but the camp had become eerie. She felt a sudden urge to run back to the cottage—and yet somehow her legs wouldn't carry her.

But then Arthur said something that made everything much better: "It must have been Nutmeg."

Lucy felt her breath come back again. Of course it was her! For who else could it have been? She must have followed them from the cottage, and when she saw that they couldn't light the fire and that they didn't have a can opener she must have crept up and put everything right.

"It would be just like her," Arthur said.

"But how could she have opened the cans?" Lucy asked. "I mean—well, she's very small, isn't she?"

The children had never set eyes on Nutmeg, and they did not know that she was a mouse. In her letters to them, she had called herself a fairy, so that's what they thought she was. And they knew how tiny she must be, for they had found a pair of her slippers in the dollhouse, and each was no bigger than a ladybug.

"Oh, she'd have found a way," Arthur replied confidently. "Think of all the things she's done in Rose Cottage—sealing windows, and lighting boilers, and unblocking sinks. Opening a can of macaroni and cheese must have been easy compared to all that."

"Where do you think she is now, then?" Lucy asked.

"Oh, I don't know." Arthur shrugged. "I suppose she's hiding in the grass somewhere."

"Goodness," Lucy said. "And there we were, thinking it must have been a ghost or something."

"*You* might have thought so, but I don't believe in ghosts," Arthur said grandly.

"Oh, all right, I know," Lucy replied. She was feeling much too relieved to argue about who believed in what. "Come on, now the fire's lit we might as well have supper. I'm starving."

The two children hurriedly set about preparing their food, for they had eaten nothing since lunch. But supper did not take long to prepare. They poked the fire with a stick, making a flat patch to cook on. Then they fried the sausages and eggs in oil and heated the macaroni and cheese in a saucepan. Everything got a bit burned. But when you are sitting by a campfire watching the sun sink over a meadow, even burned food doesn't taste too bad.

As night gathered, the stream started to fill with black shadows. But when they looked back across the meadow the children could still see Rose Cottage, silhouetted against the darkening sky. Presently a dim gleam appeared in the downstairs window as their father turned on the kitchen light. Suddenly Lucy wished she was back in her comfortable attic bed.

"Let's wash up in the morning. It's too dark now," she said when they had finished supper. And Arthur agreed, for he had

also noticed how black the stream had become. It would be much too frightening to wash up in it now.

"We might as well go to bed, seeing as it's getting dark," he said.

"All right. But remember the tent's too small for two—you're sleeping on the grass," Lucy said teasingly. Arthur's face fell. "Oh, come on," she laughed, "We can both squeeze inside."

The Nutmouses and the General, who were still finishing their enormous dinner, watched as Arthur and Lucy crawled into the tent. Arthur had turned his flashlight on and they could see the children illuminated through the canvas. It was clearly a terrible squish.

"Another sliver, anyone?" Nutmeg asked, offering around the cheese board.

"Not for me, dear," replied Tumtum, who had eaten the lion's share of the pie—and half the apple tart. "I don't know about you, but I'm ready to turn in. All this fresh air has gone to my head. And hadn't you better be getting home, General?

Mrs. Marchmouse must be getting worried about you."

"Oh, poppycock! Mrs. Marchmouse knows better than to worry about me," the General replied breezily. " 'If I'm not home by bedtime, just leave the door on the latch,' I said. So you see, Nutmouse, I am a free mouse tonight! And I intend to camp out here, with you!"

Tumtum and Nutmeg looked taken aback. You have to be very fond of a mouse to let him share your tent. And fond as they were of General Marchmouse, they weren't as fond of him as all that.

"I'm afraid you would find it rather uncomfortable, General. Our tent is only equipped for two," Tumtum said tactfully.

"Oh, fiddlesticks! I'm not going to sleep in *that*," the General replied. He stood up and pointed toward Arthur's toy boat, *Bluebottle*, which was standing beside the children's tent. "I shall sleep in there!"

"Don't be a fool, General," Tumtum said. "Imagine if Arthur finds you on board. He might take you prisoner again!"

Not so long ago, the children had found the General exploring their dollhouse, and there had been terrible

consequences. For they had put him in a biscuit tin, then taken him to their school and rehoused him in a cage full of pet gerbils. The children had thought the General would be happy there, but in fact he had been miserable. And if the Nutmouses hadn't rounded up a troupe of daredevil ballerinas to rescue him, he would never have escaped.

You might have thought the General would have learned his lesson. But the sight of *Bluebottle* had thrown him. Unbeknownst to the Nutmouses, he had been dreaming about her all through supper. In his mind's eye, he could see himself as *Bluebottle*'s Captain, coursing down the stream and harpooning salmon from the deck.

The little blue boat had stirred a fierce longing in his heart. He *had* to spend the night on board.

"Do stop fussing, Nutmouse," he said, slinging his kit bag onto his shoulder. "I won't let Arthur find me. I just want somewhere to lay my head until dawn."

Then the General was gone.

"Well if he wants to go, we can't stop him," Nutmeg said as they watched him disappear through the grass. "Anyway, I can't see he'll come to much harm if he sleeps on *Bluebottle* tonight. We'll just have to make sure he disembarks before the children wake up."

"Hmmm. I suppose so," Tumtum said. He couldn't face running after him now, for he was too tired for an argument. But the thought of the General strutting about on Arthur's boat made Tumtum very uneasy.

While the Nutmouses retired to their tent, General Marchmouse stole on board. He climbed up *Bluebottle*'s finely crafted rigging and dropped down onto the moonlit deck, rubbing his paws with glee at the sight of the toy cannon, the crow's-nest, and the shiny wooden steering wheel. It was a proper old-fashioned war vessel—and he was in command!

With a trembling heart, he took out his flashlight and crept down the narrow stairs leading below deck. And here lay more delights—a storeroom full of plastic cannonballs, and a tin soldier, and a master cabin with a bed and dressing table and dresser. Everything was mouse-sized.

The General sat down at the dressing table and preened his whiskers in the mirror, thinking what a handsome Captain he would make. Then he closed his eyes and started to dream. He fancied he could hear the spray lashing his cabin window and the waves crashing on the deck. Oh, what adventures he could have if only he were out on the open water, instead of being stuck here in the grass!

It was all very frustrating. But then an idea came to him. It was a simple idea, but none the worse for that. Instead of creeping out of the boat first thing in the morning, before the children woke up, he would simply stay on board.

Arthur will never notice me, so long as I keep below deck, he thought. *I'll hide under the bed while he carries the boat down to the stream. Then as soon as he's launched her in the water, I shall rush upstairs, tighten the sails, grab the wheel, and sail away as fast as the flow will carry me. I shall take the ship. And phooey to anyone who tries to stop me!*

Delighted with his plan, the General stretched out on the Captain's bed and drifted off to sleep.

Chapter Five

Next morning the Nutmouses awoke at dawn as the light began to fill their tent. "I'll bring you a cup of tea," Tumtum yawned. Then he pulled on his robe and went outside to stoke the fire. It was a fine day, warm and cloudless, but there was a breeze rustling the grass. There was no sound of voices coming from the children's tent—and not a squeak from the General.

"Is anyone else up?" Nutmeg asked when Tumtum returned with the tea tray.

"Not yet," he replied. "Anyway, you know what the General's like. I remember when he was staying at Nutmouse Hall, he never got up before nine."

"Oh, gracious," Nutmeg said. "I'd forgotten all about him. Well, we can't let him stay on *Bluebottle* until nine. The children might find him."

"I know. But we'll have a hard job waking him," Tumtum said. "He hates getting out of bed."

"Let's take him some breakfast; that should help to get him going," Nutmeg suggested.

"All right, but we'd better hurry," Tumtum replied. "I know it's early, but there's still a risk that the children will wake up."

They quickly got dressed, then Nutmeg fried some sausages while Tumtum prepared a thermos of coffee. When everything was ready, they packed it into the picnic hamper and hastened toward the boat.

There was a ladder dangling from the stern. They climbed up it, carrying the hamper between them, then scrambled over the railing onto the deck. The breeze was gathering and batting the sail, and as the mice made their way downstairs they could feel the boat wobble.

"Here he is!" Tumtum said, finding the General in the master cabin, stretched out luxuriously on his bed.

"Rise and shine, General!" Nutmeg said cheerily, placing the hamper on the table. "If you stay in bed any longer, your sausages will get cold."

"Leave me alone. I want to sleep," the General grunted.

"Well, you shall have to sleep elsewhere," Tumtum said sternly. "If you stay here, the children will find you. Or worse still, they might not find you, and launch the boat on the stream with you still in it! And you wouldn't want that, would you?"

The General opened one eye and looked at him crossly. Of course this was exactly what he wanted, and it was awfully tiresome of Tumtum to interfere with his plans. The General rolled over and lay with his face to the wall, wishing they would go away.

But then it occurred to him that if he was going to steal the boat, it would be much more fun if the Nutmouses came, too. *Now there's an idea!* he thought. *If I can keep them on board long enough, then we can all sail away together! What a jolly adventure that would be!*

He suspected the Nutmouses would not be keen on this plan. So he had to be very crafty. He turned over and watched as Nutmeg hurriedly unpacked the hamper and laid the table for breakfast. She kept looking through the porthole, to check that the children hadn't emerged from their tent.

"Come on, General. Come and have a sausage," she said.

The General yawned and stretched each leg in turn. Then he sat up and rose from his bed as slowly as he could. "A fine morning," he drawled. Then he slouched across to the dressing table and set about grooming his chin.

"Do come and eat, General!" Nutmeg said impatiently. But when he finally sat down at the table, he did not guzzle his food as he normally did. He ate very daintily, taking tiny mouthfuls and chewing each one for ages.

So breakfast dragged on a long time.

"I have appointed myself Captain of this vessel," the General announced importantly, raising another crumb to his lips. "You can be my First Mate, Mr. Nutmouse. And you, Mrs. Nutmouse," he added generously, "can be in charge of catering."

"Don't be so silly," Tumtum said. "This is Arthur's boat, and if we dillydally here much longer he'll find us. Now come on, General. Gather your things and let's be off."

"*Captain,*" the General corrected him. "I am a Captain now!"

Tumtum sighed. This was all too silly. But then Nutmeg pointed to the porthole and let out a shriek. "The children are up!"

Tumtum grabbed the hamper, and the Nutmouses rushed for the door. "Hurry, General!" Nutmeg pleaded. But the General just sat tight, and went on eating.

"I shall not abandon my ship. You run along if you must, but I am staying here, where I belong. And I don't care if Arthur sees me!" he said.

Tumtum and Nutmeg looked at him in astonishment. Could he not see what danger they were in?

"Don't be a fool, General," Tumtum began—but it was too late, for when they next looked back through the porthole they could see Arthur's hand reaching toward the boat. Nutmeg let out a cry of terror; then suddenly the floor lurched beneath them and *Bluebottle* soared into the air.

The Nutmouses clung to a table leg as Arthur tucked the boat under his arm and carried it to the stream. They could see brief flashes of the ground through the porthole. It looked a horribly long way down.

But the General showed no fear. He was elated. Everything was going just as he had planned. "Hurrah! We shall take command of the ship and race away downstream!" he shrieked.

Then all at once the boat started plummeting through the air. The mice braced themselves on the floor—and the next instant there was a violent smack as *Bluebottle* hit the water.

The stream was flowing fast. The boat surged forward, her mast tilting to starboard as she pulled away from the bank. Then she righted herself midstream and raced away with the current.

"We're away!" the General cheered, rushing from the cabin. "All hands on deck!"

"For goodness' sake, stay down here or the children will see you!" Tumtum shouted. But the General was already halfway up the stairs.

Tumtum stumbled to the porthole and pressed his nose against the glass. He could see Arthur and Lucy chasing after them along the bank. But the stream was widening now, and *Bluebottle* had been swept out of their reach. He looked down at the rushing water and felt a dread rising in his stomach. He staggered out of the cabin and followed the General up to the deck. *Bluebottle* was going at a ferocious pace. There was spray cutting overhead, and the breeze was thrashing the sails.

"We must change course and steer back to the bank," Tumtum shouted, clinging to the mast. "For pity's sake, General! If we continue at this rate we shall be swept out to sea!"

"Hurrah!" cried the General, who could think of nothing nicer. He tore across the deck and grabbed the steering wheel. He twisted it left, then right, then left again, making the boat lurch violently. He had a mad look in his eyes.

"Faster! Faster!" he squealed as the waves crashed upon the deck.

"You'll capsize us, you fool!" Tumtum shouted. He made to grab the wheel, but the General clung on tight. Then followed the most desperate of scenes, in which Tumtum tried to wrestle the General to the ground—it was a real fisticuffs, with pummeling and slugging and cries of "Pow!" and "Oof!" and "Ouch!"

But just as they were getting into full swing, the boat suddenly slowed down, almost to a halt, and gave a deep

shudder. The mice stopped fighting and stood up, wondering what had happened. To their surprise they saw that they had left the stream behind them. And now they were floating in a huge pool of still, clear water.

"Gracious," Tumtum said. "We're in the Pond." There was awe in his voice, for the Pond was a wild place. It was bigger than a tennis court. And if, like Tumtum, you were only two inches tall, a tennis court would seem as big as an ocean.

When a mouse stood on the Pond's shore, he could not see to the other side. He could see only a long, blue horizon. As for what lay beyond the horizon, he could only guess, for no mouse had ever sailed across the Pond before. It looked so big, none had dared.

But General Marchmouse would change all that.

"The Pond!" he whispered breathlessly. "I shall be the first mouse to explore it! I'll sail over the horizon and conquer whatever lies beyond. I shall discover foreign shores and name them all after me!" The General felt a warm glow as he imagined how famous he would become.

As the boat slowed, Nutmeg ran up onto the deck. She went to the railing and stood by Tumtum's side, gazing out in dismay on the endless ocean of water. Looking back, they could still just see the children on the bank. But they were becoming smaller and smaller. The boat had already drifted well out of their reach. Nutmeg turned very pale.

"Turn us around, General," Tumtum pleaded.

"We can't turn around now," the General retorted. "If we go back to the bank the children will catch us. And you don't want that, do you, Nutmouse?" He tightened his grip on the steering wheel and stared straight ahead. He knew the Nutmouses were at his mercy, and he had an expression of intense mischief on his face.

Nutmeg looked back desperately at the bank. But it was far behind them now, and the children had become little dots in the distance. Gradually, the shore faded from sight, and in every direction, as far as the eye could see, there was nothing but water.

"We are entering the unknown!" whooped the General, punching a fist in the air.

"This is madness. We've no compass, and no clean clothes, and virtually nothing left to eat," Tumtum protested.

But the General had the scent of adventure in his nostrils and nothing could stop him now. On and on he sailed, weaving *Bluebottle* through the dragonflies and the algae, toward where the sun glittered on a ceaseless horizon.

Again and again the Nutmouses begged him to turn back. "There's nothing out there, General. We could sail on forever and never see dry land," Tumtum said when they had been afloat nearly half an hour.

But the General did not hear him. He had picked up his field glasses and was staring straight ahead, transfixed by something he had seen on the horizon. It was only a blur, and at first he fancied he might have been dreaming. But then, little by little, the object became sharper, until there could be no mistaking what it was.

For there, directly ahead of them, in those bleak, uncharted waters, lay an island. An unexplored island, upon which *he*, the great General Marchmouse, would be the first mouse ever to set foot.

I shall call it Marchmouse Island! he thought feverishly. *My name will be on every map!*

He turned back to Tumtum and Nutmeg, cleared his lungs, and shouted, "Land ahoy!"

Chapter Six

The children stood a long time on the bank, watching *Bluebottle* drift away. They had not seen the three mice on board, for they were hidden by the wooden railing encircling the deck.

Eventually, the boat reached the island and bumped to a stop. "You'll have to go in and get it," Lucy said.

Arthur made a face. The water was full of weeds, and you could not see the bottom. "Why don't you go in?" he replied.

"Because it's not my boat. And I wouldn't even if it was. I remember Pa saying the water was very deep. You'd have to swim to reach the island. Just think—if you open your mouth, you might swallow a frog."

Arthur shuddered. He wasn't going to risk that. "So what

shall we do? We can't just leave it here," he said, for *Bluebottle* was one of his favorite toys.

"I wouldn't worry if I were you," Lucy replied. "It's bound to drift back to the bank eventually. We can come and check this afternoon. But now we'd better get a move on. We promised we'd be back for breakfast."

Lucy suspected that their father would not notice if they broke this promise. But she wanted breakfast all the same.

"Okay," Arthur said reluctantly. "But will you definitely come back this afternoon?"

"Of course," Lucy said.

They walked together back to the campsite and started packing everything away. They did not notice the Nutmouses' tent, nor their campfire, which was still burning away beneath the nettle clump, small as a penny.

Meanwhile, *Bluebottle*'s predicament was much worse than the children had feared. As the boat approached the island, the General had tried to steer her into a little pebbled cove he had spotted on the shore. But there was some litter drifting about, and when the boat was less than a ruler's length from the bank she had collided head-on with a milk bottle that gouged a hole in her hull.

The mice felt the deck heave as water started seeping into the hold. They had sprung a leak. It was a terrible disaster. But the General seemed remarkably unconcerned.

"Marchmouse Island!" he declared, blowing a kiss toward the shore. "And all discovered by me!"

"General, our boat is going to sink," Tumtum said pointedly.

"Oh, never mind that," the General cried. "We shall have plenty of time to build another one. Now, come on. Let's get out and explore!"

Tumtum looked exasperated. But when he and Nutmeg went below deck to inspect the damage, they found the Captain's cabin already flooding. There was nothing they could do. *Bluebottle* had been battered beyond repair.

They retrieved the hamper and hurried back upstairs. "We're shipwrecked," Nutmeg said miserably.

She turned a moment and looked back across the vast pond. The mainland was far from sight, lost beyond the horizon. And before them lay a wild, unknown shore. She shivered. Even the silence felt hostile to her now. She wondered if they would ever see Nutmouse Hall again.

"Cheer up, my dear lady, for we shall be shipwrecked in great style!" the General said cheerfully. "We are the first settlers on this island, and we shall set the highest standards. We shall build a colossal villa—Villa Colossus, we'll call it— and it shall have verandas and fountains and fancy colonnades. And we shall dine every night on fresh tadpole fillets, roasted on an open fire!"

"Oh, poppycock," Tumtum said crossly. "The only thing we need to worry about is building a boat so that we can all get home."

"All in due course, Nutmouse. All in due course," the General replied. "Our first priority is to chart out the island so that when we do return to our native land, we can tell everyone exactly what we've found. Imagine how astonished our friends will be to learn that there is a whole new country, right here, in *the Pond*!"

The General slung his rifle over his arm, then he clambered over the side of the boat and slithered along the milk bottle to the shore. "The first settlers have arrived!" he cried, marching onto dry land.

He could not see the rest of the island, for the cove was ringed with a tall forest of bracken. He picked his way over the pebbles and dumped his satchel on a patch of moss. "We shall establish ourselves here. We can set up camp first, and explore later," he declared.

"All right," Tumtum said grudgingly, for if they were going to be stuck on the island overnight they would need somewhere to shelter. "Nutmeg and I will gather some twigs, then we can make a lean-to," he said.

"I want a villa, not a lean-to," the General replied stubbornly. Tumtum sighed. The General was being very difficult. But then Nutmeg solved the problem.

"We shall make that your villa!" she declared, pointing to an ice-cream tub washed up on the far side of the cove.

"It's pink!" the General protested.

But once they had dragged the tub over to their campsite and turned it upside down, even the General had to admit that it looked rather smart. It was tall and round like a tower, and there would be ample room for three beds inside. Tumtum hacked out a door and two windows using the bread knife from the picnic hamper, then he carried three pebbles inside to use as chairs.

On the outside of the pot were the remains of a faded label that read Vanilla. "We shall call it Villa Vanilla," the General said. It wasn't big enough to be a Villa Colossus. They could make one of those later.

Presently, Tumtum lit a fire, and Nutmeg prepared a late lunch from the odds and ends left in the hamper. It was a meager meal, for she rationed everything very strictly. They were each allowed one sausage roll, half a centipede pasty, and a chocolate mint for dessert.

They were finished eating in no time.

"Well then, General," Tumtum said. "We had better start building a boat."

"Not now, Nutty," he replied. "I'm going exploring first. We can begin our boring old boatbuilding tomorrow."

"Well, don't be long," Tumtum said. "And if you fall down a mole hole, don't expect us to come and rescue you."

"Mole hole, pah! I tell you, we are the first rodents on this island. I can feel it in my bones," General Marchmouse said confidently. Then he slung his satchel over his shoulder and strode into the bracken.

The ferns were very thick, and soon it became so dark the General had to grope his way with his paws. But after a while the wood cleared, and he found himself at the foot of a steep bank covered in cow parsley. He started climbing, hoisting himself up by the plant stems until he came to a long flat ridge. He was on the crest of the hill, high above the level of the pond. He could see the whole island stretched before him.

And what a magnificent island it was! The coastline was wild and rugged and full of pebbled cliffs, and there were jungles

of thistles and bulrushes. In the middle of the island was a lake, more than two feet long, surrounded by swathes of buttercups.

The General peered through his field glasses, searching for any sign of habitation. But there was not a soul to be seen, not even a dragonfly. Everything was eerily still.

He took a swig of water from his hip flask and prepared to press on toward the lake, hoping he might at least unearth an exotic beetle or two. But suddenly, in the corner of his eye, he saw something flickering—then all at once there was a brilliant flash of light on the far corner of the island.

He grabbed his field glasses and peered along the shore, trying to find where it had come from. But there was nothing there. He could just see the nettles rippling in the breeze.

He looked again, searching the rushes along the water's edge—and then suddenly a dark shape appeared in his lens. He steadied his paws until he could see it clearly. It was a black ship with gold sails and the name LADY CROSSBONES painted in bloodred letters on its side.

The General reeled back in horror. He knew to whom that boat belonged. The Rats had arrived on Marchmouse Island.

Chapter Seven

The General ducked behind a buttercup, fearing he might be seen. Then he crouched there very still, staring at the ship through his field glasses.

It was the first time he had set eyes on *Lady Crossbones*. But like every mouse he knew her name, for she had inspired many a bloodcurdling legend. She belonged to the Rats, who were the most feared rodents in the entire county. The Rats were not just any old rats. They were a small minority of rats, who gave themselves a capital *R* and behaved especially badly.

They were pirates, which meant that all their nice things—their crystal glasses and their soup tureens and their silver candlesticks—had been robbed from other rodents' boats. As far as the Rats were concerned, robbing was a sport, and they prided themselves on being the very best at it.

When they saw another boat coming, they would sail straight at it, then charge on board, howling and screeching and firing their muskets in the air, and shouting, "Your money or your life!" And if any hapless vole or field mouse refused to hand over his valuables, the Rats would throw him overboard and set fire to his boat. That's why everyone feared them.

There was a time when no mouse would dare go sailing on the stream for fear of being attacked. But that was long ago. For the Rats had not been seen in these parts since the General was a cadet. Everyone assumed they had moved on downstream, to terrorize another community.

But now they were back.

The General had seen many a chilling photograph of *Lady Crossbones*, but she looked much more sinister in real life. She was huge, three times the length of *Bluebottle*, and at her bow there was a figurehead of a snarling cat. She was anchored about a foot from the shore beside a cove surrounded by thistles.

At first, the General could not see anyone on board. But

then a trapdoor opened on the deck and a big gray Rat emerged. Almost at once, a black Rat slithered out behind him. Then a brown Rat appeared, then a white one, and then came a Rat with only half a tail.

There were five Rats in all. The General swiveled the lens of his field glasses until he could see them more clearly. They looked very menacing. Each was dressed in a black cape, with tall leather boots rising to his knees. Four of the Rats had red handkerchiefs tied around their heads. But the gray Rat, who was clearly the Captain, was wearing a black felt hat, and he had a dragonfly perched on his shoulder.

All the Rats were carrying swords. And when they spoke to each other, the General could see their fangs glinting in the sun.

When they were all gathered on the deck, two of the Rats lowered a thin raft down over the side of the ship. Then they all clambered overboard and squeezed into it and began rowing in to the shore.

The General scrambled to his feet. He knew he must get back to camp at once and warn the Nutmouses of what he had

seen. As he tumbled back down the bank, he could feel himself trembling. But now it was as much from anger as from fear.

"How *dare* those savages land on Marchmouse Island!" he raged. "It is *my* island, and no ship may enter its shores without *my* permission! I wouldn't be surprised if they don't claim they got here first and discovered the island before me. Well, just let them try!"

He was so indignant he felt ready for anything. He would wage a war. He would show the Rats what he was made of! He would pelt them with mud pies from Villa Vanilla and sink their boat! It would be the greatest victory of his career.

But of course Tumtum might not play along with it. He was such a peace-loving mouse, he wouldn't like the idea one bit.

The General had been gone all afternoon, and the Nutmouses were very relieved to see him back. They fell on him with questions, wanting to know everything he had seen.

Little by little, the General told them about the wild shoreline, the forest of thistles, the plains of buttercups, and the glimmering lake—all theirs for the taking.

"It is a first-class island, a true jewel," he concluded. "If I were a businessmouse, I'd turn it into a holiday resort."

"And you are quite sure there is no one else here?" Tumtum asked, for the General had seemed a little cagey on this matter.

"Well, no—er, that's to say, no one except—"

"Except who?" Tumtum interrupted.

"Oh, just a few other rodents," the General said hastily. "But, er, they don't live here, you see—no, no, they're just visiting. They've moored their ship in a cove on the opposite shore. I saw it when I climbed to the top of the hill."

"But what good fortune!" Nutmeg cried, surprised the General had held back such vital information. "We must go to them at once and ask them for a lift back across the Pond."

"Er, I'm not sure that's such a good idea . . . ," the General stammered. "You see, they are . . . well, they're—"

"Who are they?" Tumtum asked sharply, wondering what the General was trying to hide.

The General looked at the ground and scuffled the earth with his shoe. He suddenly felt a prickle of shame for having landed his friends in such danger. There was a long silence. Then he said sheepishly, "They are the Rats."

"*The Rats?* Are you sure?" Tumtum asked. "I thought they'd moved downstream."

"Yes, I'm sure," the General said reluctantly, expecting Tumtum to be very cross. "They're on that infamous old ship of theirs, *Lady Crossbones.* There are five of them, so far as I could see."

The Nutmouses looked stunned. It was such dreadful news, it took awhile to sink in.

"Now look here, my friends," the General began, trying to jolly them up a bit. "This is our island, and we can't let those vagabonds frighten us. We shall make Villa Vanilla our fortress and fight to the last!"

"*Us?* Fight the Rats? Don't be a fool, General, we'd be eaten alive," Tumtum snapped. He could have boxed the General's ears for landing them in such trouble—but luckily for the General he had more important things to do.

Tumtum looked around him, quickly taking stock of their situation. They had no boat to escape in, and no time to build one, for the Rats were sure to explore the island soon.

"We must hide," Nutmeg said anxiously. And Tumtum agreed.

"Yes. We'll have to bury all traces of this camp, then take cover in the bracken," he said. "With any luck they'll sail away in a day or two."

Tumtum started throwing earth on the fire, while Nutmeg hurriedly replaced their picnic things in the hamper.

The General stood and watched. "I am going to stay here and defend my villa," he announced stubbornly.

"But you haven't a chance, General," Tumtum said. "They'll pelt it with pebbles and knock it down flat, and when you come running out squealing they'll pounce on you and tear you to shreds. Now come on. Let's make ourselves scarce."

"I shall *not* hide! You can run away if you like, but I'm staying here. I am an officer in the Royal Mouse Army, and I shall face them like a mouse!"

To prove his intent, the General picked up his rifle and slung it over his shoulder. He had no bullets left, for he had used the last round on the macaroni and cheese. But the gun felt reassuring all the same.

"You do know that the Rats make their prisoners walk the gangplank?" Tumtum said, remembering the stories his father had told him when he was little.

But not even a threat as terrible as this would change the General's mind. And in the end, after a good deal more threatening and pleading, Tumtum and Nutmeg were forced to go and hide on their own.

They took the hamper with them, but they gave the General more than half the rations, including the last sausage roll. All the same, they felt wretched leaving him. When they reached the edge of the cove they turned to wave him good-bye, but he was busy barricading Villa Vanilla with pebbles.

"The Rats are sure to capture him," Nutmeg said forlornly.

"Well, it's no good us being captured, too," Tumtum replied. "Anyway, I reckon he'll feel less brave when it gets dark, and come running after us."

"Hmmm. I hope you're right," Nutmeg said. But she was not so sure. "Oh, if only we had a boat, then we could sail away from this beastly island."

"I told you, dear, we'll make one," Tumtum said.

"But how? We don't know anything about boatbuilding. And we haven't even got a saw."

Tumtum wished he could think of something reassuring to say. But they both knew that the situation was very bleak. They walked on silently, deep in thought. As they were about to enter the bracken Nutmeg turned and looked back at the Pond, searching the water as if by some miracle a friendly boat might suddenly have appeared. But all she could see was some rubbish washed up on the bank—an old wine bottle and some ancient bailer twine that had drifted from the farm buildings further down the stream. Beyond it the water was empty. There was nothing moving save for the tiny ripples buffetting on the Pond's surface.

Then she noticed that since they had arrived on the island the breeze had changed direction. It was blowing away from them now, back toward the far-off bank from which they had come. She stood very still, watching the water. Then she looked back at the wine bottle, studying it more closely. It was empty, and its label had been washed off. But it still had its cork.

She bit her lip. She had thought of a plan.

"Tumtum," she said suddenly. "I've had an idea."

"What is it dear?" Tumtum asked hopefully. He knew that Nutmeg's ideas weren't always sensible. But given the crisis they were in, he felt that any idea was better than none.

"We can write Arthur and Lucy a letter, telling them that we're in trouble and asking them to send out another toy boat to rescue us," Nutmeg explained, clapping her hands with glee.

"*Write to them?*" Tumtum replied. "But my dear wife, you seem to forget that we are shipwrecked on an island. There is no postal service here." He looked at Nutmeg tenderly. He supposed that all the heat and excitement must be making her muddled.

But Nutmeg wasn't muddled a bit.

"That will be our postal service," she said, pointing to the rubbish on the bank. "We can put a letter in that bottle, then push it out onto the Pond and let it drift back to the shore. Look, you see the way the tide's moving; it's sure to get there. And then when the children come back looking for the *Bluebottle*, which they're certain to do, they might just notice it."

"Goodness," Tumtum said, trying to take it all in. "But how will we seal the bottle?"

"Look," Nutmeg replied triumphantly. "It's still got its cork."

"Well, I suppose it's worth a try," Tumtum said. "But what shall we write on? We'll need a very big piece of paper if there's to be any chance of the children seeing it."

"There," she said, pointing toward an old paper caught in the grass on the bank. "We can write on that."

"Well, I suppose it will do," he said. "And have we anything to write with?"

"Look in your pockets, dear," Nutmeg replied. "You've usually a pen buried somewhere."

There followed an anxious moment as Tumtum emptied out his jacket pockets, where an assortment of candy and paper clips had gathered.

"Here!" he said finally, pulling out a nibbled black pen.

They flattened the paper on the ground, then Nutmeg took the pen and knelt down to compose an SOS.

Tumtum stood over her, reading out loud as she wrote:

The Island, the Pond

Dear Arthur and Lucy,

I accidentally got swept away this morning in your boat—but alas, she collided with a milk bottle and is now damaged beyond repair, leaving me shipwrecked on the island. I am so terriby sorry, my dears, but I do not think your beloved <u>Bluebottle</u> will ever sail again. I will try to replace her in time. But for the moment I must ask your help. You see, I am in some danger, because a band of pirates has arrived here, too. They are savage creatures, who steal and bite and carry swords, so perhaps you would be kind enough to help me escape before they find me. I need you to find another toy boat and float it out to the island as soon as you can, so that I can sail home in it and come and visit you again in the attic.

Love,

Nutmeg

She did not mention Tumtum, as in her previous letters to the children she had only ever referred to herself. As far as Arthur and Lucy were concerned, they had one fairy in their attic, not two.

"Good. Now let's get it in the bottle," Tumtum said impatiently. They had been dallying in the open for a long time, and he was anxious to get under cover.

They rolled the letter into a cylinder and carried it to the water's edge. Then they wrenched the cork from the neck of the bottle and eased the letter inside. When they had finished, they pressed the cork back in as tightly as they could. They pushed as though their lives depended on it, sweat pouring down their coats.

When everything was in place, the Nutmouses both braced themselves against the side of the bottle and pushed on it hard until finally it rolled down the bank and plopped into the water.

They waited a moment to see if it would drift out from the shore. But then suddenly they heard a terrible noise coming from the other side of the island. It was the sound of braying and shrieking—then a piercing squeal, like a creature being pounced on.

"Come on!" Tumtum said, tugging Nutmeg by the arm. "The Rats are on the move."

Chapter Eight

Toward the end of the afternoon, Arthur and Lucy set out for the Pond, hoping to get their boat back. But in the last few hours water had been steadily seeping into the *Bluebottle*'s hold, and by the time the children arrived she had sunk without a trace.

"She's gone," Arthur said miserably. "She can't have gone," Lucy said. "She's probably just drifted around the island. Come on. Let's go and look."

But when they reached the other side of the Pond it was not *Bluebottle* they saw, but *Lady Crossbones*, lying black and motionless by the island shore.

She was nestled in among the rushes, but they could see her

quite clearly. They stood in silence a moment, dazzled by her gold sails and her cold beauty.

"Who do you think she belongs to?" Lucy asked eventually.

"I don't know. But with a name like *Lady Crossbones* it must be a pirate ship," Arthur said. "And look!" he gasped. "It's even got a gangplank!" He felt his heart quicken. It looked much more real than any of the other toy pirate ships he had seen.

There was nothing stirring on the deck. But they could see the Rats' lantern hanging from the mast. And there was light coming from one of the portholes.

"Maybe it sunk *Bluebottle*," Arthur said.

"Don't be stupid," Lucy replied. "Toy boats don't sink each other."

"But this boat doesn't look like a toy," Arthur said. "It looks real."

Lucy shivered. It did look real—and it had a sinister air. Its owner must be here somewhere. She looked around the Pond fearfully, as if expecting some vile creature suddenly to burst out from the water. But everything was very still. Then she noticed a small gleam of light, as the sun fell on something tucked into the rushes just below where she was standing.

Lucy knelt down on the bank and hurriedly brushed aside the plants, wondering what it could be. But then she saw that it was just an old bottle. *It must have been washed up the stream*, she thought, and yet something about it caught her eye.

She leaned down and picked it out of the water. "Look at this," she said, showing the bottle to Arthur.

He shrugged. It didn't look very interesting.

Lucy brushed the glass with her sleeve. "There's a piece of paper inside it," she said.

"*A piece of paper?*" Arthur asked, suddenly intrigued. "Here, let's have a look."

Lucy passed it to him, and he held the bottle close up to his face and peered inside.

He pulled out the cork and shook out the piece of brown paper. Then he unrolled it and held it flat.

The writing was too small for the children to read, and

the ink had become smudged. But they recognized the strange, loopy pattern of the letters, and knew at once that it was in Nutmeg's hand.

They both gasped. Whatever was Nutmeg doing sending them a letter in a bottle? That meant she must be on the island. But why? Could it be that *she* had something to do with the sinister pirate ship?

"We must work out what it says—she probably knows what's happened to *Bluebottle*," Lucy said urgently.

"Try this," Arthur said, pulling a small magnifying glass from his penknife. It was not very strong, but when Lucy held it over the paper she could make out most of what was written. She read the letter out loud to Arthur, guessing the words that were too faint to see.

Arthur listened in astonishment. When he heard his boat had sunk he looked close to tears. "So it was Nutmeg who took *Bluebottle*!" he said in dismay. "Well, she can't be much good at sailing if she let it sink. Now we'll never get it back."

"Why are you still worrying about *Bluebottle*?" Lucy asked

scathingly. "It's Nutmeg that matters now. Have you got another boat we can use to rescue her?"

"Not really," he said, feeling a little chastened. "There's only the plastic one in the bathroom, and that leaks."

"Then we'll have to make one," Lucy said. "There must be something at home we can use. Come on. If we hurry we can get back here before supper."

The children ran back to Rose Cottage and started turning out the kitchen cupboards, looking for something boatlike. There was a bread pan, but it was too rusty, and there was a yogurt cup, but that was too deep. There was a wooden salad bowl that might have worked, but a woodworm had eaten through it.

Then Lucy found an old margarine tub that was being used to keep rubber bands in. "That'll do fine," Arthur said. "It will be just Nutmeg's size."

What they did next was very clever. They attached two twigs in a cross to make a mast, then tied on one of Mr. Mildew's handkerchiefs for a sail and stuck it in the tub with Blue Tack. Then they put in two teaspoons for Nutmeg to use as oars, in case there was no breeze. When they had finished, they ran straight back to the Pond. They had been gone nearly two hours, and dusk was gathering. But the pirate ship had not moved.

"I hope we're not too late," Lucy said, looking at it with apprehension.

"I wouldn't have thought so," Arthur replied confidently. "It's getting dark, so maybe the pirates will have stopped pirating for today. And by the time they start up again tomorrow, Nutmeg will have escaped in our boat."

They walked to the water's edge and launched the margarine tub from the bank opposite the ship. Arthur poked it as far as it would go with a stick. Then they stood and watched as the breeze played in its sail, nudging it toward the cove where *Bluebottle* had sunk.

Chapter Nine

Back on Marchmouse Island, events were developing at quite a pace.

The Rats had roasted a frog for their dinner, and they were full of rich food and high spirits. As the night drew in, they began rampaging across the island, slashing the heads off dandelions.

Tumtum and Nutmeg lay trembling in the bracken, buried deep under a pile of ferns. They were well hidden, but they were frightened the Rats would sniff them out. Nutmeg wished she had applied less perfume that morning.

The Rats came closer and closer, until they were so near the Nutmouses could hear the leaves rustling under their feet. When they were but an inch or so from where the mice were hiding, the Rats stopped a moment, wondering which way to go. Then they gave another cheer and rampaged on.

The Nutmouses waited until the wood had gone quiet again. Then they poked their noses out of the ferns and took a deep breath.

"That was close," Tumtum commented.

"They sounded the most awful savages," Nutmeg said. "I do hope the General doesn't do anything too silly. If he goes taking potshots at them from his villa they'll tear him to shreds."

"He wouldn't dare," Tumtum said confidently. "He'll be feeling much less brave now that we've left him on his own. I'll bet the last hair on my tail that he's gone into hiding, too."

If only he had. For then the Nutmouses' ordeal might have ended rather sooner. But the General was not hiding. Far from it. At this particular moment, he was standing outside Villa Vanilla, stoking his campfire and roasting a snail for his supper.

And he was thinking the same defiant old thoughts—such as, "I'll show the Rats who owns this island!" and "Hah! They won't get rid of me!"

But trouble arrived sooner than he might have expected.

For by now the Rats had emerged from the bracken and were clambering up the bank behind the starlit cove. When they reached the top, they sat down a moment to admire the view. They were very still, with the dragonfly perched motionless on the Captain's shoulder.

Then they saw the General's campfire flickering on the beach.

They suddenly jumped to their feet, enraged and astonished. Until then, they had believed they had the whole island to themselves.

"Who the devil's down there?" snarled the Captain, whose name was Captain Pong. He grabbed his telescope and glared down the bank. His dragonfly clung to his shoulder, giving an angry flap of its wings. It was a brilliant night, and the Captain could see Villa Vanilla gleaming a soft pink in the moonlight. Then he saw the General, illuminated by the campfire.

"Well, look at that! It's a mouse!" he said.

"*A mouse?*" the others cried. "How dare there be a mouse! This is our island. It's *Rat* Island. Let's see him off!"

"Hang on a minute," Captain Pong snapped, twizzling his

lens to get a better look. "I've seen that mouse before. It's General Marchmouse!"

"General Marchmouse? It can't be!" the others said. The Captain gave them each a turn with the telescope so they could see for themselves. And then there could be no doubting it.

None of the Rats had met General Marchmouse before. But they recognized him at once, for he was very famous. They had seen his picture time and again in the *Mouse Times*, and there had been posters of him on some of the boats they had robbed. Not so long ago, he had even had his face on a stamp.

The General was a legend of his time. And now here he was, cooking his supper on their beach!

They all sucked in their breath. The Rats were jealous of the General because he was the only rodent with a reputation as big as theirs.

"Ha! Who does he think he is?" the black Rat snarled.

"Stupid little squirt," snorted the Rat with half a tail.

And going through all their minds was the same nasty thought: *Here is the chance to bring the General down a peg or two.*

"Let's tie him up and paint him purple!" said one.

"Let's make him walk the gangplank!" said another.

"Let's make him ride a frog!" said a third—and so they went on, suggesting more and more horrible things they might do.

"Shhh!" the Captain hissed, fearing the General might hear them. "Come on—we'll take him unawares."

The crew stopped squeaking and slithered silently down the bank. When they reached the cove, they hid behind a clump of nettles, watching as the General turned his supper on the spit. Then they crept up to Villa Vanilla and crouched in the shadows, waiting to pounce.

The General was taking his time, for he liked his meat well cooked. Eventually, when the snail was brown all over, he took it from the fire and made back toward the villa. His mind was wandering, recalling all the battles he had won, and he did not hear the Rats sniggering. But as he put out his hand to open the door he felt a cold paw on his neck.

"Gotcha!" the Captain said.

The General kicked and nipped and squealed, but he was no match for five Rats. After only the briefest of struggles, he was knocked out cold. Then he was slung over the brown Rat's shoulder and carried back across the island to the ship.

It was perhaps just as well the General was unconscious, for it was a long hike, up hill and down dale, and through a swamp and a thistle forest.

Had the General been awake, the Rats would have made him walk. And he would have hated every step. But as it was he was carried along like a sack of Smarties. He was still unconscious when the Rats heaved him onto the ship and locked him in a cabin below deck.

When the General finally came around he felt very stiff. He sat up painfully, trying to work out what had happened to him. He was on a bare wooden floor in a small room furnished with a stool and a bookcase full of silver plates and candlesticks. On the wall above him was a porthole, letting in a pale dawn light.

In a rush of shame, he remembered being ambushed outside Villa Vanilla and realized the Rats must have imprisoned

him on their ship. It was a glum awakening.

He stood up and rattled the door shouting, "Let me out!"—
but no one came. He shouted until he was worn out, then he
collapsed on the floor and sat with his head in his paws, brood-
ing miserably.

Finally, he heard a key in the lock. As he jumped to his feet,
the door was flung open and the black Rat and the white Rat
walked in.

The black Rat had a ring through his nose, and the white
Rat had only one fang. They both had scars on their faces that
made them look even more ferocious.

"Sit on the stool," the black Rat said. And the General did,
because the Rat was much bigger than him. Then both Rats
stood in front of him, looking at him very hard and asking lots
of questions. This was called an interrogation, and it was not at
all pleasant.

"How did you get here?" the black Rat snarled, leaning over
the General so close their noses were almost touching.

"I arrived on *Bluebottle*," the General said, trembling.

"Where is she now?"

"She has sunk. She collided with a milk bottle and sprang a leak."

"Who else was with you?"

"No one," the General lied.

"Were there any valuables on board?" the white Rat asked, drooling.

The General was so nervous he started to babble. "Valuables? Gracious, no. *Bluebottle* was rather basic, you know. The only thing of any possible value was Mr. Nutmouse's silver picnicking crockery—it was rather fancy, you know, blue and white, with impressions of bumblebees. . . . Anyway, he and Mrs. Nutmouse took that with them when they went off to hide in the—"

The General suddenly realized what he had done and clapped a paw to his mouth. "Oops," he said.

But it was too late. At the mention of Tumtum's name the Rats' ears had gone as stiff as cardboard. For the Nutmouses were rumored to be fabulously rich, with a huge mansion full of expensive furniture. They should surely demand a king's ransom if they kidnapped Tumtum and Nutmeg, of Nutmouse Hall!

"Where are they?" the Rats growled.

"I don't know," the General gulped.

"Yes, you do! Now tell us where they went to hide!"

"I tell you, I don't know!"

"Yes, you do!"

"No, I don't!"

"Yes, you do!"

"No, I don't!"

There was no danger of the General giving in, of course, because a General would never betray a friend. But nonetheless, his voice had started to waver.

Then the door opened again, and the other Rats appeared.

"What's going on?" Captain Pong asked, giving the General a menacing glare.

"He sailed here with Mr. Nutmouse—you know, that stinking rich fellow who lives at Nutmouse Hall," the white Rat explained. "Their ship was sunk, and now Nutmouse and his wife are hiding somewhere on the island." The Rat paused and pointed at the General accusingly. "He knows where they are. *But he won't tell us!*"

"Then throw him overboard," Captain Pong said.

"Throw him overboard!" the others cried, delighted with this plan.

The General leaped from his seat, punching and squealing, but he was overpowered in no time. They tied his paws behind his back, marched him up to the deck, and then hoisted him onto the gangplank.

It was a thin, springy gangplank, and it struck the General that it went on a very long way. He could feel the tip flapping.

"Go on!" the Rats sneered, prodding him in the back with a candlestick. "Walk!"

The General looked down at the dark water and thought he could see the shadow of an enormous fish. He felt his legs wobble. He could hear the Rats chanting—"Walk! Walk! Walk!"—but their voices had become faint and echoey, as if coming from a cavern far away. The General had never known fear like this.

He could not go on.

"Oh, please, sirs!" he quaked, his face reddening with shame. "The Nutmouses are in the bracken wood!"

439

Chapter Ten

Had the Rats been truly horrible, they might have made General Marchmouse walk the gangplank all the same. But in most creatures there is a shred of mercy. So once the General had given them the information they required, they pulled him down, cuffed his ears, and locked him back in his cabin.

The General watched from his porthole as the Rats clambered back onto their raft and rowed to the shore. He could hear them as they made their way across the island, screeching bloodthirstily as they went to track Tumtum and Nutmeg down.

He knew there was no hope for the Nutmouses now. Soon they would be prisoners, too, and it was all *his* fault for betraying them. He sat on his stool, seized with remorse. It gave him a hot, tickly feeling to think how cross Tumtum would be.

Before long, two dreadful squeals rose from the depths of the island, and he knew his friends had been captured.

Presently, he heard the Rats clattering back onto the deck. "Lock them up below!" one of them shouted. And next thing the door to the General's cabin was opened, and Tumtum and Nutmeg were flung inside.

They were a sorry spectacle. Their clothes were torn and scuffed, and they had burrs in their hair. And Tumtum's watch was broken. But their spirits were still intact.

"These Rats are savages!" Nutmeg cried. "You should have seen what they've done to Villa Vanilla, General. They've battered down the walls and gnawed a big hole in the roof. Oh, it's a pitiful mess. And they stole our last slice of ginger cake—and smashed the picnic glasses!"

"Did they ambush you in the bracken?" the General asked sheepishly. But to his relief Tumtum did not suspect him of betrayal.

"They caught us in the cove, just as we were trying to sail away in the margarine tub," he replied. "If they had only arrived a minute later, we'd have been able to escape."

"*The Margarine Tub?* Who's she?" the General asked, thinking this a curious name for a boat.

"She is a margarine tub, as her name suggests," Nutmeg said.

"But a cut above most margarine tubs," Tumtum added proudly. "She has a fine cotton sail and oars made of solid steel."

The General looked even more bewildered. But then the Nutmouses started at the beginning, and told him all about the SOS they had sent to the children; and how they had crept down to the cove that morning as soon as it was light and found the margarine tub washed up on the pebbles, like an answer to a prayer.

"And we were just pushing it out to water, about to set sail, when the Rats sprang out of the bushes, shouting, 'Who goes there?'" Nutmeg went on. "And then they searched the boat and found a letter in it from Arthur and Lucy. It was clearly addressed to me, but the Rats read it all the same. And it was just

an innocent letter, explaining that I should be careful with the sail, as it was attached with putty and might wobble a bit. But of course the Rats made a terrible fuss about it and wanted to know who Arthur and Lucy were. So we told them they were only human children who meant no harm. But then the Rats' eyes went all narrow and greedy, and they asked us if the children were rich. And Tumtum laughed, and said, 'Oh, dear me no. They're not rich at all. Quite the contrary: they're so poor, they can't afford jam for their bread.' But the Rats wouldn't believe it. And they sent the boat back to the shore, with another letter in it—a letter from them to Arthur and Lucy. And . . . and—"

"And what did the Rats' letter say?" the General asked impatiently. But Nutmeg had started sobbing and couldn't go on.

"They informed Arthur and Lucy that they had taken Nutmeg hostage," Tumtum said. "And they said that if the children send the boat back to the island by tonight, filled to the brim with gold, then they will let her go. But if the Rats do not receive the gold before darkness falls, they will make her walk the gangplank."

"And what about you and me?" the General asked self-centeredly.

"We don't feature in the letters, because the children don't know we're here," Tumtum replied. "But the Rats advised me that if they make Nutmeg walk the gangplank, they'll make us walk it, too."

The General grimaced. "Do you think the children will meet their demands?" he asked.

"How can they?" Nutmeg cried. "They haven't got any gold. Not a pound coin between them."

"In that case we're in a spot of bother," the General said.

Lucy awoke early that morning expecting to find that Nutmeg had visited the attic in the night. But the midnight feast of milk and biscuit crumbs that the children had left out in the dollhouse was untouched. And there was no note from her on the dresser.

"Arthur, wake up," Lucy cried. "She hasn't been here."

"She's probably still making her way back from the Pond," Arthur grunted, pulling the covers over his head. "Now, go away and let me sleep. It's not fair being woken up this early when we don't have school."

"Oh, *please*," Lucy said. "I want to go down to the Pond now. If we can find the margarine tub then at least we'll know if Nutmeg got away from the island." She got up and opened the curtains. It was already light. "Come on. If we go now we can be back for breakfast."

"Oh, all right, " Arthur said, for he was curious, too. The children got dressed and tiptoed downstairs, so as not to wake their father. Then they let themselves out of the garden door and ran across the meadow.

It felt cooler today, and the Pond was scattered with a thin, feathery mist. The pirate ship had not moved. It was still lying motionless beside the island, its deck deserted and its portholes unlit. But the margarine tub was nowhere to be seen.

"It can't have just disappeared," Lucy said.

"Maybe it's sunk," Arthur suggested glumly.

"Of course it hasn't sunk," Lucy said. *Bluebottle* sinking was bad enough. The margarine tub couldn't sink, too. It would be too much bad luck.

She started around the bank to look again, brushing aside the weeds with her hands. And then suddenly she saw the little boat floating on the water, just a few yards from where she was standing. It had appeared as if by magic. It had mist in its sails, and it looked gray and ghostly.

There was no one on board.

"Arthur, look. It's here," she called. "Can you get it?"

"Hang on," he replied. He found a long stick, then he lay on the grass and gently pulled the margarine tub onto the bank.

Lucy lay down beside him and reached it out of the water.

"There's something in it," she said, taking out a tiny can, as small as a thimble. (It belonged to the Captain. He always carried a can in his knapsack, in case he found a delicious bug he wanted to take back to the ship to fry for his supper.) Lucy pried off the lid with her thumbnail. And inside the can she found a piece of paper, folded several times.

"It must be another letter from Nutmeg," Arthur said. But the children got a fright when they unraveled it, for the writing looked very sinister. The page was smudged with black ink, and the letters were all botched and coarse. It was quite different from Nutmeg's handwriting.

"What does it say?" Arthur asked.

Lucy read it out loud to him. The Rat's handwriting was much bigger than Nutmeg's, so she did not need a magnifying glass to decipher it.

Rats' Island
The Pond

To Arthur and Lucy,

Ur boat arived to late to save yor belovid Nutmeg. Weve taken her prisoner, and were goin to show her wot hapins to any1 who tresparsis on R island. We wil sail out to were the Pond is deepist, and were there R giant fish in the waters. Then we will make her walk the gangplank, with her paws tide behind her back.

But if U are good children, and return The Margarine Tub to the island bye nightfal, filed to its brim with gold, then we wil set

Nutmeg free, and let her sail back to the shoor. But remember, we

must get the gold by nightfal. Or U wil never sea Nutmeg again.

From,

The Rats

Arthur and Lucy were stunned. It was a very frightening letter to receive.

"They can't really be rats," Arthur said. "Rats can't write."

"Well, these Rats can hardly write—look at their spelling," Lucy said. "But whoever they are we've got to get Nutmeg back before they do something awful to her."

"But what can we do? We haven't got any gold to send them."

"Then we'll have to tell Pa. Maybe he can swim out to the island and rescue her."

"Don't be silly. Can you imagine Pa swimming? I shouldn't think he's ever been swimming in his life. And I hardly think he's going to throw himself into the Pond in order to rescue a fairy who's been captured by Rats. If we tell him that, he'll think we're just being silly."

Lucy looked thoughtful. Arthur was right; their father would never believe their story. No one would believe it. It was much too strange. They were going to have to rescue Nutmeg themselves. One way or another, they needed to find some gold.

Then Arthur had an idea. "Listen, you remember those chocolates that Aunt Ivy gave us at Christmas—the dark ones with goo in the middle?" he said excitedly.

Lucy nodded. She had tasted them and they had made her feel quite sick. They contained a disgusting syrupy substance called liqueur, which made her eyes water and her throat sting. Chocolate liqueurs are very potent. If you eat too many, you start to feel drunk. But they are so revolting, not even the greediest person would want more than one.

No one had liked Aunt Ivy's chocolate liqueurs. So they had been sitting in the pantry since Boxing Day, gathering dust.

"What about them?" Lucy said.

"Well, you remember what they looked like? Each one was wrapped in gold paper and shaped like a brick. If we pack them all into the margarine tub, the pirates will think we've sent them

a cargo of gold bullion!"

Lucy thought this was a wonderful plan. "And we can write them a letter, saying we'll send over a second load as soon as we've got Nutmeg back," she said cleverly. "That way they'll be sure to keep to their side of the bargain. Come on, quick! Let's go and find them."

Lucy picked up the margarine tub and they ran back to Rose Cottage. Then they took the chocolates from the pantry and polished each one with a tea towel until it shone. They packed them into the boat two layers deep. And then Lucy found a piece of paper and sat down at the kitchen table to write the pirates a letter.

Dear Rats,

We are sending you these bricks of gold as a ransom. In return you must release Nutmeg AT ONCE, and let her use the boat to return to the shore. If you let her go tonight, we will send you a second cargo of gold in the morning. But if you keep her prisoner, we won't send you anything else, ever.

From,

Arthur and Lucy Mildew

Rose Cottage

Lucy folded the letter tightly and wedged it beside the mast. Then they went straight back to the Pond. Lucy carried the margarine tub, covering it with both hands to make sure the chocolates didn't fall out.

They could see signs of life on *Lady Crossbones*. There was a feather of smoke coming from a little stove on the deck, and a black flag had been raised on the mast. The children stood on the opposite bank and pushed the margarine tub out onto the water.

"Now all we can do is wait," Lucy said.

Chapter Eleven

The mice spent a horrible day locked up in their cabin. They were given nothing for breakfast, and lunch was just a piece of cheese—the sort of stale, rubbery cheese used in mousetraps. It was supper time now, but no supper had been served.

"If we don't escape soon we'll starve," Tumtum said.

"I told you, escape is out of the question," the General replied sharply. "Even if we managed to break out of this cabin, our only hope of getting away would be to jump overboard. And then we might be eaten by fish."

"Well I'd take a chance on it," Nutmeg said. She had been away from Nutmouse Hall for two whole nights, and she was so homesick she felt she would risk anything to get back—even an encounter with a carp.

But the General had been badly shaken by his experience on the gangplank the morning before and was feeling less brave than usual. "We must wait and see if the children come up with the ransom money," he said. "This is no time for foolish heroics."

Tumtum was tempted to point out that if it hadn't been for the General's foolish heroics last night, when he was so determined to defend Villa Vanilla, they might not have been captured at all. But he didn't.

"There is no way the children will raise the ransom," he said instead. "Last time I crawled into their piggy bank, it only had five pence in it. And five pence pieces are made of silver, not gold. Anyway, it will be dark soon. Our time's running out."

The General shrugged. "If no ransom arrives, we shall just have to negotiate with the Rats as best we can. Perhaps you can offer them Nutmouse Hall in exchange for our release," he suggested.

Tumtum looked at him scornfully. Give the Rats Nutmouse Hall? The house his great-great-great-grandfather had built! He would never do that.

And he was about to say as much. But then Nutmeg looked out of the porthole and let out a cry. "The children have sent the boat back! And it *is* full of gold! Oh, Tumtum, look! It really is!"

Tumtum and the General rushed to the window and saw the margarine tub floating toward them with its cotton sail billowing in the wind. There was no one on board, just a great heap of gold bullion, glinting in the twilight. It was a strange and wonderful sight. The tub was heavily laden, and it had taken it the best part of the day to drift this far. It did not take long for the Rats, who were eating supper on the deck, to notice it, too. Their jaws dropped. At best, they had expected that the children might send them a few gold coins. But there was enough treasure here for them all to retire on.

"We'll never have to rob another boat again," the brown Rat drooled.

In his mind's eye, each Rat pictured the new life he would lead. A life of palaces, hot baths, soft beds, long naps, and

banquets that went on and on. Oh, it would be a fine thing to be rich!

"Come on. Let's pull her in!" Captain Pong said. The mice watched from the porthole as the Rats rowed out to the tub in a raft, then carefully looped a rope around the mast and started towing it back to the shore.

They went very slowly, fearful one of the gold bricks might topple from the pile. When they reached the bank they dragged the margarine tub out of the water and rested it in the mud. Then they all gathered around it, looking rather tense. The gold was the most beautiful sight they had ever seen. But a sense of rivalry had developed between them, with each Rat already fussing about whether he'd get his fair share.

"Don't touch it!" Captain Pong rasped, sensing a fight might break out. "I'll count the bricks. And *I'll* decide who gets what."

This caused alarm, for Captain Pong was not best known for his sense of fair play. But he had a paw placed meaningfully on his sword, so the other Rats hesitated to challenge him.

The Captain leaned over the tub and tried to lift one of the bricks to see how heavy it was. It felt like concrete, for

the chocolates were very stale. The others watched avidly as he raised it with both arms—then they gave a greedy cheer when they saw the second layer of bullion underneath.

"Hang on, what's this?" the Captain said, seeing the children's letter peeking out from the wrappers. He dumped his chocolate back on the pile and yanked the letter free. Then he laid it flat on the ground and stood at the bottom of the page, reading it out loud.

The Rats sucked in their breath as they heard the children's offer:

... If you let her go tonight, we will send you a second cargo of gold in the morning. But if you keep her prisoner, we won't send you anything else, ever. ...

"More gold!" they said dreamily. They were beginning to feel dizzy. At this rate, they would be the richest Rats in the whole world.

"Well then. We'd better hurry up and unload this stuff, then let Mrs. Nutmouse go," the Captain said. And everyone agreed, for they didn't want to miss out on a chance like this.

"What about Mr. Nutmouse and the General?" asked the white Rat, who spoke in a much squeakier voice than the others. "The children make no mention of them. If we keep them hostage we might be able to demand a third load of gold later on."

Captain Pong considered this for a moment. The prospect of a third load was certainly tempting. But he was worried Nutmeg might not be able to manage the margarine tub on her own. And if she capsized and drowned while crossing the Pond, there would be no more gold at all.

"Nah," he said eventually. "Let 'em all go. The wind will be against them. She'll need the gents to help her row."

"Good riddance to them," the other Rats said, for they were sick and tired of taking the prisoners lumps of cheese.

"So where shall we hide all this gold?" the black Rat asked. "It weighs a ton. It's going to be an awful sweat hauling it all up onto the ship."

"We'll need a pulley. It will be hard work, that's for sure," the brown Rat said.

"All right, all right. Let's not worry about that now," said the Captain, who hated work of any kind. "We can take it onto the ship tomorrow, once the second load's arrived. We can leave it here for now. It's not as though there's anyone to steal it."

"But we can't just leave it out in the open. The birds might take it," the black Rat said.

Captain Pong muttered crossly. But the black Rat was right; the treasure had to be moved. They all looked around for somewhere sheltered. Then the Captain pointed to a small cave at the rear of the cove, formed where two stones had toppled against each other.

"We can move it in there," he said. "It will be perfectly safe for a day or two." He turned to the white Rat. "You. Go back to the ship and fetch the prisoners. The rest of us will stay here and unload."

So the white Rat rowed back to the ship in the raft while the other Rats started hauling the gold out of the margarine tub and lugging it across to the cave.

When they had moved about half of it, the white Rat returned to the beach with the Nutmouses and the General.

464

"Get out," he squeaked, bumping the raft to a stop against a pebble. The mice clambered nervously onto the beach, where they were addressed by Captain Pong.

"Those children of yours have met our demands, so when we've finished unloading our gold you can sail this margarine tub home," he said mercifully. "I need only have released Mrs. Nutmouse—but I have decided to let you all go." It made him feel very powerful setting them free.

"Oh, how generous you are, Captain!" Nutmeg cried. She was so happy she could have kissed him.

But then there was a sudden shriek—and looking around they saw the brown Rat trip head over tail on a twig. The gold brick that he had been carrying fell from his paws and crashed against a pebble.

"Careful! You'll dent it," the Captain snarled. But something much worse happened. The precious treasure split and cracked down the middle. Then a foul-smelling goo began to ooze out from inside.

"Woah," the other Rats said. No one could understand it. Gold shouldn't behave like this.

But the Captain was trembling, for a terrible suspicion had stirred in his mind. Leaning over the broken brick, he drew his sword and slashed off the wrapper.

"This isn't gold. It's chocolate," he said.

Chapter Twelve

For a few glorious moments, the Rats had believed they were rich. So the discovery that their gold was fake came as a savage blow.

"I could eat those children alive!" roared the Captain. He was so cross the tip of his nose had turned purple.

He suspected that the mice had somehow colluded in Arthur and Lucy's trick. He turned and glared at them, determined to make them pay.

"Do you still want to let them go?" the white Rat asked stupidly.

"*Let them go*? Of course not, you fool! Do you think I intend to let them go after *this*? Pah! We shall take them back to the ship, lock them in a cabin with no porthole, and keep them there for as long as they live on a diet of bread and water. Or maybe just water. That will teach them to try and make a fool out of me!"

Tumtum gulped. "I say, Captain, we really didn't know anything about . . . I mean to say, we didn't—"

"Quiet!" the Captain snarled, baring a pair of yellow fangs. He turned to his Rats and started giving orders. "Load these filthy chocolates back into the margarine tub and cast them adrift. I want the children to find them, so they know we haven't fallen for their wicked ploy. If they want their mangy little mouse back, they'll have to come up with a better ransom than this."

Tumtum and Nutmeg listened in horror. Events had taken a terrible turn.

"We must try and reason with him dear," Nutmeg trembled. And yet Captain Pong looked so cross that somehow they both felt tongue-tied.

The Nutmouses were so frightened they did not notice the excited expression on General Marchmouse's face. Until now, he had been behaving very feebly. But he was suddenly

looking at the chocolates very intently, and his brain had started to whirr.

"What sort of chocolates do you think these are, Mrs. Nutmouse?" he whispered.

"They must be liqueurs," Nutmeg said. "Aunt Ivy gave Mr. Mildew a box of them at Christmas, and no one liked them, so they've been hanging around Rose Cottage ever since. The children must have dug them out of the pantry, thinking they could play a trick on the Rats."

"Liqueurs, eh?" the General said.

"That's right," Nutmeg said. "You know the sort, General. Your humans have probably got some in their pantry. They're dark and sickly, with revolting alcoholic drinks in the middle."

The General's eyes gleamed. "Yes, yes, I know what a liqueur is, Mrs. Nutmouse," he said impatiently. "And if these are liqueurs, then we must persuade the Rats to eat them. We must ensure they eat *every single one*."

"What good will that do?" asked Tumtum, who had been listening to this exchange.

"It will get them drunk!" the General hissed. "And have you ever seen a drunk rat, Nutmouse?"

"I don't believe I have," Tumtum replied. But the General was more worldly. He had seen many strange things during his army days.

"Well, you've missed a thing or two, for a drunk rat is a sight to behold," he said knowingly.

"What are you getting at, General?" Tumtum asked, thinking this was no time for silly games. "What's so special about a drunk rat?"

"I shall tell you what's special about a drunk rat, Nutmouse. A drunk rat can't chase after you. *That* is what's special about a drunk rat!"

The Nutmouses caught their breath, as what he was saying suddenly began to make sense. "You mean to say—" Nutmeg began.

"I mean to say that if we can persuade the Rats to eat enough chocolates, then they'll fall down flat and start wriggling their legs in the air, and hiccuping, and giggling, and—"

"And we can run away!" Nutmeg finished excitedly.

"Ah, but we won't run," the General corrected her. "We shall sail. As soon as the alcohol has taken its effect, the three of us will jump onto the raft and row out to *Lady Crossbones*. Then we'll climb on board, pull up anchor, and sail away—leaving the Rats stranded on Marchmouse Island!"

"What a heavenly plan," Nutmeg said admiringly.

But Tumtum was foreseeing problems. "Nutmeg and I tasted the chocolates once, and I can vouch that they're truly disgusting," he said. "Do you really think we could persuade the pirates to eat them?"

"Of course. Rats will eat anything," the General replied confidently. But then the conversation was suddenly cut short by Captain Pong. "What are you muttering about?" Captain Pong barked. "Planning your escape, eh? Hah! You won't be so lucky!"

The Rats had already finished loading the chocolates back into the margarine tub. And now they were dragging it to the water's edge. "Cast her adrift!" Captain Pong shouted.

"I say, hang on!" the General cried.

The Rats glared at him. "What do you want?" they snarled.

"Well, I suppose I don't want anything really," the General replied, looking at the chocolate longingly. "That's to say, well— I was just thinking what a shame it would be to let all this lovely treasure go to waste."

"It isn't treasure. It's *chocolate!*" the Captain screeched. He was puce with fury. His disappointment was horrid enough as it was, without the General rubbing it in.

"But my dear Captain, these aren't just any old chocolates," the General persevered. "They are Chocolate Liqueurs. Liqueurs, Captain. *Liqueurs!* Beautiful, rare, priceless things. Forget about gold, Captain. Oh, phooey! A whole boatful of gold is worth nothing compared to one Chocolate Liqueur."

Captain Pong had not heard of chocolate liqueurs until now. So this was very puzzling to him. "What's so special about them?" he asked.

The General feigned surprise. "Gracious, Captain! What a sheltered life you've led. Why, liqueurs have magic centers. If you eat enough of them, anything becomes possible. I've known mice who would sell their own young for a single bite!"

The Rats had all gathered around and were looking at the General suspiciously. More intelligent rodents might have dismissed these wild claims straightaway, but the Rats did not know what to make of it. They had never been to school and had not been taught to question things.

Nonetheless, they were not completely taken in.

"Is there enough magic in them to make me rich?" Captain Pong asked greedily.

"Why, of course, my dear fellow!" the General exclaimed. "Hah! You could become the richest rodent in the entire county, if you ate enough of them. Mr. Nutmouse here owes his entire fortune to a chocolate liqueur, don't you, Nutty? One of his ancestors found one dropped under a Christmas tree, and—sensible mouse that he was—he bolted it down before anyone else could snatch it. And while he was bolting, he made a wish. 'I wish I had a grand house with a billiards room, and a ballroom, and a banqueting room, and a butler's pantry full of expensive china plates,' he said. And next thing he knew, he owned Nutmouse Hall."

"Is this true?" the Captain asked, turning to Tumtum.

"Quite true," Tumtum replied.

Nutmeg caught her breath, for it was the first time she had heard him lie. Tumtum was surprised at himself, too. But then he remembered that Captain Pong was threatening to lock them up in a dark cabin for the rest of their lives on a diet of bread and water. And sometimes, when a threat such as that hangs over you, only a lie will do.

"My advice to you, Captain, would be to seize your chance and scoff the whole lot," Tumtum said. "And remember, the more you eat, the richer you'll become," he added encouragingly.

Captain Pong looked at Tumtum very carefully. Everyone knew that Tumtum was a learned mouse. It was rumored he even had his own library. So perhaps his advice was worth taking. Besides, the thought of being rich made the Captain feel gloriously reckless.

"Pass me a chocolate," he said.

Chapter Thirteen

There followed the most revolting scene. Tumtum had told the Rats that the more liqueurs they ate, the richer they would become. So they weren't going to let Captain Pong scoff the lot.

It was each Rat for himself as they all fell upon the boat, tearing the gold wrappers off the chocolates and frantically sinking their fangs into the dark shells. The chocolates were thick and hard, and the Rats had to gnaw like crazy to reach the magic centers. As the Rats finally chewed through to the middle, each chocolate released a torrent of sickly syrup. Soon the whole beach was awash.

The Rats stood back in fright, for the liquid was giving off an overwhelming smell. It was like burned sugar, but

much more intoxicating. It was so strong it made their eyes water.

"It's petrol," one of them declared, holding his nose.

"It's poison," another Rat said.

Their suspicions were mounting. And the General's trick might easily have fallen through, had it not been for Tumtum's quick-wittedness. He could see that the Rats needed encouragement—so he fell to his knees with a groan of delight and started slurping.

"Oh, heavenly nectar!" he cried, briefly coming up for air.

In actual fact, Tumtum was only pretending. He was not swallowing anything at all. But the Rats were fooled. And at the rate Tumtum appeared to be drinking, they feared there would be nothing left for them.

"Get out of there, you greedy brute!" Captain Pong grunted, hauling Tumtum aside by his collar.

Then all the Rats fell on the ground and started spooning up huge pawfuls of the mysterious brown syrup. They ate with bitter rivalry. Not a word was exchanged. There was nothing to be heard but the *smack*, *smack*, *smack* of their jaws.

The mice watched anxiously, waiting for the first signs of silliness.

But the Rats just went on gorging.

Presently, however, Captain Pong rose to his knees, his face the color of beets. He could sense a great giggle rising in his stomach. He was usually a very serious Rat, but now he felt dizzy and carefree. It was as if all his Ratty pride had been stripped away, and his head had been filled with mush.

He turned to Tumtum, who looked a little fuzzy, and gave a loud hiccup. "Good morrow to you, Mr. Nutmouse," he said. And of course it was a silly thing to say—but you'd say something silly, too, if you'd been gobbling chocolate liqueurs.

Without waiting for Tumtum to reply, the Captain staggered to the margarine tub and pulled another chocolate from the pile.

Then the white Rat lurched to his feet. He was also flushed, and there was syrup oozing down his chin. He made to follow Captain Pong. But he was walking very strangely. For every step he took forward, he went three steps back. Finally he fell over and landed on his bottom.

The other Rats had got up now, and they were having a fine old time of it—stumbling about in the mud and giggling until the tears coursed down their snouts. Then one of them grabbed another's paw, and soon they were all prancing in circles, braying their boating song to the moon.

Rob, rob, rob the boats,
Cruelly down the stream,
Greedily, greedily, greedily, greedily
Life is but a dream.

When they had finished, they all fell down.

Tumtum and Nutmeg looked on in astonishment. The General was right. A drunk rat was a sight to behold.

"Come on!" the General hissed. "Now's our chance to escape."

Chapter Fourteen

It was a glorious night to escape. The sky was a deep blue, and the moonlight was catching on the Pond's surface, making it beam. The mice slunk silently across the beach and clambered onto the raft. Then Tumtum and the General took the oars and started pulling out toward *Lady Crossbones*.

Nutmeg kept glancing back, fearing the Rats might suddenly pounce after them.

"I shouldn't worry if I were you," the General said carelessly. "They're in no state to chase us now. I tell you, they're so drunk, it will be morning before they even notice we're gone!"

They rowed around the ship's stern and drew up on the far side out of sight of the cove. The General tied the raft tightly to the guard rail, for they would need it when they had crossed the Pond. And with both the ship and the raft gone, the Rats would be stranded. They still had the margarine tub of course—but they would never be able to sail away in that. It was barely big enough for one Rat, let alone five.

When the raft was secure, the mice scrambled up the side of the ship and dropped down onto the deck. The lantern was still lit, casting a forlorn glow around the mast. There was a woodworm nibbling the water keg, and the remains of the Rats' supper—fly fillets and mashed slugs—had been left strewn on the stove.

Tumtum quickly began hauling up the anchor. But the General was too excited for such practicalities. Ever since he was a small boy, he had dreamed of having his own boat. And now he did. "She's mine!" he cried, strutting the deck with delight.

"Steady on, General," Tumtum said. "We're only using her to escape in. You can't *keep* her. She's much too big for you."

"Of course I can keep her," the General replied. "She shall become my private yacht. I shall repaint her and replace that horrid cat with a handsome figurehead of myself. And I shall give her a new name, such as . . . well, such as *Lady Marchmouse*. Yes, *Lady Marchmouse* has a pleasant ring to it."

"But what will you do with her?" Tumtum asked. He was tugging down on the sails, anxious to be off. "A yacht is a big responsibility, you know."

"Oh, fiddlesticks," replied the General, who seemed in no hurry to set sail. "I shall moor her along the stream— somewhere nice and tucked away, where the moles and the otters won't find her. And then, whenever there's a nice sunny day, I shall come *rap-tap-tapping* at your door, Mr. Nutmouse, saying, 'Do join me for a cruise on the *Lady Marchmouse*,' that's what I'll say. Then we shall wave our wives toodlepip, and off we'll go on our pleasure boat—just you and me, titans of the stream, waving royally to all we see!"

Neither Tumtum nor Nutmeg liked the sound of this. But their bigger concern was getting home. "Come on, General. Help me tighten the sails," Tumtum grunted.

Neither mouse was an experienced sailor, so much of what followed was guesswork. They heaved down on various ropes and pulled on this lever and that—until suddenly they felt a great force above them. The mast heaved. The cloth strained. Then the gold sails flared out in the breeze.

The General ran to the wheel and wrenched it down until the ship was pointing away from the island. They were free at last, slicing silently toward the moonlit horizon. And they might easily have escaped unseen, for the Rats had not noticed the ship pulling away. But the General could not resist a chance to show off.

"Take the wheel," he ordered Tumtum, then he grabbed the lantern down from the mast and raced back to the stern. The ship was inching on fast, but he could still see the Rats dancing on the shore. He leaned over the rail, filled his lungs with air, and shouted, "Cheerio!"

The Rats heard the General's voice echoing around the cove. They wobbled to a halt and looked stupidly over their shoulders. Then they turned toward the Pond and finally noticed their ship blowing away.

"Oiy," they all cried. They stumbled to the shore and waded drunkenly into the water. Their joy had given way to a terrible rage.

"Come back or we'll eat you alive!" Captain Pong roared. But his threats were empty now, and *Lady Crossbones* sailed on heedlessly into the night. Soon all the Rats could see was the silhouette of the great General Marchmouse, waving gloatingly from the stern.

"We're free!" Nutmeg said rapturously, grasping Tumtum's paw. And even Tumtum let out a whoop, so relieved was he to have escaped.

But their trials were not over yet. For the voyage was long and grueling, and *Lady Crossbones* proved devilishly hard to control.

No sooner had she blown six feet from the shore, than she was caught by a fierce headwind, which sent her buffeting around in circles.

Tumtum and Nutmeg tugged with all their might on the sail, and the General tried to wrench the wheel, but the gusts were too strong for them, and *Lady Crossbones* refused to go on.

"Blast this vessel," the General fumed. "What's the use of a ship that dances around in circles?" He had already burned his paws pulling on the sail ropes, and he was in a foul humor. Being in command of such a big ship wasn't turning out to be nearly such fun as he'd expected. He wished he had a smaller, nimbler boat—like *Bluebottle*. But *Bluebottle* was no more.

Eventually the swell eased, and the breeze caught in the sails again, nudging them on. But when they had gone a little farther, a freak wave smashed over the deck, tipping the boat to starboard and nearly washing Nutmeg overboard.

"Aagh!" she cried, clinging for dear life to the mast. Tumtum and the General both rushed to her side and held her tight. When the ship steadied they all collapsed on the deck, soaked through and exhausted.

It was a miserable voyage. And to make matters worse, there was no fresh water and nothing to eat but the rancid remains of the Rats' supper. And there weren't any comfortable beds.

It was many hours later, and almost light, when *Lady Crossbones* finally approached the main bank of the pond. "Lady ahoy!" the General cried weakly, guiding her in around a clump of weeds.

By the time the ship reached dry land, even General March-mouse was fed up. "I'm not sure *Lady Crossbones* is the right boat for me," he said.

"Hmmm. What did I tell you?" Tumtum replied. "Well, never mind, General. If you don't want her we can just abandon her here on the bank."

"We can't do that," the General said. "If we leave her here the Rats will reclaim her—they're sure to find their way back from the island one day. And once they've got *Lady Crossbones* back, they'll be able to start pirating again."

Tumtum considered this a moment. The General was right; without their ship the Rats would be much less dangerous.

"I've an idea," Nutmeg said. "Why don't we give *Lady Crossbones* to the children, as a present? It was our fault that *Bluebottle* sank, so now we can make it up to them. I can leave them a letter in the attic tonight, explaining what's happened, and telling them that if they come down to the Pond as soon as they've had breakfast, they'll find a new boat waiting for them. Imagine how delighted they'll be!"

"That's a splendid plan," Tumtum said.

"We can warn them that she'll need a good scrub," Nutmeg went on. "And I'll tell them to repaint her and give her a new name, so everyone will know she's not a pirate ship anymore."

"Well, that's settled then," the General said, relieved to have the ship off his paws.

As the three mice lowered the sails, ready to disembark, the General looked back a moment at the Pond, searching through the weeds and the rushes for one last glimpse of Marchmouse Island. But it was invisible now, lost beyond the vast horizon. He felt a stab of longing. It was *his* island, his alone; and one of these days he would go back there. But the Pond looked so big, he wondered if he would ever find it again.

He turned back to the shore and saw the dawn rising beyond the meadow. With a sudden start, he realized that he had been away from the gun cupboard for three whole nights. He had given Mrs. Marchmouse clear instructions not to worry about him—but he suspected she might not be following them.

"I had better be getting home," he said.

Chapter Fifteen

A few hours later, Lucy woke up. She wanted to find out if Nutmeg had come back. But suddenly she felt afraid. Instead of rushing out of bed, she turned her face into the pillow and lay with her eyes shut tight.

A minute went by, then she pulled herself together and sat up. Arthur was still sleeping. Quietly, so as not to wake him, she walked over to the dresser. And with a rush of relief, she saw a tiny envelope propped against her hairbrush.

"Arthur, she's back!" she cried. While her brother was still rubbing his eyes, she found the magnifying glass in the drawer of her bedside table and read Nutmeg's letter out loud.

Dear Arthur and Lucy,

Thanks to your wonderful trick, I have escaped. But events took quite a turn and went much better than we might have planned. In the end, I stole <u>Lady Crossbones</u> from under the Rats' very snouts, and sailed her home by the light of the moon, leaving the pirates marooned on the island. It was quite a night!

But we must never allow the pirates to reclaim their ship—for then they would start pirating again. So from now on, <u>Lady Crossbones</u> belongs to you. She will need a wash, of course, and a fresh coat of paint, and perhaps a dab of superglue on her rudder. But for the most part she is in good shape, and I believe you will find much to admire in her. I have moored her on the southern bank of the Pond, near the tree stump with moss on it.

Now hurry, my dears, and claim her before someone else does.

Love,

Nutmeg

P.S. I would not send the Rats any more chocolates if I were you. Rich food has a bad effect on them.

The children were overwhelmed. At best they had hoped they would get Nutmeg back. They hadn't expected a new boat as well.

"Come on, let's go and find it," Arthur said.

They got dressed then hurried downstairs and let themselves out into the garden. It was very early. The village had not yet stirred, and the grass was still covered in dew. They shut the back door quietly, so as not to wake their father, then ran across the meadow to the Pond.

The children did not know which way was south, but they soon spotted the tree stump that Nutmeg had described. It was on the far side of the Pond, where the grass had been trampled by sheep. They ran over to it, and when they parted the weeds they found *Lady Crossbones* moored against the bank.

She did not look so menacing at close range. Her huge gold sails had been tied down, and there was a snail snoozing on the deck. The children carefully lifted the boat from the water and stood it on the grass. Then they knelt down and peered through the portholes, examining each cabin in turn.

Everything looked very real. There were rugs on the floor, blankets on the beds, and clothes spewing from the dresser. And there were paintings hanging from the walls—big gloomy portraits, mainly of rats—and silver candlesticks on the bedside tables.

Arthur felt no regrets for *Bluebottle* now. This was the best toy boat he had ever seen.

"Nutmeg's right, we should repaint her. Black's too sinister," Lucy said. "And we should give her a new name. *Lady Crossbones* sounds silly."

"Let's call her *Lady Nutmeg*," Arthur said. Lucy agreed to this. So *Lady Nutmeg* she became.

"Do you think the pirates will be stuck on the island forever?" Lucy said.

Arthur shrugged. "I don't see how they'll get back without a boat."

It was strange to think there were pirates on the Pond. But many strange things had happened to Arthur and Lucy, so they supposed it must be true. They longed for a glimpse of them—but when they looked across to the island, all they could

see was the margarine tub upturned on the bank and a few gold chocolate wrappers scattered along the shore.

"I wonder if we'll ever see them," Lucy said.

"I should think we're bound to one day," Arthur replied. Though he wasn't sure he wanted to. He'd had enough of pirates for now. "Come on. Let's take *Lady Nutmeg* home and start painting her," he said.

They lifted the boat between them, for it was very heavy, and turned back toward the cottage. But had they watched the island a moment longer, they would have seen something stir. For just then Captain Pong, who had slept all night under a crisp wrapper in the cove, rolled over and gave a loud belch.

And there is not much more to say about the Rats. The Captain had become quite frenzied when he saw the mice escaping in his ship and had tried to chase after them in the margarine tub. But it was much too small for him, and he had capsized a few inches from the shore.

The other Rats could say nothing to console him that evening. But next morning, when they all took stock of the situation, things didn't seem so bad. For it was a glorious day, and they still had lots of chocolates left. And now that General Marchmouse had gone, the island was all theirs again. Which made them feel quite rich in a way—for as Captain Pong rightly observed, it's not every rat who has an island in the sun.

Meanwhile, the General had returned home to a tearful reception from Mrs. Marchmouse. Just as he feared, she had been worrying about him nonstop. The General often went off exploring on his own, but it was most unlike him to stay away for as long as this.

She was beginning to feel sure something awful must have happened to him. And she was just putting on her bonnet, ready to go out and summon help, when suddenly he burst through the gun cupboard door.

"Marchie!" she cried weakly, throwing herself upon his mousely chest, and the General was so touched by her concern that he promised he would never go adventuring again.

This would have come as welcome news to Tumtum and Nutmeg, who felt the General had embroiled them in quite enough trouble as it was. The last few days had been a terrible ordeal, and it was a wonderful moment when they finally crept back into the broom cupboard and saw their beloved Nutmouse Hall again.

They had been away so long that everything looked dusty and neglected. A fly had knocked over the milk jug on the kitchen table, and there was a spider bathing in the sink.

Nutmeg was too tired to tackle these upsets now. She had barely slept all night, and she could feel herself fading. Tumtum suddenly noticed how drawn she looked. "You sit down and I'll make some breakfast," he said.

They both felt much better when they had eaten some porridge. Then Tumtum made a pot of tea, and they sat at the table for a long while, mulling things over.

"What is it with us, Tumtum?" Nutmeg asked. "No sooner is one adventure over than another seems to come along."

Tumtum leaned back in his chair, considering this problem. What they both liked most of all was peace and quiet, so all this

excitement did seem rather bad luck. But then it occurred to him they might not appreciate their peaceful days nearly so much if there wasn't the occasional adventure to interrupt them.

And he was about to explain this to Nutmeg, but he dozed off while thinking how to phrase it.